THE HEN'S HOUSE

THE
HEN'S HOUSE

A NOVEL

Peter Israel

G. P. PUTNAM'S SONS   NEW YORK

PRINTED IN THE UNITED STATES OF AMERICA
By American Book–Stratford Press, Inc.

The quotation on page 68 is taken from *The Serpent of Paradise* by Miguel Serrano, published by Rider & Company, London.

Contents

THE HEN'S HOUSE

1   The Solitaire

❧

He laid out the deck for Canfield, snapping the face-up cards, squaring the six stacks beside the lead card as if neatness and symmetry would help his chances. He did not always play Canfield. Sometimes he tried the doubledeck game, which was so difficult to win he didn't measure it in terms of wins but only relative successes. He didn't know its name, if it had a name, only that his chances of winning must have been no better than one in a thousand, one in a thousand after the laborious doubledeck shuffles, the long layouts. The pleasure of a win, of working through the dwindling decks and sensing victory at long last after endless failures or "relative successes," the cards playing themselves out as if a master logician had organized the complex doubledeck patterns so that victory was not only possible but inevitable—the pleasure of a win was so great that he stayed with the game despite the dismal odds, despite the preliminary labors. He had probably played more doubledeck than Canfield, all in all. Canfield was an easy win, a game for old ladies of dwindling concentration, not for a man with time on his hands. A gambler's game, true, but whom did he have to bet against? His left hand against his right hand? (In fact, he had done it, countless times. He would call his left hand the house, his right the player, but after a sequence of layouts the left hand would usually be so rich there would be no point in continuing. He would lose track and start over, changing roles, or turn to double-deck.)

Still, this morning—or what he called morning, which was the same thing, it made no difference, a given period of time could be labeled morning because you woke up in it—this morning, waiting for the summons to the Hen, waiting for the door to slide open, gliding silently on its runners, gliding open with that professional, noiseless ease he associated with the functioning of the Henhouse, that "Swiss professionalism," as he called it, waiting for the little functionary with the slick, lightly oiled hair who always escorted him through the maze of corridors to the Hen, waiting for the summons to the Hen, which sometimes came early in the morning (right when he came awake the little functionary would be standing in the doorway) and sometimes late, irritatingly late, after he had exhausted the possibilities of Canfield and doubledeck and merely sat by his table, watching the doorway, waiting for the summons—(Actually he had long since accepted the fact that the summons was always on time, that the fluctuations in the waiting period were caused by irregularities in his sleep)—this morning, then, waiting for the summons to the Hen—(He cursed himself for his mental divagations, he never could think straight in the mornings, his mind awash with contradictory snatches of ideas, a bit of this and that, fragments of memories, of past Hen dialogues and events, of dreams, fantasies, no cohesion, none of the smooth professional processes he

had sought to cultivate, which only came after the first
dialogue with the Hen and the first meal, when he could
slow down, reorganize and begin to function again in the
orderly style he had set forth for himself)—this morning,
then, waiting for the summons to the Hen, the regular
morning summons—at last!—he wanted a quick victory. So
he chose Canfield over doubledeck and snapped the up-
cards and squared the stacks as he dealt.

Before finishing the layout, he decided to allow himself
his special treat. He had learned to separate his treats so as
to savor their pleasures fully. They lost savor when he
squandered them. He saved them for mornings of extreme
irritation, mornings of craving, when the wash of contradic-
tions, the mindrace, threatened to spill over if he didn't
answer the craving. The special treat was gambling at Canfield, but not left hand versus right hand. Not left leg vs.
right leg, either, nor heart vs. stomach. In the special treat,
he was the gambler. He, not his left hand or his right hand,
sat before the layout on the player's side, chips in front of
him.

And the banker, in the special treat, was the Hen.

This morning he didn't need the treat. It wasn't essential.
He could stand the craving, surmount it, master it, stop the
mindrace without the treat. Nevertheless he decided to
allow himself one, just one whim. That was it: whim, a
chance fancy. If the Hen asked him to explain why, he
wouldn't be able to. Not at all. He didn't need the treat. It
was a whim this morning, a fancy, frivolous, a chance
occurrence without cause. A squandering, which he might
pay for tomorrow morning if he should really need the treat,
and therefore pleasing.

He studied the layout, satisfied as he selected the currency
for the game, for there were at least three immediate plays,

one an ace, before he even opened his pack. He could bet
with any currency he chose. The Hen allowed it. The Hen
accepted whatever he had, whatever he chose to risk. He
chose Swiss francs. He had had luck with Swiss francs. He
counted out fifty-two chips, the price of the deck, pushed
them past the layout toward the Hen, watched the Hen's
fingers nimbly arrange them into stacks of five each, with the
two left over. It was the two that counted. The two were for
the house. They represented the house's profit over the long
run of deals, the extra two which meant that over the long
run he, the player, was bound to lose, though if he could
keep himself to short runs he could connect with a lucky
streak, a string of victories which would stack the chips
before him, which would have the Hen shoveling chips
across the baize-covered table where he, in turn, could take
his time stacking them, in piles of five or ten or twenty as he
chose, or just loosely amassed in a mounting heap, if that
was what he decided, or even, as the streak continued, some
of each.

Cautiously, flexing his fingers as he studied his moves, he
began the play, conscious that the Hen was watching him
but unruffled, confident, automatically turning over the first
three cards of his pack before putting out the ace and
making the two transfers. Three times through the pack,
three cards at a time, that was how he and the Hen played
Canfield. Five Swiss francs for each card scored (already five
Swiss francs back in his pocket for the first ace), meaning a
loss on ten or fewer cards scored, a profit on eleven or more,
a clean profit of 208 Swiss francs for scoring the entire deck.
You could go all the way in Canfield often enough; that was
what lured the gambler, that was what lured him to gamble
with the Hen, even though in the long run those extra two
francs, which meant a loss even on ten cards scored, would

wear him down, wipe him out, leave him at the mercy of the house.

He squared the rows and stacks as he touched them, then proceeded slowly through his pack, three cards at a time, making the plays as they occurred: red ten on black jack, two to the ace, transfer the king to the vacant row and open the down card, then three more from the pack. As he reached the end of the first round, his confidence rose. He allowed himself to glance at the Hen, seeking a reaction. There was none. What did he expect, after all? Still, he knew the deal was promising. A deal with a chance. Four cards had been scored, three aces and a two, which already gave him a cushion against disaster, and he knew where two more scoring cards were, they would surely appear in the next round with the change in order in the pack. But most important of all was his chance for the whole deck, the sweep, the clean 208-franc coup. He knew from the number of plays he had made, from the developing pattern of the layout, that there was a chance. More than just a chance in fact, a good chance.

Turning the pack over, he began the second round. Quickly he found the two scoring cards as he had predicted: a three for the two and a two for one of the aces. Then, uncovering a stack, he found the last ace and the deuce to accompany it, which gave him eight cards scored, a maximum possible loss of twelve Swiss francs and still almost two rounds to play.

He needed a black eight. How he needed a black eight! The black eight was the key to the game, he felt it in his bones, the black eight would open the deck, would play on the red nine and allow the red seven to leave the last fat unplayed stack. And he had seen the eight of clubs in his own pack!

In his excitement he missed a move. Or almost missed a move. The Hen would have said he missed it, for the Hen pointed it out, indicating the red nine which would play from an empty row onto a black ten. The Hen. The wise, omniscient Hen. Goddamn the Hen! He'd seen the nine, hadn't missed it at all, a professional didn't miss moves at Canfield and he was a professional at Canfield. No, he hadn't missed it, even though he was turning the cards faster, even though the stacks were now irregular, his own dwindling pack unevenly piled before the layout. But why the nine, O Wise Hen? Why play the nine when there was no king to go in the empty row and a red nine still to come from the pack? Why rush out with the nine? He hadn't missed the move at all, and he turned three more cards to prove it. There was the other nine, the other red nine, the diamond nine. He placed it on the black ten, placed it neatly, squaring the line of cards, looking briefly into the Hen's eyes, straight into the Hen's impassive eyes. Then he turned three more cards and came upon a king. Under it lay the eight of clubs, his coveted eight of clubs, the lovely eighter, the key to the game.

How had the Hen known? No, the Hen hadn't known, it was chance, the mere chance of Canfield, the fall of the cards, no one could have known it, not he, not the Hen, not the most astute gambler. The point was: because he had played the diamond nine and not the heart, now the king wouldn't play. There was no empty space for it. His eight of clubs was lost for another round, lost maybe forever, and the game with it. Who knew? Who could tell? But that was cards, that was gambling. That was the way it went sometimes when you ventured fifty-two Swiss francs against the Hen at Canfield. In the long run it had to be a losing proposition.

There was the third round to come. He could still catch the eight in the third round, still score the whole deck, still catch the 208 Swiss franc coup. There was a chance for it yet, the cards could give him his one last shot. That was Canfield too. You always had your shot.

He dealt through the third round and missed the eight again. Various cards played, but he found no more scorers. In the end his pack reduced to six cards, six cards only, one away from an open pack, for that was the rule: reduce the pack to five and you could open it. An open pack usually meant the sweep.

But he didn't have five, he had six in his pack, one too many for opening, and the irony was that in a hypothetical fourth round the pack would reduce to five, the third card would play, and he could have his eight of clubs. He wondered if the Hen would allow him a fourth round, just this once. It would be cheating, against the rules, surely it would be cheating, against the Canfield system to which he and the Hen subscribed, but how often did he miss opening the deck by one card? And maybe if the Hen hadn't rattled him he'd have made the winning play—not the correct play, the correct play was to take the diamond nine from the pack over the heart nine from an open row just as he had done it, but the correct and the winning play are not always the same in cards. And what after all did the loss of 208 Swiss francs mean to the Hen and the Henhouse compared to the pleasure winning them would give him?

He considered a fourth round. It was cheating, no way around it. He had cheated before, but not against the Hen, only in the games of left hand versus right hand and then only occasionally, and only for a change of luck in the midst of hopeless streaks. How would the Hen react? He had no idea.

He knew it made no difference then, none at all, whether he cheated or not, whether he lost twelve Swiss francs or won 208, for there were no Swiss francs, no chips, no gambler's baize over his bare table, maybe there was not even a deck of cards before him, maybe he had imagined them too.

Nor was there a Hen sitting across the table. The special treat was over. In place of the Hen, standing in the doorway, the door having slid open without his having heard or noticed, was the functionary in his usual gray suit, his thinning hair lightly oiled and slicked, come to summon him to the Hen, as usual, in the morning.

2   To the Hen

𝕾

He knew the way to the Hen by heart. He had walked the corridors in his dreams: the red-tiled floors, the white walls broken regularly by doors, the striplights down the centers of the ceilings. Twice a day the functionary turned his key in the lock and the door slid open. Twice a day, he followed him through the three corridors to the Hen, in the mornings before the first meal and again in the afternoons, except on special days when no afternoon sessions were held. For a time he had assumed the special days were Sundays, that the Hen kept Sunday afternoons for himself, until he began counting and failed to find a pattern to the intervals, only that, sometime between every tenth and sixteenth session, every fifth and eighth day, an afternoon session would be omitted.

He had long since ceased trying to disrupt the Henhouse system. None of his tactics had worked. The Hen, or whoever planned routine and system for the Hen, had thought of every contingency. He had only succeeded in thwarting himself, as the Hen pointed out. That was the reality, the sole product of his destructive, disruptive impulses: that he only succeeded in thwarting himself, inflicting needless injury on his case, in—he could parrot the Hen's very words, the mechanical intonation of words uttered repeatedly, even the punctuating sighs of impatience—slowing his progress, introducing new cycles of self-destructive behavior into his situation. These ideas of his, these impulses, were inaccurate. He had to recognize them as inaccurate. "Inaccurate" was a favorite Hen word, uttered with clipped, pedagogic precision, or slowly, in a low-pitched drawl, depending upon the moment—but always emphasized, always followed by a silence in which the two of them could contemplate its relevance. Ideas were never good or bad, true or untrue. An idea existed, whether or not one approved of it. Once it had been thought, it existed; once it existed, it had to be brought to light. That was the problem: to bring his ideas into the open, to consider them in the bright light of reality, so that they, he and the Hen, could determine which ideas were accurate and which inaccurate. Inaccurate ideas were at best useless. Those such as his attempts to thwart the Hen and the functioning of the Henhouse were useless, their futility self-evident, but they were also self-destructive: they impeded the progress of his case.

In the end, he could but agree.

Nonetheless, he still concocted his inaccurate ideas, though he had ceased putting them into action. He couldn't help himself. They were his fictions, largely petty notions of baiting the Henhouse, of throwing it offstride, disrupting its routines. He had abandoned the more serious schemes which once had plagued his mind—plans for passive resistance, physical violence, or even escape—but what could he do when a new device, an impulse, popped into his thought processes like a surfacing cork except pursue it to its conclusions? To the Hen, it made no difference whether these devices were fictional or practiced. They were mental games, the Hen said, indulgences like solitaire and his child-ish fantasies about gambling, harmless pastimes perhaps if they had nothing better to do. But he had meant it, hadn't he, when he had said he wanted his case to progress? If he had been lying, of course, then they must reappraise his situation, they must seek a different view. No? He hadn't been lying? He genuinely wanted to progress? Good. All to the good. If, then, he genuinely wanted his case to progress, perhaps he ought to give up these childish pranks and misdemeanors, these inaccurate little ideas of his, no?

Once he had refused to go to the Hen. When the door slid open in the morning and the functionary appeared, he had simply remained on his bed, his hands linked behind his head.

"It is time, Mr. _____," the functionary had said, which was what the functionary always said when he did not respond immediately to the opening of the door, this or the longer variant: "Mr. _____, it is time for your meeting." There were no other variations to the same set speech, uttered in an even, unaccented tone like a recorded an-nouncement: "It is time, Mr. _____."

He had lain there on his bed, his hands behind his head, unblinking, smiling inwardly at the chance to use silence, the needle of silence, the Hen's favorite technique.

After an interval the functionary spoke again: "Mr. _____, it is time for your meeting."

The functionary disappointed him. He merely waited in the doorway, expressionless, as if in his experience he had encountered every form of reaction from inmates of the Henhouse, as if nothing at all could surprise him, much less

this basic form of rebellion. Was the functionary giving him
a chance to reconsider? If so, was he acting out of his own
kindness, or was this normal procedure in dealing with
recalcitrant members: to give them another chance? Let him
wait. He could wait all he wanted.

The functionary left and the door closed.

Then it had been his turn to wait, to let the waiting and
the silence prey. He had expected a reaction, some sort of
reaction, he knew not what. In his mind he watched the
functionary walk the corridors alone, his heels clicking on
the red tiles, watched him open and close the doors which
joined the corridors, heard him deliver the message in the
Hen's office. What would the Hen do? How did the Henhouse deal with recalcitrants? Let them use force. Let them
send their team of functionaries tiptoeing down the corridors to spring on him unexpectedly. He was ready for them.
He would not resist. He had prepared himself not to resist.
In any case he would be subdued. But they would have to
drag or carry him to the Hen, it would take four of them to
do it from those he had seen, and not even all the
functionaries the Henhouse could muster could force him to
talk. Then at last this sham of cooperation, this hypocrisy of
membership, of working together on his case, would be done
with once and for all and the lines drawn.

So he had waited, sifting possibilities, steeling himself
against the tension.

And still they did not come.

When he first began to sense what was happening, he
couldn't be sure of it. He needed confirmation. It was difficult for a man alone in his cell—Goddamn them, he was
going to call it a cell whatever euphemisms the Hen used!—
to keep track of the passage of time when there were no
clocks, no daylight to be observed, no external measure-

ments possible, only the calculations and estimates of the mind. The mind tricks itself. The mind loves to play tricks on itself. When left to its own resources, the mind is a charlatan. Maybe hours had elapsed. Maybe only minutes. He had long since left his bed to sit at the table, to pace back and forth from one wall to the other, but how long had he lain on the bed? Had it been an hour or five minutes? And had he paced the floor, this way and that, fifty times or one hundred times? Or only eleven times? Or had he dreamed the whole episode?

He only knew positively when the door opened again and the functionary reappeared.

"It is time for your meeting, Mr. _____," the functionary said.

This time he arose quickly and stormed after the functionary, outraged at the form the Hen's retaliation had taken, barely able to contain his anger as he followed close on the functionary's heels and waited impatiently outside the Hen's office, ignoring the chair in which he usually sat, until the other functionary with the thin neck and the face wizened like a prune came to escort the inmate who preceded him. Hardly had the door slid open and the other inmate passed through it than he was inside, waving off the Hen's habitual greeting, the proffered chair, shouting at the bald head, which shone red in the chandelier light, focusing on the pate, the glistening dome.

"This is your treatment! This is your way of punishing us! You starve us when we don't obey, when we don't do precisely what you want! We are *prisoners* then. Why don't you stop your pretenses and admit it? We are *prisoners* and you will simply starve us when we don't obey you!"

All that had happened was that the first meal, which always followed the morning session, had not been served. As

simple as that. Usually he was back in his room only a few
moments after returning from the Hen when the door slid
open again and the waiter wheeled in his tray. He had
refused to go to the Hen this one morning, and the Hen had
merely canceled his meal. As simple as that. Had he refused
the functionary's second summons, he supposed the second
meal would have been denied him as well. And so on. Which
explained why meals were never served in the Henhouse
until after sessions—a simple, easy technique for controlling
the prisoners. Yes, they were *prisoners*. The recognition of it
infuriated him anew, so that he continued shouting.

"Please," the Hen interrupted, removing his glasses and
rubbing them with a handkerchief. "Please to calm yourself
and take a seat."

"No, I will not calm myself and take a seat!" he shouted at
the ruddy dome, shaking his fist in the air. "We're *prisoners*
here against our will, *prisoners!* Even so, we won't be denied
our food, you can't starve us into submission. All this talk of
cooperation . . . 'If you are that concerned about your future . . . ' " he quoted, mocking, mimicking, wanting to
throw the words in the Hen's face, remembering bitterly
how the Hen constantly sidestepped all his questions about
his status. "Well, we see now who is concerned with whose
future, and we'll see who'll cooperate with whom!"

In the silence which followed, the Hen continued to rub
his glasses, gazing steadily at him with those eyes, the
overlarge watery eyes which often looked fatigued, and
suddenly he became aware of the incongruity of his words,
of his posture. Still standing, his arm still raised in the air, he
felt awkward, inappropriate, an orator rehearsing before a
mirror, as if his speech, the accusations he had prepared,
had been shouted in an empty room and echoed around him
absurdly. He dropped his arm and, responding at last to the
Hen's motion, subsided into his armchair.

Another Hen silence ensued. The Hen was allowing the perception of his own absurdity to work on him. Then the thick rimless glasses went back over the watery eyes, and the inevitable question came, which stiffened him despite his anticipation of it:

"Please now, can you tell us why you refused to come here when you were summoned?"

He could not answer. There was nothing to say, no explanation.

"Of course not," the Hen answered for him. "Of course you cannot. You know, you talk so much of the others . . . the other 'prisoners,' as you call them. It is true there are other members here, you have seen them for yourself. But they are no concern of ours, we need not worry ourselves about them." Then, with the corners of his mouth lifting: "And in addition, we have our hands full worrying about just your own case, is it not so?"

"But you don't deny that you seek to punish us?"

"Us?"

"Me then," he said angrily. "You can't deny that you punished me by keeping the first meal from me."

"Yes. And I can deny it, and I do," the Hen said in his soft, steady voice, accompanied by a Hen gesture, the placing of fingertips together in a steeple. "Punishment is for children, and you are not a child, even though your refusal before was a childish act. As both of us know, we have certain systems, certain patterns, certain requirements in the society which exist because they have to exist, because they are for the benefit of all members, for your benefit as well as mine. When the pattern is broken because of the willfulness of one of our members, we have no choice but to respond. That is the way any society must function.

"No, I am sorry," the Hen continued, "but I cannot agree that you were punished, any more than you succeeded in punishing me by refusing to come here. That is what you wanted to do, isn't it, like a child punishing a parent? You must ask yourself why. For what? After all, what would you gain by punishing me? Is there anything you want? You know you have only to ask and, if it is possible, it will be granted you. Isn't that the way it has always been between us? Tell us now, what have you been denied that makes you so want to punish me, except for this unfortunate incident of the meal?"

He started to retort: Yes he *had* been denied—but lulled by the reasonableness of the Hen's words, the soothing, reasonable sound of the voice which invariably flowed over him like a wash of warm water, the limpid, watery, open gaze, the slow tapping of the smooth-skinned fingers on the polished wood of the desk top, he sensed the futility of argument. Within the framework of the Henhouse—and what other framework was possible for him?—how could he argue? Already he felt the pangs of remorse which always followed such incidents and dialogues. How could he be so childish? Why did he cause such trouble? Why did he inflict himself so on others, on the Hen, who had far more on his mind than one member's petty frustrations? Once, in a similar situation, he had asked these questions aloud, and the Hen had reassured him, as he did now:

"You know, you don't have to suffer over causing trouble to me or to the society. We are here to help you, to serve you as long as you are among us. It is only unfortunate that you cause such trouble to yourself, is it not so?"

Yes, he nodded. Yes. He was back where he had started, the cycle complete. Then the knife pangs began to be assuaged by the only relief they recognized: a flush of gratitude for the Hen's generosity, his kindliness.

Later, when his functionary led him back to his own door,

he found that his meal had already been wheeled into position, of itself an unusual occurrence, and he fell upon it ravenously.

This incident, however, did not have the desired effect on him. It provided no object lesson. The feelings of gratitude, purge, exhilaration, which accompanied him from the Hen's did not last. Soon enough, in the routine, they disappeared: fugitive, then forgotten.

The argument that he and the Hen were inexorable enemies taunted and spurred him like a demon. He could not escape it. Having experienced the Hen's method for handling recalcitrants, it remained for him to demonstrate that he was no common prisoner, no groveling lackey whose docility could be insured merely by feeding him well. In this way the idea of strike occurred to him, and once having occurred, a thought among many thoughts, it sprouted rapidly into an obsession. He had to strike. He had not only to ignore the functionary's summons, but the functionary as well.

The Henhouse must be banned, excommunicated.

The Henhouse must be banished, must cease to exist.

He could not predict the outcome of the new tactics, knowing only that the Hen wanted him alive, that he was being maintained and prepared for some end. Did not the same motif continue to crop up in the sessions: the references to "case" and "situation" and "progress"? Therefore, he did not fear the Hen's retaliation—what could the Hen do? —but only his own weakness, which was the real enemy. He would have to hold out against himself. If he succeeded, there would be perforce some change in his status, some clarification, some resolution. The Hen would not let him starve himself, but he had to convince him of his intention to do so. His will was his best weapon. He had to impose it, not on the Hen but upon himself.

The critical point, when the temptation to yield almost broke his resolve, came the second morning. Like an officer busying his troops he had prepared himself well, had worked out a schedule of activities to buttress his will, to lure his mind and body away from the battlefield. He had learned the first day that no new retaliatory measures would be used against him. Except for the meals, there would be no denial of privileges. His books would not be taken from him, nor his writing materials, both of which formed important elements in the schedule. He was left alone. Twice the first day the functionary had appeared in the doorway and said: "It is time, Mr. ————," or his variant statement. Twice he had waited, totally ignored, repeated the statement in the same monotone, waited again, then closed the door with his key.

The meals had not arrived. He rejoiced in the knowledge that the Hen and the Henhouse were less flexible than he had thought. They were playing his game, unwittingly perhaps, but playing it nonetheless. He followed his schedule rigorously: certain estimated hours for reading fiction, others for study, others for card games, an extra time length for writing in the assorted papers which he called his notebook. He performed his exercises at regular intervals: the push-ups, the sit-ups with his ankles anchored under the rim of his bed, the running-in-place, the organized pacing of his room.

The fasting was simple. He had only not to think about food. When, the first evening, the cravings nagged at him, coaxing him to pound on the door, to demand to be taken to the Hen, he confronted them directly, fought them face-to-face, conquered them, mastered them. His mind was only playing tricks on him. It was unoccupied. He had to occupy it. He occupied it. He stayed away from the door. Finally he fell asleep.

When he awoke, however, the morning of the second day, he had no time to consolidate, to control, to organize, to buttress. The mindrace had him in its grip. His will was defenseless. The functionary was already standing in the doorway, and his will almost crumbled before the image.

"Get away from me," he called out, defying his own resolution of silence. "Leave me alone. I've told you I'm not coming."

"Mr. _____, it is time for your meeting."

The functionary was baiting him. He stood there, exhaling, inhaling, lingering longer than necessary. Doubtless that was what he had been instructed to do: to wait and continue to wait, to tempt by his presence. How he detested the man, how he loathed the very sight of him! He never smiled. He would never laugh if you tickled him, never wince if you screamed at him, never whimper if you struck him. He only went about his business, he only lingered in the doorway.

"No, I'm not coming! Just leave me alone!"

Did the functionary know how many times he had slaughtered him in his imagination, how he had slashed into him, clawing at his face, slamming that placid, imperturbable face with his fists, blood spurting from the mouth and nose, shrieks of pain spurting from a man who never shrieked? When that impeccable, imperturbable mien had embodied all that he suffered in the Henhouse, Yes!, he had slaughtered him, annihilated him! And the Hen looming invisibly behind him, the Hen's smooth fingers crooking at him, the fatigued brown eyes saying: You have only to get up and follow your functionary. Come now, let us proceed together with your case, forgetting all that has happened. The Hen, his arms spread wide like a candidate for office.

"No! Tell him I'm not coming!"

Still the functionary had lingered, baiting him.

In the end it was not his will that saved him. His will was no good at all. It was the image of the Hen. For he found that he dreaded conversation with the Hen more than solitude and hunger, dreaded the extended arms, the reasonable words, the sad brown eyes with their tacit accusations, their tacit recriminations, and his own guilt, followed by his own remorse. The Hen, the clever Hen, who would contrive to turn him back on himself as he always did. He could not face the Hen. No. He could not face him.

The functionary gave up. He left, closed the door behind him.

Had the functionary really stayed longer than usual? No, probably he had not. It was just his mind tricking him again, just his imagination. And realizing this, he also realized, to his relief, that his worst test was over, that he had won.

As the second day passed and the third began, he tended to forget about food entirely. He could go for days, he thought, without it. The second night he suffered intermittently from headaches, a pain behind his eyes which was no worse than annoying, but then the headaches passed and he experienced in turn a kind of giddiness, a light-headedness, as if gravity had suddenly ceased and he walked on the moon, jumped, soared, free-floating.

The functionary came and went, the hours came and went, virtually unnoticed. Sometime, however, he began to neglect his program of activities. What were books, he thought, to a man in his situation? Why should he waste his time reading? The idea of reading was suddenly so funny that he laughed out loud, and then he was laughing uncontrollably. He put aside the books, the course of study he had outlined. Then, writing in his notebook, he could no longer concentrate on a flow of thought. In the midst of a sentence, he would forget the beginning. Contemplating a verb, he would lose the subject. His sentences elongated, clauses multiplying upon clauses, words stretching out to permit other words to enter like soldiers in expanding ranks. His thoughts came out like diarrhea, in dribs and drabs. The paper filled with streams of disjointed fragments, huge sentences composed of fragments which made no sense to him. His exercises too. His exercises made no sense to him. Slowly he lost the energy for them, even on a reduced regimen. His body was lapsing into lassitude, and though he knew it, he found it increasingly difficult to rise from his bed, not only because of the physical exertion, but because he saw in the effort no point whatsoever.

Where was the functionary? Had he come or gone? Or was he about to come? It made no difference. He would come and go, and then he would come and go again. That was the functionary for you.

Then he was sitting cross-legged, head bowed, on the floor of his room. It had many sides. Its walls were white wood panels of uniform width, its sole source of light a cone in the ceiling. How many times had he sought the way out? Many times, he thought. That was his impression, his definite impression. First he had passed his hands at random across the smooth panels. Then he had covered each inch of wall space, every last inch from top to bottom and across, prodding, tapping, searching for the place or combination of weak places. Then he had worked at the panel joints with an implement, picking, scoring, trying to force a crevice. If he worked at it long enough, surely he would force a crevice or find the mysterious combination. He just had to keep at it, working at the panels, tapping and prodding. Yet he had known all along, hadn't he, that the only way out was to gather his strength for one concentrated effort, hoarding his

strength like a discus thrower, then to hurl himself against
any of the panels? It made no difference which one. Why
should it make any difference? He saw himself bursting,
lungs swelled beyond their capacity, through the flimsy
wood of the walls into the bright cold air of the world
outside with its crisp greens and blues, its sunshine, its
rolling fields of soft, resilient grass. There he would stand on
a slight rise, hands on hips, sides heaving from exertion,
sweat drying fast in the cold air. Sooner or later, he knew, he
would have to try it. Why not try it? Was there any reason
why he shouldn't?

With the knowledge that he would try it, however, came
the vision of what would happen, the vision of the sham.
Yes, he stood in the center of the many-sided room, in the
center of the white panels. Yes, he picked his panel of wood,
his white panel. Yes, he turned away, his muscles coiled,
tense, like the discus thrower coiling for the toss. Yes, his
own body uncoiled, and yes, it hurtled like the disc itself
toward the white wall. But the panels did not smash and
shatter. No. Not at all. They only drifted backward, errati-
cally, as if propelled by some counter-magnetic force in his
own body. He ran toward them in frantic haste. Then his
feet met the soft grass. Encouraged, he ran on, but the
panels of wood were even faster, darting, swerving over the
undulating landscape until they disappeared, invisible pres-
ences, behind the distant hills. Where was the bright blind-
ing sunshine? It did not exist. Nor was the air invigorating.
It was moist, stagnant, almost tangible. But at least there
was the grass, soft and green as he had envisioned it, and as
long as he ran, the panels remained hidden, lurking, floating
unseen beyond the hills of the horizon. He was running in
circles, running on tangents which doubled back on themselves, running at cross-purposes, this way and that, crossing

and recrossing his steps. Eventually, exhausted, he sank
down, his legs resuming their cross-legged position. There,
sure enough—hadn't he expected them?—over the horizon
and the hills, came the white panels of wood, drifting,
floating, darting toward him like kites on gusts of wind,
increasingly discernible and increasing in size, bigger and
closer, bigger and closer, until at last their sides could join
again, reforming the crevices, shutting off the vista, reforming the many-sided room, the cone of light in the ceiling, the
familiar red-tiled floor. He arose in protest, but there the
walls were, together again, close enough to touch. So he
started all over, seeking the way out, prodding and tapping,
working at the crevices.

Then he saw himself from incredible height. He was way
up, way way up, propelled and sustained by jets of air. Far
below, no bigger than an ant, flattened as if by a boot, his
body lay spread-eagled on a vast white plateau which extended far beyond the horizons of his vision, a plateau flatter
than a pancake, flat as the world had first appeared flat. He
saw nothing else, only the flat plateau as vast as the world
itself, a plateau devoid of all objects, all shadows, save his
own antlike body on its back.

He saw the functionary, several times. The functionary
was beckoning to him, talking to him, but he only saw the
lips move, he could not make out the words. He wanted to
curse him. He had a message for the Hen. He wanted to give
him the message for the Hen, and curse him. But he couldn't
speak. He couldn't make the connections between his tongue
and the words which flickered through his mind. It made no
difference anyway. The functionary was gone and already he
was on his hands and knees, under the bed, groping in
darkness for the entrance to the narrow passage. He knew it
existed. He was sure of it. He groped for it, crawled for it,

found it. Then he lowered his feet into it, wriggled his hips and shoulders in shudders to avoid touching its slimy sides. With a last deep breath, he let his body fall into the pliant arms of the swamp. Twining vines rose through the mist to greet him, licking at his face. The red mouths of serpentine creatures sucked at his calves, his knees, his thighs, gently tugging him deeper into the ooze. With his hands he parted the reeds and marsh grass which wiped at his eyes like cobwebs, but then, with one further step, the undulating slime yielding beneath his weight, he lost his balance. As his body plunged, he heard the swamp creatures bleating in pleasure. Frantically, he flailed with his arms, seeking support. He reached for a vine, grasped it, and, choking, pulled himself toward it. Its strength sapped by wet rot, the vine quietly disintegrated in his hands. His cry was stifled by the slime which filled his mouth. His body was sinking, swallowed whole by the maw. Unable to breathe, unable to hold his breath, unable to sustain the pounding in his brain, he opened his mouth and nose at last to the slime, which rushed in to claim the organs ripe inside his body. In his last instant of consciousness he felt an overwhelming relief, while his body sank to the bottom, flopped slowly on its back on the bottom, and the clusters of red mouths began to feed. Bubbles of corpse gas eddied gently toward the surface. The swamp had commenced his decomposition with rhythmic efficiency, and soon it would be sated, soon it would recline once more in graceful sleepy coils.

He was in a hospital. A cone of light shone in his eyes. He was on his back. He turned his head to avoid the light, saw the white walls, the huge bottles, the thick tubes descending into his arm. A head leaned over him, a hand touched the skin beneath his eyes. He could not see the head, only the outline of the head. It was the Hen. The Hen had intervened

at last. The Hen. He smelled the hospital smell. Then he was
sinking again, back down, down into the swamp.

But he had not been moved to a hospital. The hospital had
come to his room. The hand touched the skin beneath his
eyes, and he started to sit up, had time only to see his
writing table before the hand, gently, firmly pushed him
down.

"You are still very weak. Please lie back again."

The voice was not the Hen's, nor was the face. It was a
doctor, that's what it was. He was weak. He was weak, as
the doctor said, so weak, he had never before felt so physically helpless, he could only lie in his bed and watch the
comings and goings, watch the doctor and attendants, watch
the administering.

He had failed. He knew it right away, without the Hen.

He recovered. He was on his feet, eating with his own
hands. When, one morning, the functionary came for him,
he felt no impulse to refuse the summons.

The Hen agreed with his appraisal.

"Yes, it was a failure. Although, whatever your attitude is
today, there must have been moments recently when you
felt ennobled by your courage, by having proved to yourself
that you have a will. You must even have enjoyed it." The
Hen had risen from his desk and strolled about his office,
back and forth in front of the heavy drapes behind his desk,
twirling his glasses by an earpiece, signaling a speech. "You
have learned, you see, the secret of martyrdom, or passive
resistance if you will, the reason it has survived all the ages
as a technique of rebellion. The passive resistant, once
started, need not care about consequences, results, the effec-
tiveness of his actions. He becomes absorbed in testing his
own will, he rejoices in the discovery of his own will, the

proof of his will. Martyrdom or passive resistance is an
enjoyable occupation, and, once started, it is easy. I have
never understood why history has so sanctified its martyrs.
Examine the motivation of the martyr carefully, and you
will find only selfishness. Perhaps no breed of men has been
more selfishly motivated, though the martyrs parade their
selflessness.

"In certain instances passive resistance has even proved
effective. It has spurred a particular society to action,
though in the process the particular society is duped into
sanctifying the resistants. But in your case?" The Hen sat
down. "What have you accomplished after all? In a society
such as ours, passive resistance is meaningless. We are here
only to help you. That is our purpose, and you have not
succeeded in changing our resolve. All you have accomplished is to inflict some temporary physical damage on
yourself. Fortunately it was only temporary. Yes, too, you
have managed to delay the progress of your case by some
days, but though this may be unfortunate, it is no great loss,
not permanent. We will catch up.

"So what is left? Yes, you proved to us that you had a will
of your own. This is a valuable piece of knowledge, surely,
that a man has a will, but has it not been self-evident all
along? Did we ever doubt it? Did you really have to go to
such drastic lengths to demonstrate it?"

The Hen paused, then smiled at him, shaking his head
slowly in faint disapproval. "Didn't we know it all along?
Surely you must see it now: that this idea of yours, this
demonstration of will, this hardy passive resistance, was, in a
society such as ours, unnecessary, not to say inaccurate."

3 The Hen's Anteroom

The walk to the Hen, this morning of the Canfield, took him through familiar corridors and doorways. The functionary opened the doors with keys, inserting a key in the slot to the right of a door to open it and making a corresponding insertion on the other side to close it. Five doors separated him and the Hen, although the last door, on the other side of the Hen's anteroom, was never opened by key.

His own corridor was short. Twenty normal paces took him to its end. He had covered the distance in seventeen paces but his average was twenty. The other end appeared equidistant from his room, but he had never walked that way, had never turned right upon leaving his room, and could thus only trust his visual estimate.

The walls of the corridor were white, like all the Henhouse walls save those in the Hen's office. The floors were red tile. The lighting was a fluorescent strip down the center of the ceiling. Set in the walls on both sides were doors like his own. He assumed they opened onto the rooms of other "members," although his schedule had been so arranged as to

minimize contact with his fellow inmates. He had never seen
the other doors of his corridor open. It might have been that
many of the other rooms were vacant, pending departures
and arrivals. In fact, it had to be. They couldn't all be
occupied. The Hen had only so many hours in his day. No
matter how diligently he worked, no matter how arduous a
schedule he undertook, he could still accommodate only so
many inmates.

Unless, that is, there were inmates on programs different
from his own. Or unless there was more than one Hen in the
Henhouse.

He had rejected both possibilities. How could there be
inmates who never saw the Hen? With the passage of time
he had become convinced in the eventuality of his own
progress, though he knew neither when it would start nor
the direction it would take. Thus he couldn't conceive of a
different situation, of inmates merely living in the Henhouse,
subsisting, existing, without progress, without purpose,
spending purposeless day after purposeless day without the
leavening of the sessions. If he had not yet started to progress, nonetheless he would. He could not believe otherwise.
He would not.

As for the second alternative, yes, theoretically there
could be more than one Hen. Possibly the Henhouse was a
vast roost of functionaries, inmates, and Hens. Yet, knowing
the Hen, how could this be? The Hen was the Hen. The Hen
was unique and idiosyncratic, uniquely powerful, with the
unique ability to determine his destiny. He could no more
accept the existence of two or more Hens than he could
believe that inmates belonging to another species lived and
breathed in the Henhouse. For that is what belief in the
existence of other Hens would have required of him.

No. There could be but one true Hen, his Hen, and so he
had concluded wryly that the Henhouse had vacancies, that
some of the rooms on his corridor—if they were rooms—not
to say the two other identical corridors he and the functionary traversed four times a day, coming and going, were
empty. He had even tested the theory. He had paused in the
corridors to knock on some of the doors. The functionary
had never interfered. He had merely stopped on the red tile
floor and waited. There was never a response to his knock-
ing, never an acknowledging knock, never an answering
sound of any kind, merely the functionary, true to his style,
waiting for him without patience or impatience.

But the other rooms, like his own, were soundproof. That
must be the explanation! Perhaps his knocks were unanswered only because they were unheard!

Perhaps so. He could not deny it. Any argument had its
converse argument, and an agile mind could present and
uphold either side as convincingly as its opposite. In the
end, abandoning the useless dictates of logic, a man had to
believe what he chose to believe. That was the way it was
with his progress. Supported by the Hen, he believed in its
eventuality, and yet he could not demonstrate it. On the
contrary, in accordance with the facts, he saw his own
history increasingly in terms of the curving, tangential
circle. There was just one road for him to follow, this idea of
the circles said, if he was to develop, and though this road
doubtless began nowhere and ended nowhere, he nonetheless had to seek it and follow it loyally. It was futile to try to
advance at once on a number of roads, to extend his search
prongs in multiple directions. Like a man revolving in the
middle of a vast square, dazzled by the possible avenues
open to him, he too had experienced the thrill of multi-

plicity, the prospect of infinite options. But multiplicity was a deception, at least for him. Perhaps some future evolutionary form, more amorphous than he, would be capable of developing in numerous directions at once, but he was only a linear man, he had only two legs, he could only walk. To seek multiplicity meant only that he would remain in the square, revolving, beholding. Which was an impossibility. Whether he liked it or not, it was human nature to be in constant motion, to change, however imperceptibly, from day to day, minute to minute. Only when he died would he attain stability. To remain in the square was to die, to non-exist, to become finite. As long as he existed he had to leave the safety of the square. He could never linger for more than a moment or two. He had no choice.

But whenever he found himself on the open road, it was not long before the road itself began to curve, as in some theoretical attitudes a straight line is an impossibility and sooner or later becomes a curve. He continued to follow the road because to his vision the curve was imperceptible, because his motion was taking him from some place to some place, from one point to another. The idea of progress, of advancing in space, however, was illusory, for as he walked, the curve sharpened, and soon enough he perceived the square ahead of him, the same square he had left, with the same fountains and kiosks, the same demarcations of light and shadow, and then he would be in it once more, revolving and beholding.

He believed that the curves were of his own making. Somewhere the straight road existed. He had only to persevere. He would find it, he would follow it, and it would lead him ever further from the square and the city which harbored the square. Meanwhile his own mind blinded him from this straight road, convincing him that the curving tangents he followed were the straight road, which, though in reality it extended right before him, was masked by mirages of buildings, cul-de-sacs, and similar obstructions concocted by his mind. And how could he argue with his mind when he saw the road before him with his own eyes? How could he doubt his senses?

He was, he thought, continually betrayed by his timidity, by his unwillingness to venture very far from the neighborhoods he knew by heart, from these avenues which emanated from the square. With all other men, few of whom ever really left the neighborhoods in which they were born, he must share this fear of unfamiliar buildings and streets, of dialects and languages he couldn't understand, of regulations the very existence of which he ignored. Yes, he told himself, men would travel, would venture forth, because they had to, but how long would they stay away, how long before their minds would propel them homeward? His own mind, confronted with the choice of what it was and what it might be, had always opted for the familiar.

Was he only a pattern man? Were all men only pattern men? He could not disprove it from the evidence. He changed, yes, because he was alive, and being alive, he had to leave the square, but his changes always followed the pattern of the circling tangent, were invariably characterized by equal measures of forward and retrograde motion. Viewed from a distance, his whole life had been a series of little circling motions of similar length and duration, beginning and ending at the same central point. He was always back where he had started. He was always back with himself. And if the Henhouse was any different, it was only because of its absence of illusion, of pretense. The road to the Hen was straight. It began and ended. He walked its length every day, twice a day, and he returned its length twice every day.

If life was more than a series of repeated patterns, of circular adventures and returns, if his straight road existed, wouldn't he once have seen it? At least once, on all his starts and returns, wouldn't his mind have been sufficiently lulled or diverted to allow his eyes to perceive it, if fleetingly? In fact he had never once seen it, though he had looked and would continue to look, having no choice but to leave the square by one or another of its avenues. He believed intuitively in the road's existence. He assumed that it was there, to be found, though eventually, if the process remained futile, he supposed he would tire of the effort, the spirit which kept him in motion would wane, he would leave the square less and less frequently, preferring to loiter among the fountains and kiosks in the company of other old men, and at such a time he would be dying.

Perhaps a different kind of effort was required to find it. This had occurred to him too. Perhaps no one man was capable of it, and only a community of men, searching all the avenues simultaneously like the scouts of an advancing army, could determine once and for all if the road existed. Yet he doubted the efficacy of such an enterprise. Somehow it would fail. He would not join it. If by chance any group of men happened to discover the road and travel it, they would only desecrate it with the trappings of groups, and as far as the Henhouse was concerned, he had learned that he could not count on the help of his fellow inmates.

He would continue to look, however, walking back and forth each day to the Hen. He had no choice. If, as he sometimes suspected, its existence was illusory, the illusion could neither be proved nor disproved, and in any case, he would never know, never know for certain, if somewhere, lurking behind some mirage of buildings or corridors, was not the road he sought.

His contact with other Henhouse inmates had been so minimal as to be meaningless. He met them only in the Hen's anteroom, the small room at the end of the third corridor where he and the functionary waited for the Hen, or where the functionary waited for him at the end of sessions. He saw the same two inmates every day: the one who preceded him and the one who followed. In all his days in the Henhouse, he had encountered only three other inmates, and always at the same place: the small, white-walled anteroom with the red-tiled floor and the four metal chairs, two against each facing wall.

If he was Inmate Y, then the other three inmates he had seen were Inmates X, X^1 and Z. In his early Henhouse days Y was preceded at the Hen by X and followed by Z. Twice each day he saw X on his arrival and Z upon leaving. The routine never varied until one morning, when he arrived in the anteroom, he found the Hen waiting for him, his door already open. Immediately he had begun speculating on X's whereabouts. He could not ask the Hen. The Hen would only sidestep. Of course there were obvious explanations, any number of them. Perhaps X was sick. Perhaps X too had decided to resist the Hen, though, from what Y already knew of the man, that was unlikely.

No session had taken place that afternoon, which was not of itself unusual, but the following morning, he had been astonished to encounter a man he had never seen before in the Hen's anteroom, the stocky blond-haired inmate he was to refer to as X^1.

Z was waiting outside the Hen's door when his own

session ended that morning, old Z, who always wore a tie
and jacket. Old Z. Y and Z were the long-termers, the old
Henhouse hands, the veterans. Though in fact Z must still
have been in his twenties, though he couldn't have been
much older than X or X^1, he nonetheless had a way of
looking old, as if he had vaulted straight from diapers into
the clothes and demeanor of a respectable man of affairs. He
was virtually indistinguishable from the Henhouse functionaries themselves. Implacable Z, imperturbable Z, old Z, the
kind of man who, if you suddenly accosted him, if you stood
toe-to-toe in his way and shouted obscenities at him, would
only say, "I'm terribly sorry," as if you had asked him the
time of day and he was apologizing for not carrying a watch.
Y and Z. After X's departure, they became linked in his mind
as the Hen's trusties, or his incurables or at least his regulars,
a comical picture for he could not imagine a less likely
combination of twins. Taken together, they attested to the
democracy of the Henhouse, the catholicity of the Hen's
selections.

Yet what had happened to X?

X did not return. He kept expecting to see him, yet
knowing all the time that he would not see him. X's disappearance gnawed at him, not because of the man himself—
after what X had done to him he could not concern himself
over his fate—but because of the mystery of it and just
because any break in the Henhouse pattern, from the
slightest procedural variation to the disappearance of an
inmate, filled him with an unanswerable anxiety. Where had
X gone? Or: How had they disposed of him? Was he dead?
It was preposterous to assume that he was dead, but was it
that impossible, couldn't it have happened? Or had he contrived to escape? Had he really found a way out through the
maze of doors and corridors? For wasn't that what the

Henhouse consisted of, wasn't that it: of corridors upon
corridors, of doors opening onto still other corridors and
corridors ending in doors? The callous indifference of the
Hen and the functionaries, the way they proceeded as if X
had never existed, only deepened his anxiety and finally
drove the subject of X into the open.

"Why do you concern yourself so about the other members," the Hen had replied finally, after Y had asked his
questions and speculated endlessly on the possibilities, after
a whole day, two whole sessions, in which the Hen had said
virtually nothing, as was his wont, as was his clever way of
letting silence work on Y, drawing Y out of himself by
silence, "when you know perfectly well they need not concern you? You see, you are wandering again, cluttering your
mind with extraneous materials. No? Is it not so?"

So that X's disappearance remained a mystery. He would
not have expected X to escape or to try to escape, not after
what had happened between them, not X, the slender, ath-
letic youth with the shock of auburn hair which always
seemed about to fall into his eyes, who reminded him on first
impression of characters he had encountered in various
novels, the kind who always manages to be three places at
once, flitting tirelessly about his fictional world on errands,
ubiquitous, prying, all-knowing. That was X, with the small
dark eyes set close together which darted about the anteroom, taking in the three faces—the two attendants and Y—
in a single, darting glance. X who had betrayed him.

The idea of trusting X, of confiding in him, of seeking a
collaboration with him, had come to him as an impulse one
morning, which was when all his bizarre notions attacked
him, when the mindrace was in full force, when he had little
control over his mental processes, little perspective, when
small fancies loomed as reality and the real world of the

Henhouse diminished into an unperceived background. His
mind had been describing tangents and circles for him,
setting actual points in space in motion so that they curved
and circled, this way and that, here and there. He had been
thinking about the road, the actual road which he could
trace with his finger on a map if he could only find the map,
when the impulse struck him. Hastily, before the functionary appeared, he scribbled on a piece of paper which he
then crumpled into a wad and concealed in his fist. When, in
the anteroom, the Hen's door slid open, he arose immediately so as to pass X as near to the doorway as possible.
Quickly, exultantly, he thrust the wad of paper into X's
hand, so quickly that he was certain neither of the functionaries had noticed.

He had chosen X as his confidant over Z not because he
trusted X but because he did not trust himself. How could
he pass an entire session with the Hen and successfully
conceal his possession of the wad of paper? Once he had
written the note, once he had crumpled it into a ball, once
he had carried it on his person, he had to rid himself of it at
the first opportunity. Then too, he had put himself into Z's
position. How would he himself react if someone thrust a
wad of paper into his hand, a foreign, unexpected object,
just before he entered the Hen's office? Could he conceal it?
No, of course not! Nor, in all probability, could Z, despite his
imperturbability, his functionary's demeanor, for how could
anyone, even Z, remain imperturbable before the Hen?

It had had to be X then, X with the darting eyes, whether
he trusted him or not.

When he entered the Hen's office that same afternoon, the
first thing he noticed was the crumpled piece of paper
spread out absurdly on the dark polished wood of the Hen's
desk top. It was his paper. He recognized his own writing. In

it, he had merely stated his name, had written that he lived
on the third corridor from the anteroom where they met. He
did not know how long he had been in the society, he had
said. He would appreciate any information on why they
were there, to what end they were being held captive.
Finally, he had wanted to know what the recipient thought
of their captor.

He had hesitated so over that last word, over how to refer
to the Hen. The Hen was his own name; he had never used
it; it would mean nothing to X. None of the titles he could
think of—interrogator, administrator, leader—was sufficiently inclusive. The Hen was all of these, yet he was more.
At times the Hen's manner resembled a doctor's, or a psychiatrist's, but Y was not a patient, the Hen himself had insisted
that he not consider himself a patient. He had thought also
of *professeur*, but discarded it lest the intended irony
confuse X. Finally, fearful that the door might open and the
functionary appear at any moment, he had settled on
"captor."

If his reflex on seeing the piece of paper was to fear the
Hen's reaction, to anticipate reprisal, the gleam of humor in
the Hen's eyes and his accompanying chuckle reassured him.
The Hen was only amused: by the formality of the note's
expression, by its assumption that any other member of the
society would automatically know more of the society's
functioning than Y himself. He was sure the Hen would
resent the "captor," the repeated implication that the inmates were being confined against their will, that they were
pitted against him as prisoners against their jailer—the Hen
referred to them too often as a society of members for him
not to resent it—yet this time, if he felt it, he kept his
resentment to himself.

Instead he had focused on Y's anger toward X, an anger

which surged in him from the moment he saw the paper on the Hen's desk, a fury at X's betrayal. Not that X, as he called him, need concern him at all, but why, the Hen had wanted to know, was he so angry?

"After all," the Hen had mused, in his reflective pose, the spectacles twirling between thumb and forefinger, the bald dome glistening in chandelier light, "what would you have done in such a situation? Put the case this way. Suppose, let us suppose, that an utter stranger, a man perhaps you had seen before but someone you didn't know, not at all, suddenly thrust a piece of paper into your hand without warning, and in a moment which you, yourself, would consider precarious. Wouldn't you tell about it to a person you knew much better, a person you were accustomed to confide in, a person who knew more about you than anyone else?"

"No," Y had replied confidently. No. No, he would not. He did not yet believe in betraying others. Maybe his own time would come, but not yet.

"Please to think about it, though," the Hen had persisted. "Wouldn't you at least want to? Wouldn't a part of you, some part under your skin, feel a desire to tell about it?"

He hadn't answered.

"Well," the Hen had sighed finally, "perhaps you would think about it. I am not so sure you know what you would do. It is not always so easy for us to say what we would do in such a hypothetical circumstance. And do you know"—the Hen had looked into his eyes, the corners of his mouth lifting into a smile—"I really do think you might tell me about it after all."

Later, after X had been replaced in the Hen's schedule by X^1, it occurred to him to link the two incidents, the note and X's disappearance. He surmised that, at the time of the message, X's case had advanced to such a point, X had made sufficient progress, to enable him to hand the paper over without qualm. That was what the Hen wanted then, lackeys as docile as X. X's disappearance was thus merely a sign that he had graduated, that his case was over, to be disposed of by whatever method the Hen employed to rid himself of his graduates. Nonetheless, he kept expecting to see X again, coming through the anteroom door, and he could never recall him, could never summon forth the darting, calculating eyes, without a resurgence of anger. Never again, after the incident until the day of X's sudden disappearance, had he looked him in the face, much less exchanged the hesitant nods of greeting which were characteristic among the inmates.

The idea was not inaccurate, however, the idea of communication, of collaboration. The idea was sound. It began to tease him. The road remained to be found, did it not, his elusive road? He resolved to try again. His choice had been stupid, that was all. X had been too far advanced to be of use to him, X, the well-trained betrayer. Then why not the newcomer?

But in the end he had abandoned the scheme. He got as far as writing the message, a few well-considered words, before realizing that the picture of him seeking to hand it to X^1 was unalterably ludicrous. He had watched X^1's bland blue eyes. He could see them as he handed him the note suddenly widening in utter astonishment, his hand recoiling as if goosed by a live wire, his whole body quivering like a startled cat at the very idea of someone touching him. For that would have been Y's own state of mind back at the beginning, apprehensive at every gesture, every advance.

That the scheme was unfulfilled made no difference, however. The details of it had inevitably come to light before the

Hen. Just as if he had actually handed the note to X^1, just as if, as had occurred in fantasy, X^1 had dropped the paper in terror, and as if the Hen, rising from his desk to greet him as he rose this morning of the Canfield and at the beginning of every session, and, rising, saw the exchange, the piece of paper, and grasped their significance, so the Hen had offered the same laughing comment at the end of Y's exposition:

"I see, then, that we are up to our child's play again."

4   The Hen

ω

"Come in," said the Hen, the morning of the Canfield, rising behind his desk, waving in the general direction of the two armchairs.

Y half expected to see the wad of paper uncrumpled and stretched out on the desk top between the pipestand and the pads. It was not there, of course it was not, but that was what the Hen had done to him. The Hen had taken him by the shoulders and turned him around so that his mind now described tangential circles in his past, so that, for example, when he saw X^1 leaving the Hen's office, the message incident recurred in all its details.

No matter how many times he had performed the ritual, he was never able to enter the office without anxiety: not merely because he was confronting the Hen again and thereby, like a student in oral examination, putting himself on display, but because of the contrast between the office and the rest of the Henhouse. His own room, the corridors, the anteroom, were purely functional, institutional. The office, with its muted wallpaper, its carpeting, its chandelier, had a personality, almost a cosmopolitan flavor, as if its owner were indeed what Y called him in sardonic moments: the refugee from Vienna. The desk was weighty and huge, adorned with heavy carvings and scrollwork. Its top, dark and polished, was invariably bare save for the familiar articles: the pads and pencils neatly arrayed, the large ashtray, the pipestand and tobacco jar which was sealed or opened by a metal disc, the Hen's glasscase and penknife, with which, at times, he scraped at his pipe bowls. The wall to the right was lined with glass-fronted bookcases. Behind the desk hung heavy damask drapes, ceiling to floor, wall to wall. What these drapes concealed Y had never determined, but, by another of his choices which had nothing to do with logical argument, he liked to think there would be windows behind them, windows which perhaps gave out on the vista he had seen: the grassy, undulating landscape. Still, there were other times when he was absolutely certain the drapes hid nothing but a blank, papered wall, that they were a Hen trick, an illusion.

The office symbolized his ambivalent attitudes toward the Hen. It was a station on his cyclical wanderings, the point at which tangents began. He walked the straight line to the office just as he walked the straight line to the Hen. But the office constituted the terminal obstacle of his route, an obstacle he could not breach. Here he was diverted, turned around, reoriented toward his room, reoriented toward his past. As much as he wanted to believe the Hen, to believe in the Hen, a part of him could only resent him, resent the proof the office itself gave that the Hen's insistence on "membership," and its corollary implications of equality and the happy family of the Henhouse, were sham. In the course of sessions, as his initial anxiety evaporated, he might begin to enjoy his surroundings, lulled by the intricacies of desk

carvings, the patterns of light reflection from bookcase glass
and desk top, the ever-twirling spectacles, which even now
as he sat down began slowly to twirl. But sessions ended and
sessions began, and the change, the abrupt contrasts between the twin poles of room and office, jerked him back to
the reality of his situation. Invariably he entered the Hen's
office with mixed apprehension and resentment, a combination which could erupt into belligerence, were it not for the
miracle of the Hen's performance, the miracle by which Y's
most intensely felt emotions were lulled and soothed and
transformed.

"Yes," the Hen said. "How is it today?"

A usual opener, Y reflected, annoyed by its very famil-
iarity, a favorite selected from the Hen's quiver of openers.
Even the openers had to be calculated, as the effects of
everything the Hen did or said were calculated. He sat in
silence. He tried to count minutes, but soon he gave up. The
Hen waited for him, idly twirling his spectacles, waiting for
him to begin, to start the display once more. He watched the
smooth skin of the plump fingers as they manipulated the
spectacles, watched the spectacles themselves, the light
glinting from them at several points on their circuit, then
abruptly fixed his eyes on the top of the Hen's head, the
ruddy bald dome.

"We played solitaire this morning," he began, blurting out
the confession, "you and I. One round of Canfield. Then the
functionary came. I used Swiss francs." He laughed. His
words were always so stilted when the Hen made him begin.
His laughter fizzled. He waited for a reaction, but the Hen
said nothing. Did the Hen know what he was talking about?
Had he described the game for his benefit? Yes he had. Of
course.

Irritated by the silence, which led him to wonder if the

Hen was listening, he continued: "Oh, I know what you're going to say so you don't have to trouble yourself to say it. Childish games. I'm wasting my time with these childish games. Yes, they're childish. I admit it, and it's worse than that. Yes, worse. There I go again, you'll say: pitting myself against you, that's what you'll say, setting you up as my rival and enemy, even in these imaginary childish games of solitaire. Solitaire. Yes, it's childish. I know it.

"Well, it can't be helped. If that's what I'm doing, it can't be helped. I can't help it, and that's all there is to it."

He would have liked to convince himself that there had been at least an element of doubt as to his intention, that the Canfield might be of negligible significance. But there could be no doubt. The Hen was never wrong. He had to admit that what he had wanted more than anything was to best the Hen, to annihilate him, even if it was only at Canfield. Black eight on red nine and the clean 208-franc coup. That was what he had wanted, and he wanted it again right now, and over and over again until the Hen's resources were wiped out, all the way to the last chip. He wanted that last chip too. Black eight on red nine.

He remembered the cheating, then, but the cheating was irrelevant, there was no need to talk about it, he didn't want to mention it, so he hastened on: "Well, what you'll want to know now is why I persist in this childishness, in these silly games and this pitting myself against you like two adversaries. I know all the time that it is just foolishness and inaccurate. So how can I keep doing it? Isn't that it?

"Yes . . . Well, I'll tell you. If you insist, I'll tell you the truth. I've been thinking again about it, about leaving. In fact, it's all I can think about. I want out. I want to get out. I want it, I still want it, it's all I want. And I don't think anything you can say or do is going to change me."

He looked at the Hen's eyes, first in challenge, then quietly in apology for what he had said, but the eyes merely continued to study him in that familiar, sad gaze, the spectacles twirling in the air. He looked back at the bald dome.

"I suppose it sounds crazy . . . I know it does, it almost embarrasses me to say it, but it's your fault for insisting on knowing everything . . . Damn!" He hated himself for this stalling, for his constant apologizing. He stopped, mentally stiffened, then started again. "You'll want to know the connection between the Canfield and the leaving. As crazy as it sounds, it was on my mind that, if I won a few times, if you paid me the two hundred and eight francs a few times, if I got maybe a thousand francs ahead, I could quit and buy the ticket to somewhere. Yes, that was it! The ticket! It would have been like buying the ticket! *That was my fantasy!*"

He emphasized the last sentence, wanting to insist upon its truth. Then, anticipating the Hen's next question—how many times had he heard it already—he hurried again to answer it before it could come: "I know, nowhere."

He looked back into the Hen's eyes, but the eyes said nothing to him. Damn them! Damn the Hen! Why did he always find himself in the position of carrying on both ends of the dialogue?

"I know, I have no place to go.

"And it is true," he went on. "You always ask me where it is I want to go when I'm talking this way, even though you know perfectly well what my answer is going to be: that I have no place, nothing I can point to that I want to do or see, no pressing business, no waiting family.

"So why all the rush? Why am I always in such a rush to go?

"Don't you see, though? Really, come now, surely you see that it doesn't make any difference, that the urge is the same, that I feel it anyway—Yes, I still do feel it—and that not all the talking we do will change the feeling."

He might be lying to a degree. He did lie some, sometimes. He might be trying to persuade himself as much as the Hen.

Of course, he realized, of course he was lying! That was it! That was what the Hen was waiting for him to discover! And confess! He wouldn't have stopped at a thousand francs, the price of a ticket. Not for a minute! He had wanted it all while he was at it, all the Hen's chips, every last one. The ticket be damned!

But the other urge still existed. Oh yes. Given the chance, he would still walk right out of the Henhouse. He wouldn't hesitate two seconds.

It was only that some of his old fervor was gone. He was an old-timer now, a veteran, like Z. He and Z were the regulars, and regulars were not like newly captured animals who would stop at nothing to escape the bars of their cages. He and Z were zoo beasts, domesticated.

Or perhaps, he reflected, it was that when you wanted something over a long-enough period of time, and the wanting was repeated constantly to the point of obsession yet remained unanswered, some of the sting went out of it, the act of wanting itself degenerated into ritual.

"Did you win?"

The Hen's words, his first since the beginning of the session, jolted him.

"What?"

"Did you win?" the Hen repeated. "In the solitaire?"

He shook his head.

He was unwilling to admit his defeat, even though he knew it could not make the least difference to the Hen.

"No," he said, at last, his voice subsiding, "it cost me

twelve francs. Still, I had every chance to win, and in fact I came that close." He indicated the margin with thumb and forefinger. "About as close as you can come without winning."

Then, despite his earlier reluctance, the whole story of the cheating came out, as if drawn from him by a magnet. He told it honestly, going into all the details of the game in explanation, from the character of the initial layout to the critical point, omitting nothing from his account save the issue of whether or not the Hen had distracted him into committing the crucial error. He left that out. It might be taken as an apology, an excuse, a shifting of blame, even though it remained possible in his mind that the Hen had deceived him into defeat.

When he had finished, the Hen asked: "What do you think about it?"

"About what? About what in particular?"

"The cheating."

"The cheating? Yes, the cheating. I thought you might not mind, not really. It was only a question of two hundred and eight francs, no great sum to you. After all, I wanted to win. As silly as it sounds, it was important to me to win, whereas you wouldn't particularly care."

"Why *didn't* you, then?"

"Why didn't I cheat?" He stopped, momentarily puzzled, having to relive the scene. "Why, because the functionary came for me. I was debating about how you would react, and then the door opened. The functionary was waiting. There was no time to finish."

"Well? But suppose you had had the time? Suppose he hadn't come? Or let us suppose that, right now, we ended this session so that you could continue your game. What then?"

It was typical of the Hen to worry a subject like a terrier. That was the Hen's way, always attacking the most trivial subjects, always relentless when something petty caught his attention. He hadn't even wanted to bring the cheating up, and there it was, impaled on the desk like a choice specimen.

"No," Y said, disappointed by his admission, "I guess I wouldn't cheat anyway. I'd cash in the cards and start another shuffle."

"Even if it meant your ticket, a free ticket to wherever it is you want to go?"

There it was then.

The idea of the ticket was not new. He'd imagined it before, the whole story, but he had never talked about it. It embodied the left hand of his ambivalence toward the Hen as much as the office signified the right. The Hen was going to give him a ticket, the Hen really intended to, if only he gave the right answer. Sometimes the answer would be Yes, sometimes No. It didn't matter. Like a magician conjuring a rabbit from thin air, the Hen was going to produce a stamped piece of paper, complete with the Henhouse seal: his ticket, his diploma. With a flourish the Hen would sign it. They would shake hands. Off he would go, by himself, descending far down into the bowels of the Henhouse, which had grown incomparably vast for the occasion, deeper into the earth than any inmate had ever ventured, to a huge underground station. There he waited on a long, empty, windy platform until, far off, he saw the locomotive slowly wheezing and steaming around the last curve, dragging the line of coaches behind it.

Seeing the coaches, he saw the rest of the story, and knew what his answer had to be.

"No," he said quietly, "I wouldn't. Not even then."

He hated the rest of the story, he hated to think about it.

It made him wince, for it nullified everything he professed to
believe about his situation, and it proved the Hen right. But
he had started it, and it sped through his mind again like the
landscape flickering past the windows of his train. It was
this landscape which always defeated him, this landscape he
hated to look at. Always he tried to close his eyes, but he
couldn't. He couldn't resist the temptation, once the train
had left the underground station.

The countryside grew increasingly familiar, but he saw, to
his astonishment, that it had been horribly mutilated, as if
an army of monsters, sweeping across its length and breadth,
had deliberately and meticulously defaced it. Its houses
were shells, gutted, emaciated, clustered together like refu-
gees in deserted towns. The streets of the towns were empty,
except for clumps of abandoned vehicles. Traffic signals
blinked and changed absurdly. And the names of the towns!
He couldn't read the names!

Between the towns, acres of empty burnt fields, forests of
gnarled trees, whizzed past his window, extending under a
sunless gray sky which blanketed the world. On the tele-
phone poles which clicked past, the lines hung askew,
dangled, drooped. As always, he turned to shout at his
fellow passengers, to question, to protest, but his voice
would not function. He couldn't speak above a whisper, and
his whispers were unheard. They must be used to the landscape, he thought. Having seen it many times, they didn't
even bother to look. They read their newspapers, chattered
at each other, ate their lunches, as the train sped on. Finally,
to his relief, it slowed. Finally it stopped, in the city he
thought he knew, but when he had left the train and entered
the station, he saw that all the signs—the billboards, the
directions—were printed in a strange, indecipherable language, and he realized immediately that all the chatter he

had been hearing in the coach and all the hubbub of voices in the station were totally unintelligible to him.

The whole sequence of images never lasted more than a few seconds, and there, this time, was the Hen's voice summoning him from his reverie, but once more he was overwhelmed by what he had seen. It was like an old, recurrent piece of mindrace which haunted him, a fragment of mindrace experienced at breakneck speed: this chatter, this mutilation . . .

"Good," the Hen was saying softly, calling him back to the subject of the cheating, "good. You see, we are perhaps making some progress after all."

Suddenly he felt tears begin to well in his head, as if the Hen's words had released an emotional trigger in him. It was not just shock, however, at the Hen's praise which brought on the emotion. Was this what he expected to find, this mutilated world which used a language he couldn't speak, this landscape which had turned barren and foreign in his absence? Or was this what he thought he had seen, long ago? How long ago was it? Or what? What was it the mindrace was trying to tell him? But that was just the way the mindrace worked, that was what drove him to Canfield or doubledeck or other mindless pursuits in the mornings: this confusion of images, this doubt, this indecisiveness, this lack of wholeness, this jumble—all at a dizzying pace, like the train itself.

He had answered truthfully, and the Hen was right, he reflected. Yes, he had made progress. But the reflection was tinged with bitterness. Time was, had he been asked the question about the cheating, he might likewise have answered "No," but only in deception, only as part of a tactical maneuver. Well, now he was done with tactics. He had progressed. Or time was he would have answered "Yes." Yes, he would have cheated for a ticket out of the Henhouse, he would have done anything for it, and he would have answered accordingly, with his head raised in defiance, seeking to stare down the soft brown eyes. Time was the question would never have been asked, for the answer would have been self-evident to the two of them. But he had progressed. Or they had progressed. If certain circumstances remained in which he still might cheat, no, he could no longer cheat the Hen.

The Hen was busying himself with his pipe, a pot-shaped pipe selected from the pipestand. The plump fingers were tamping tobacco inside the bowl, then fumbling with matches. The pipe was all that mattered. He might just as well not have been present.

That was the Hen's way too. The Hen used silence expertly, like a pianist, or a chess master toying with his opponent. He used it sparingly, for maximum effect. In other sessions he rushed Y through his catechisms like a prosecutor attacking a reluctant witness. But the silences worked best, a realization which never failed to unnerve Y, as it did now, when, at what appeared to be a point of breakthrough, or at least a widening of the circle, the Hen could think of nothing better to do than fiddle with his pipes. When he'd first encountered the silences, when he'd entered the office and sat and waited, and continued to sit and wait while the Hen twirled his glasses or fumbled with his pipes, he hadn't known how to react. He had tried to stare the Hen down in silence, to outgaze the sad eyes behind the glasses, but he had never succeeded, no matter how he goaded himself. Always he would avert his own eyes, and then the tension would start to build. (He felt it now. He realized he was turning his eyes away that very moment, but he couldn't help it. He realized what was happening, he knew the process backward and foward, and *still* the tension built!)

No, he could never outwait the Hen. The "refugee from Vienna" was an expert, a professional. If Freud had discovered the efficacy of silence, had codified it into a system, the disciple had nonetheless outstripped the inventor. He had found in the end that his only way of handling silence was to ignore it, to go on talking as if the dialogue were still in progress, even if it meant manipulating both prongs of the dialogue himself without the Hen's help, to talk about anything which struck him, anything whatsoever which entered his mind—which was precisely what the Hen hoped to achieve.

He understood the technique, knew that the erratic vacillation of his emotions during the sessions was caused by these very silences, the Hen allowing him to be tricked into gratitude or anger by his own mind careening in silence, and therefore he loathed it. The fact that he understood only heightened his antagonism. As efficient as it was, it was yet a cruel device. The Hen was tricking him. The Hen was a master of deception, adept at cheap devices. What he would have given for a device of his own, a means of shaking the man's aplomb, his cool, appraising gaze, his damned impervious patience!

"Well, let me tell you something," he said harshly, no longer able to sustain the unequal competition. "Listen to me now. Maybe I have made some progress. You would have me believe that the fact that I wouldn't cheat you signifies progress in many areas, and maybe you are right. Maybe I have progressed, maybe I've changed. All right, I'm willing to admit it. I admit it.

"You've changed me then. You've won. I won't cheat to win. I'll no longer pay any price, and that's just what you

want, isn't it? To be able to set the asking price higher than
what I'll pay, to know my limit and exceed it, so that you
can say: 'You see? When it comes down to it, you didn't
really want to leave all this time. Is it not so?' "

The bitterness implicit in his mimicry surprised him, and
yet, imprisoned by the bitter spirit, he plunged on:

"So. You've succeeded in changing me. Bravo! But let me
tell you something else: I'm not proud of it. Not for a
minute. Not at all. I wish I wasn't what you've made me. I'd
rather be what I used to be. I was a child, you'll say, oh yes,
I was a child, I did childish things, I rebelled like a child
against the status quo, just because it was the status quo.
That was my cycle, my habit. And now it is different. Now I
accept the status quo. Now I'm the good soldier.

"Well, you've won. I congratulate you. It's worked, all of
it, and I congratulate you on your skill and prowess. I only
hope you're satisfied with what you've produced."

Suddenly he felt exhausted by his effort, as if his bitterness
was warm water washing him toward sleep. He had nothing
more to say. He wanted only to leave, to regain his room as
quickly as possible, to lie on his bed. Dimly he recognized
again the extent to which these sessions were a microcosm of
his emotional sequences, that all the shifts and divagations
of his emotional life could be crammed into the short timespan of the session like gifts into a Christmas stocking.

The aplomb with which the Hen had listened did not
alter. Swirls of smoke rose from the Hen's pipe, eddying
slowly in wreaths around the chandelier to settle in stratus
layers under the ceiling. The Hen puffed in the silence,
filling the air with the aromatic scent of his tobacco. Then
he put the pipe down on the desk, balancing it carefully
until it stood by itself, and then at length he spoke:

"Just two observations, or two groups of observations.

One: you are angry with yourself for feeling gratitude toward me. This is old business, isn't it? I won't dwell on it, only to say that the anger is inaccurate." Here the Hen paused, as he always paused after the use of the word. "You were honest, and I complimented you for your honesty. Whatever you may think, that is not at all like a dog being petted by his master. On the contrary. You were honest with yourself, which pleased me and should please you. It is scarcely a crime for us to thank ourselves for our own honesty, is it not so?

"But we have talked this through before, and I need not say anything about it.

"The other is that your unwillingness to cheat in the solitaire indicates, as you pointed out, that you are not now in such a hurry to leave us as you once thought you were. This is a new idea to you, it frightened you, so you were compelled to defend yourself. But new ideas have frightened people from the beginning of time. If they are accurate, they frighten people all the more. People have to get used to them.

"Let me say this: we have still a long way to go before your case can be concluded, but we have time, time to use the progress we have made. And we have made progress, perhaps further than you realize. And still we have plenty of time.

"Or let me put it another way for you. Let me use your own idea, this impression of yours of the cycles, the circular motions. Perhaps this time, of all times, you have walked *past* the point where you always turn around, where the circling always starts. You have gone a little farther. You are farther away from the center than ever before, and still the road has not begun to curve, as far as you can tell. Good! All to the good!

"You see, I don't wish to belabor the point. But might it not be that we are on your road at last, and that the farther we walk the straighter it will become?"

In spite of himself, the Hen's voice had soothed him. He subsided further. Often it affected him this way, lulling him merely by its timbre. Impelled by the silence, he had worked himself into a fever of excitement far beyond the boundaries of reality. The silence had caused him to lose his grip on his own stability, to struggle in the swamp of his own ideas. Just a word or a few words from the Hen had brought him quickly back to dry land.

Had he found his road? Why not? After all, why not?

Before the Hen had even finished, his anger had evaporated into myriad particles. It had been the mindrace which had plagued him, which had driven him to anger, the mindrace and the morning, when his grasp on himself was never secure, when the naked fragments of the mindrace darted uncontrolled through the corridors of his mind until he could only clamp the corridors shut by force of will. The silence had reopened the corridors; the silence had driven him to resentment.

Seized then by a craving which arose from he knew not what source but which attacked him with a gnawing intensity, he was suddenly wide awake, his mind hyper-alert, and he was asking the logical question, the one question which mattered:

"Then can't you tell me something about why I am here?"

"Yes," the Hen said, smiling.

Before he could recover from his surprise, the Hen went on: "Yes. I will tell you something, though unfortunately you have heard me say it before. You are going to live with your guilt."

His initial excitement and surprise were quickly dispersed.

Not only had he heard the words before, but, as he realized again in pondering the statement, whatever meaning it contained was hidden in the oracular phrasing of which the Hen was so fond, a phrasing at once cryptic and hopelessly elusive.

5 The Mindrace

⟨⟩

He was walking through a vast hall of mirrors and myriad pillars, larger than all the halls he had ever seen or even imagined, with entrances and exits and corridors leaving and entering at asymmetric angles. He was walking slowly, strolling, in slow motion.

The hall was infinitely populated. Throngs of people hurried through it, rushing among the pillars in groups, in pairs, singly, on a variety of errands, their numbers multiplied further by their mirrored reflections. In color and feature, they represented the human races. They wore the clothes of all the ages of history. There were Romans draped in togas, monks from the Middle Ages, English children out of Gainsborough paintings, Japanese in Western business suits as well as kimonos, astronauts in space helmets. At times the races and ages were incongruously mixed. He saw Negroes dressed like Greek orators, Nordic women in saris, Orientals in the robes and headdresses of American Indians. Wherever he turned, and he turned constantly as he progressed through the hall, revolving slowly in his tracks, around and

around, he saw people rushing past each other, jostling and
jostled, intent on their errands. Every man, woman, and
child was talking, employing countless languages and the
whole range of pitch possible for the human voice. Some
shouted at each other as they hastened by; others cursed the
turbulence, the masses which blocked their way. He heard
snatches of whispers, the crying of children, the staccato
chatter of an unintelligible Oriental tongue. The constant
din of the vast hall rang in his ears, yet from the cacophony
he picked out smatterings of foreign speech, never more
than a word or two or at most a few phrases before the
speaker had rushed by, to be replaced by others, scurrying
every which way, bumping into him, shouting incomprehen-
sible fragments of sentences in his ears, to be replaced in
turn by others.

As he walked through the hall, suddenly, as if everything
he saw and heard were on film and sound track, the scene
accelerated. The people began to run, their legs darting,
scurrying, as legs had darted and scurried in early films,
doubletiming at incredible speeds in and out of corridors, in
this exit, out that entrance, quick quick quick, scurrying,
scurrying, their voices rising in pitch so that even those
fragments of language he had once been able to understand
now became utterly unintelligible. At such a moment, in
spite of himself, his own legs began to move at ever-quicken-
ing speed. He couldn't resist. He was intoxicated by the
pace. He joined the darting mob, shouting words he couldn't
hear in the general din, searching frantically for an exit,
elbowing and shoving like the others, darting into this corridor, sprinting its length only to find it ending in a cul-de-sac,
backtracking, his legs aching from the strain but unable to
slow their pace, back to the vast mirrored hall, darting,
scurrying. As he ran he searched anxiously in the mirrors,

but not once was he able to pick himself out in the multi-
colored swirl of humanity.

Then the cameras increased their speed again. Individual
figures became lost in a blur of revolving colors. The noise
mounted higher still to a deafening shriek. And he was
spinning, spinning and shouting at the top of his lungs, until
what he saw became too much for him to bear and his own
agonizing howl pierced and shattered the image.

The vast hall of mirrors was one of the metaphors he had
seized upon in attempting to describe the mindrace. The hall
itself was his skull. The stranger walking through the
crowds, the observer, the self, was his mind. The throngs of
people in motion were the jumble of fragmentary ideas,
memories, colors, noises, words, which wheeled and ca-
reened through his head during the mindrace.

Yet he found the metaphor inadequate, inaccurate. He
was dissatisfied with it. It was too organized, too rational.
The mindrace was not constituted of people, of tangible
entities, but of an asymmetric mosaic of bits and pieces,
some of them recognizable, but the majority of which he
never succeeded in comprehending. The mindrace was never
experienced in slow motion. Its components could never be
frozen and examined at leisure, much less for a few fractions
of seconds. Rather they darted momentarily into his field of
perception and then fled, like electrons escaping a nucleus,
sometimes to return, sometimes to disappear forever. He
could never track the flight of any one element. Its place
would immediately be occupied by a successor, or cluster of
successors, which demanded his attention, only to be
bumped in turn from his concentration by a new batch of
intruding elements.

He had discovered that the mindrace experience was not

unique to him. Once he had read the autobiography of a
South American mystic, or aspirant to mysticism, and he had
copied down a particular passage:

> Usually these experiences took place at night, when I
> went to bed. In that half-world between consciousness and
> unconsciousness I would have the feeling that a switch
> had turned which made me lose all control of myself. The
> objects in the room where I lay would lose their equi-
> librium, and my ordinary relationship to them would
> disappear. I could see myself moving and acting at a
> tremendous speed, while inside my head thousands of
> words would gush forth at an increasing tempo. I would
> feel dizzy and helpless, and the only way I could escape
> was to fall into a deep sleep.

When he first read it, the passage astonished and exhilarated him. He was relieved to learn merely that the experience was not unique, that he was not alone in the shadowy
realms, the half-worlds, that the mindrace did not, as he had
feared, presage madness, that some other man, even if he
inhabited a faraway country, knew what he knew. Yet their
experiences were not identical. He recognized immediately
the reference to "thousands of words." In the mindrace,
thousands of words gushed into his mind, as if released
through a sluice, traveling at fantastic speeds in the sphere
of his mind, the vast hall, shrieking and reverberating
against the sides of the sphere to rebound again, thousands
of words, but not only words: nonsense syllables, letters,
snatches of phrases, and also a myriad of colors and unver-
balized elements, as if his mind were a supercyclotron capable of generating such noise and speed that he must stop
it or go insane.

There the resemblance ceased. True, his mindrace oc-

curred at night, when he went to bed, but more frequently
he encountered it upon waking, either in the middle of the
night or the morning, when, in the process of departing sleep
and dreams, that coherent world of fantasy, and journeying
toward the other coherent world of reality, his mind paused
in the shadows. Unlike the author of the passage, he could
not escape into sleep. Instead, like a stumbling climber
who desperately seizes the ledge which overhangs the
chasm beneath him, he could only flail for consciousness,
he could only destroy the mindrace by becoming wide
awake and pursuing one or another of his mindless activities.

Although he acknowledged his fear of the mindrace, the
author of the passage nevertheless awoke from the deep
sleep which followed it refreshed and "loving life." On the
counsel of his sage, the mystic who instructed him, he vowed
to pursue it to its bottomless end, wherever that might be. Y
sensed, however, that his own odyssey had to be different,
that it was his lot to emerge from the swamp of the mindrace
if he could, from the circles of mental chaos, as, it was
taught, mankind itself had emerged from the swamp.

Perhaps the mindrace was what the Hen referred to in his
cryptic comment on living with his guilt, which had now
been repeated again. Obviously the Hen relished such op-
portunities for crypticism, for oracular sentences uttered
theatrically at key moments, guru pronouncements of un-
questionable profundity but doubtful meaning. Guilt was a
Hen word, occupying at least as prominent a place as "inaccurate" in the Hen's hierarchy of language. But, though
they had often examined his feelings of guilt about such-and-
such a deed or thought, though surely in the aftermath of his
rebellious acts he had experienced guilt and remorse over
what he had done, and though the Hen had reinforced these
attitudes, still this was not guilt in the abstract, was not

what the Hen meant by "living with his guilt." "Living with his guilt" was a larger concept, as if, in his absence, he had been tried and declared guilty, and now, without knowing either the charges or the bases of judgment, had to accept the judgment, to live with it. Probably a whole series of appraisals and judgments had been made in his case without his knowledge, participation or testimony. If so, the Hen was behind it all, at once prosecutor and judge, collecting evidence directly through the sessions, or indirectly, through the apparatus of his informers—the various Henhouse functionaries, even the other inmates with whom, in the twice-daily ritual of approaching and leaving the Hen, he came in contact. The Hen never charged him. He was only studied and appraised, weighed and judged, without his knowledge or participation. And these processes were continuous. Whenever he sought answers to his questions—Why was he there? How had he come to be chosen for confinement in the society? And, most important, when would his time be up, when could he leave?—the Hen habitually turned him back on himself or, on rare occasions, responded with oracular observations: "You are going to live with your guilt." Still, even an oblique answer was an event of such magnitude, because it was so rare, that he had seized on the words with voracious appetite, masticating them like an animal its cud, turning them this way and that, saying them over and over, writing them down, considering every possible meaning his mind could conceive.

Was the mindrace, then, his guilt? Or an expression of his guilt? If so, where did it come from? What combinations of subconscious processes produced the awful sensation, the careening, the whirring, the caroms of words and particles in collision, which, when he came awake in his bed in the blackness of night or the blackness of morning, signaled that the mindrace was once more imminent?

He had not always been plagued by it, he thought. As a child he had known irrational night fears. The smallest unidentifiable sound in the night, the slightest creak or rustle, would freeze his heart. He would cease breathing and slowly, noiselessly, burrow in his bed, so that the sheets and blankets and at least a piece of pillow covered his head. The habit had lingered with him long after childhood. Even now he could not fall asleep without a covering of some sort, even now, at moments, he found himself holding his breath in the night, in bed. But these relics from childhood bore no relationship to the terrors of the mindrace. The mindrace was a more recent development, even perhaps of the Henhouse, an adult phenomenon, as if its disparate elements could only have collected together in the passage of time, fragments from childhood commingled with the stimuli of later years.

How often he had tried to sort it out, this jumble, this highspeed chaos! Sometimes he thought he recognized individual elements, pieces, for instance, of his fantasy of the ticket and the train, but had he collected and organized this coherent story from the mindrace, or had the mindrace itself, like a giant sponge absorbing all his fantastic materials, seized upon the story and broken it into particles? He had often attempted to write down what he could remember, but his memory was inadequate to the task, the very dimensions of paper restricted him, and the result, which never approximated what he had experienced, was nothing more than a bland and meaningless series of words and syllables. Perhaps electronic devices which recorded the impulses as they occurred could recreate the mindrace accurately, but he doubted that a machine had yet been invented which could capture and encompass the endless variety of constituent materials: the words, the sounds, the colors, and the indescribable fragments which were neither word nor sound nor color. The mindrace was the inchoate universe itself, unformed, unstructured, infinitely varied. And it was this impression of its infinity, together with his realization that he could never possibly absorb the infinity of stimuli delivered at infinite speed, which habitually drove him to destroy it.

But the mindrace as his guilt? Though he had read him the passage from the South American author, though he had recounted his insufficient efforts at recreation and otherwise described it as best he could, the Hen, to his disappointment, exhibited little interest in the mindrace. He listened, to be sure. The Hen always listened. But he offered no comment, his face was a mask of indifference. Unlike his dreams, which the Hen seized upon with the zeal of a psychoanalyst, the mindrace appeared to be outside the Hen's province. The Hen's provinces were the activities of sleep and wakefulness. These furnished the evidence, the raw material, he sought. But this other space between, the shadow world in which occurred a phenomenon neither unconscious nor conscious, fantastic nor real, was a no-man's-land, a limbo, into which the Hen did not choose to venture.

He and the Hen had surveyed the facts of his life countless times, those facts he could remember. Sparse as they might be, they contained no crime or intimation of crime. He had not become a Henhouse inmate, he felt, as a result of due process of law. In a legal sense, he had no cause for guilt, and even when guilt was construed as broadly as possible, so as to include acts of omission, malevolent intentions, the kind of social alegal guilt which, according to certain moralists and theologians, all men shared in greater or lesser portions as part of their inherited condition, he could not accuse himself on the evidence.

This evidence, however, was admittedly fragmentary, inconclusive. His past was viewed as through the wrong end of a telescope, or the wrong ends of telescopes, focusing on this vignette and that impression, recalling sensations, faces, snatches of conversation, scene, event. He could not have written a coherent, exhaustive account of his life, not even a comprehensive chronology. Yet how many men could? he protested. How many could produce more than the type of meaningless skeletal entry found in employment résumés and biographical dictionaries? And what did it matter if a man was born on such-and-such a date in such-and-such a place, if he graduated from these schools, worked in those offices and rose to those positions, married so-and-so, sired this son and that daughter who were christened under the following names, died on such-and-such a date at such-and-such a place?

Memory did not work in well-ordered chronological sequences. At least his memory did not. The least significant impression—the aroma of a certain meal, his score on a test, the joy he experienced the first time he saw palm trees blown by the wind—might occupy a place far more prominent than the death of a close relation. Or it might not. Or again, on a given day it might, and on the day after the given day it might not. Although at times the Hen attacked his memory like a prosecutor (even the Hen, he thought, could be driven to exasperation), his knowledge of his past remained inexact, he had not yet developed the capacity to produce precise, stable data. One session he would recall an event a certain way; another time, despite the Hen's prodding, he would cite completely different, even contradictory details. In abstracted terms, in its chaos, its jumble, his memory resembled the mindrace. But the Hen wasn't interested in the mindrace. The Hen sought facts, like an attorney marshaling evidence for a case, using words like "case" and "progress" and "situation."

The development of his memory even to its presently inadequate state had been a time-consuming task. In the main he had cooperated, delving for indisputable facts, accepting without challenge the Hen's corrections. But, although he considered himself more introspective than the generation of men which followed him—the astronauts, he called them—whose orientation was to the future, for whom days past were like stepping-stones in a stream, to be forgotten once the stream was crossed, a constant of Henhouse life itself worked against the Hen's efforts and his own. For in the Henhouse, one day's activities were like any other day's activities. Tomorrow was today repeated. And for a man mired in this sameness, the prospect of a bleak eternity of similar days passed in the same activities and postures, the same endless drone of dialogue, was intolerable. He could only cling to a vision of the future, however unrealistic, which embodied the enticements of incalculable vistas, the beckoning of barely visible beacons and beacons beyond the visible, the promise that some day, somehow, he would find his elusive road.

Yet he had changed. The Hen had convinced him, at least partially, that the way to his future traversed his past. To be sure, it remained possible that all the talk of progress was only a deception to keep him docile, that even such events as the disappearance of X were ingredients of this deception, that his future might in fact comprise nothing more than a purposeless repetition of yesterday, today, and tomorrow. Again he had had to choose, without the guidance of reason, however, for any one of his contradictory postures—the orientation to a distant future, the focus on the past as a method of attaining his future, and the third possibility: that his very presence in the Henhouse was a grisly error—could be logically supported. He had had to choose, and apparently (not being conscious of the process) he had chosen tentatively to believe the Hen. For there could be no doubt: through all the sessions and dialogues, the Hen had succeeded in turning him partway around, like a wrench twisting a reluctant bolt, had forced him to fuller introspection, to a sharpening of focus.

There remained the gaps in his memory, those areas dimly perceived as through shifting sands the droppings of an ancient civilization, and the inexplicable references to the guilt he was to live with. The gaps and the guilt. At times, to amuse himself, he explained both by concocting fictions, fantastic tales of murder, *crimes passionels*, which he concealed from the Hen because to exhibit them would only evoke lectures on his self-destructiveness, on inaccuracy, on the ways in which he impeded and delayed his own progress. Even fictions more plausible than *crimes passionels* would fail to fool the Hen. The Hen would find him out, and the Hen would be justified in criticizing him. For, it was true, in the aftermath of his fictions he became utterly convinced that his third posture was the only accurate one: You have the wrong man! I am not the man you want! It is all a mistake! I am innocent of all crimes!

To such denials the Hen listened in silence, puffing on his pipe. He had heard their recital on countless occasions. And could Y blame him if the Hen was sometimes impatient with them? In the Hen's behalf, he had to admit that not only had he never been charged, but that the idea of a criminal past was his own fiction.

6   The Triptych

The Hen had taken him back to the white house.

"Let us go over the early vignettes again," the Hen had said, forming the steeple gesture with his fingers. "Your triptych."

The white house was an old frame house near the sea which appeared ramshackle even though it had been newly painted. Its three stories rose crazily to a peaked roof. White house and wide lawn and the old shade trees and fruit trees, the slate path which led down the sloping lawn to the hedges, and beyond the hedges, the road. The gravel driveway which wound past hydrangea bushes to the garage and the small house in the rear by the vegetable gardens where he sometimes lived. The way the sun shone brightly in summer but the front of the house was always daubed in shadow. Usually he heard voices inside, male and female, and snatches of conversation which reminded him of mind-race words they were so fragmented, but nothing he could describe, nothing concrete or coherent, nothing the Hen would be interested in. Whenever he tried to seize them, the voices went away, and this session, strain as he might, he had not heard them at all. The house was quiet, somnolent. There was only the Hen's voice, questioning in dry, objective tones, and his own voice, answering, and the Hen's pencil, scratching on the pad.

The vignettes which formed the panels of the triptych had not always been linked. Consisting of three distinct episodes, only two of which connected to the white house, they had originally popped from his memory in different sessions. Only through the filter of many dialogues and repetitions, in the course of which the Hen's questions and his own responses had slowly hardened toward ritual, had they united into the triptych. Yet their union was natural, inevitable. In theme, content, and time they were so much alike that sometimes he could scarcely believe they had not occurred one right after the other in the actual chronology, and he could not concentrate on one without the details of the other two crowding into his mind.

The trouble was that he could no longer concentrate on them. In the beginning, when, out of all the subjects they discussed, the Hen had led him toward the vignettes, his stomach had invariably waved and fluttered in uneasiness. Was this where the guilt lurked, he had wondered, the guilt the Hen harped on, back beyond the murky territory of the vignettes, the same dark, shadowy terrain which awaited him, he thought, on the remote day, as far off as the womb, when he would confront his own death? Then the mixture of anxiety and remorse had evaporated, or almost evaporated. He would find himself waiting in the Hen's opening silence for the fluttering to start. The fluttering would not come. The only guilt he felt was secondary: guilt over the absence of guilt and in its place a mild satisfaction.

Finally, as in this afternoon session, he was only bored. He sought to distract himself in the scenery of the Hen's office, in the comical image of the bald pate which was all that could be seen when the Hen lowered his head and scribbled on one of the pads, in that movement at once so rapid and jerky that Y couldn't imagine how the notes could ever be deciphered or transcribed, if in fact, as he sometimes suspected, they were not being taken merely for his benefit, to be discarded at session's end. The vignettes were too banal to be reviewed or recorded still another time, too ordinary, too boring.

"Come now," the Hen had said, leaning forward in his chair, the bald prosecutor, "let us proceed. Tell us about the dog."

The Hen had wanted the dog? All right, then, the dog first. And the Hen had asked for freshness, had reminded him before to describe the vignettes as if he were doing it for the first time to a total stranger? All right, he would leave nothing out. And in truth, under the Hen's pushing and prodding, as if the bald prosecutor were himself goaded and irritated, he had seen the initial picture vividly: the green lawns surrounding the house, the summer sun which dazzled his eyes, the tall trees all around, many of them fruit trees, apple and cherry, even quince.

". . . a rambling old white frame house, but in good condition. It was where I spent some summers . . ."

There had been the dog, a newcomer, a new pet in the household, still a puppy, well-bred, black, with a shiny coat. He had craved affection, would do anything for a little affection. He had wriggled all over for affection.

". . . pedigreed, I think . . ."

But by then his recital had become automatic, his tone a monotone. He paused to look at the Hen, at the fingers back in their steeple, at the ruddy dome which had raised so that

their eyes met, at the brown eyes, limpid and large behind
the spectacles, large and watery.

The Hen sighed impatiently. "Go on," he said.

"In the morning I put his leash on . . ."

He had taken him into the backyard near the quince tree,
the quinces hanging low as if soon they would fall of their
own accord. No one else was up or around; probably all
asleep. The dog had fawned and wriggled, as usual. He had
petted him some.

"Then I started to whip him. I took the leash and . . ."

He paused. In the past, when recounting the vignette, he
had faltered and swallowed whenever he came to the image
of the leash raised in the air. This afternoon he did not
swallow, but the pause was part of the ritual, as was the
Hen's response.

The Hen sighed again.

"Please to go on."

With the end of the leash, which formed a leather loop, he
had belted the dog on the back as hard as he could, many
times, until the dog cringed in the grass as if he could cringe
straight through the earth and disappear. He had kept up
the beating until the dog began to yelp.

". . . plaintive yelps of a puppy . . ."

Then he had stopped beating him and petted him again.
He talked to him softly, to soothe him, stroked him until he
wriggled and fawned again, the way he did.

"His eyes grew so large when you stroked him."

That was all that he really saw of it now, the dog's large
black eyes which seemed to enlarge further while he looked
at them.

"And then I belted him again until he winced and yelped,
and stroked and talked to him again until he fawned."

That was the vignette, all of it. He had trained the dog to

such a fine point that all he had to do was raise the leash for the dog to cringe, to flatten out in anticipation. But not yelp. The dog never yelped until he was actually struck.

Would he erase the memory if he could? Undoubtedly. It was scarcely flattering. But was it really so important, worthy of so many repetitions? Once, in the beginning, it had haunted him but now he was only mildly disturbed, and more bored than disturbed. Was that just what the Hen wanted? But a useless question. He couldn't take it back. He could neither atone for it nor erase it. It had happened. Therefore it was, it existed. The dog was long since dead.

"How many times?" the Hen was asking. "How many times did you repeat this cycle of beating and petting?"

"I've told you before. Several times."

"And on how many days?"

"On several different days."

"Several different days," the Hen repeated. His head was lowered again. He was scribbling. In spite of himself, Y had grown irritated. What could be so important about the times and days? Nothing. They had covered it all before. He was surer than ever that the Hen was only baiting him, for reasons of his own.

"Several times," the Hen repeated, looking up once more. "And that is all you recall?"

"Yes."

"And why, then? Why did you beat him that way?"

Distracted, Y answered without thinking: "I don't know."

"You don't know?"

He shook his head. Strangely, for the words had come out involuntarily, it was true.

"You liked him, didn't you? Didn't we hear you say once that you loved him?"

Y nodded.

"Yes. You liked him, didn't you, the little black dog, but still you whipped him. Yet you say you don't know why." The Hen paused to unscrew the top of the tobacco jar, selected the pot-shaped pipe from the rack. "We've speculated about this why before, haven't we? One time you said you thought you wanted to teach him respect, and another you said you beat him because you were afraid of him. Is it not so? Even today we've heard you tell us: 'Maybe I was afraid of him.'"

Had he said it? He didn't remember it, but perhaps he had. It made no difference. He would take the Hen's word.

"But we've already decided," the Hen was saying, "that there was no reason for you to be afraid of him, haven't we? What reason could there have been?"

Y shook his head.

"He hadn't taken a bite out of you, had he? Or threatened you in any way, the puppy?"

"No, of course not."

"You couldn't really have been afraid of him, could you? 'No, of course not,' you say. Then if you weren't afraid of him, what other reason could there have been?"

He gave no answer.

"You don't know," the Hen persisted. "That is what you said. Then accordingly we may conclude today that you had no reason, that you just did it? The puppy was there. You were there. So you beat him. No reason other than that. Will we agree?"

"If you say so."

The Hen was writing again, and suddenly Y's boredom vanished. He was momentarily furious at the Hen: for the artificiality of his performance, for the absurd endless catechism, for all the trappings and gestures and theatricalities of the prosecutor—the steeple, the scribbling, the pipe—for

playing the role even to the point of putting words in his
mouth, for the usage of "us" and "we" and "tell us," as if the
two of them were members of the same prosecuting team,
contemplating the defendant together.

What did the Hen want of him? Was he to go on for the
rest of his days perfecting his recital for a performance
which would never take place? Of what importance was the
triptych? Just a trio of items from his past, one of many such
collections under the Hen's scrutiny. He had long since
decided that the shame with which he had originally regarded it was unjustified, the projection of adult criteria
onto a child's actions. The "I" of the triptych, the dog beater,
was a boy, an innocent in short pants.

The Hen was lighting his pipe. He was smiling, looking
over the pipe at Y with his large sad eyes. Doubtless he read
Y's mind, and doubtless what he saw there amused him.
Wasn't his head shaking ever so slightly in disapproval?

Just as quickly Y's anger was displaced from the Hen to
himself. He had been manipulated again, like a puppet. He
had allowed the artificiality of the catechism, the reason for
which he could not explain, to induce a reaction in him
which was itself artificial. The Hen's purposes eluded him.
That was all, and that was nothing new. If their sessions
were nothing more than elaborate endless games, he had no
alternative but to play along, waiting for their purpose, if
they had one, to be revealed to him. Boredom was his proper
state of mind. If the proceedings bored and frustrated him, it
was at least not his fault.

"Well then," the Hen went on, puffing at his pipe, "let us
proceed. What else about the white house today?"

The old frame house which appeared ramshackle even
though newly painted, the three stories rising crazily, the
slate path which followed the sloping lawn to the hedges,

and beyond the hedges, the road. He had been trying to catch the voices, to hear what they might be saying this quiet day, but there were only the slates and the ants, and though the Hen knew all about the ants, they went over them again, as if for the first time.

On the slates of the walk in the summertime, squadrons of black ants had marched, the bigger ants. Hunkered on his heels, he would watch their formations for hours, as they scurried along the lines of sand which separated the slates, climbed onto the slates themselves, hastened at doubletime pace along cracks and furrows. Contradicting what he had been told about ants, about their industry, their organization, these bigger ants traveled without apparent purpose, hurrying this way and that, like crowds in a city.

He had tested them in various ways. He had placed obstacles across their lines of march—pebbles, twigs, leaves —and watched them avoid the obstacles, often hastening away in the very direction from which they'd come. Sometimes he flipped them over on their backs, but this failed to immobilize them for very long. They merely wriggled a second or two, then flipped rightside up and scurried away, often bumping into other ants in the process, which made the bumpers flee in opposite directions. Or, standing, he would bomb them with clumps of dirt, sighting through imaginary crosshairs, dispersing them with his splatters.

He had been God to the ants. They ignored his existence. The obstacles, the flippings, the bombings, were all acts of God.

Inevitably the time would come for God's massacre, the only means of controlling the ant population of the slates. The massacre was obligatory, a social necessity. Standing again, and proceeding methodically from slate to slate, he would squash ants. Someone had once described to him the only sure technique of killing a sidewinder: to drive right over him and jam your brakes just as your wheels crossed him. To do otherwise would allow the snake to crawl away and survive. He would not, therefore, merely kill ants by stomping them; he would twist his foot as he stomped, thereby squashing them into paste. Usually he annihilated between thirty and forty before, suddenly, the slates would be wiped clean except for the corpses. The survivors, if there were any, had disappeared. Then he would rest, enormously satisfied with the slaughter.

This day, idly watching the smoke from the Hen's pipe eddy and curl toward the ceiling, he contemplated the distant vignette with a faint echo of that satisfaction, but the Hen did not allow his mind to linger. Already it was propelled impatiently to the vignette's successor which, following the recollections of the dog and the ants, formed the third panel of the triptych.

"There was this boy in school," he told the Hen, the monotone of his voice the only sound in the office. "A Greek. I still can't remember his name. Douris or Bouris or something like that. We were vaguely friends. Sometimes I walked him home in the afternoons after school. His skin was dark, very dark. His hair too, and long. He always looked dirty.

"One time he showed up in school on crutches. I think he had broken his leg. I tried to find him after school, but he had left before me, so I ran along the route I knew he had to take to go home. I caught up with him in a block or two. He was moving slowly on the crutches. Maybe he wasn't used to them yet, because he couldn't go very fast.

"When I reached him, I began to swing at him, at his crutches and legs, with my lunch box. I carried the black metal lunch box to school every day. I kept swinging it at him, as hard as I could, hitting him with it, until he cried out and fell. Maybe he lost his balance. Or maybe I knocked him down."

The same thing had happened every day. Sometimes they had left the school together, but after a few repetitions, the other boy had tried to hide from him, to leave early, or late, and thus get home safely. But Y always caught him. He had to go along that one street, and Y knew it. Dimly he saw the street again, as so many times before, pretty, lined with trees and brownstone houses and invariably empty in the middle of the afternoon. Somewhere along this street he would always catch up with him, or when the other boy tried leaving late, Y would sit on a stoop and wait for him. He never missed him.

"When he got there, or when I'd catch him, I'd start to swing the lunch box, I'd bring it up in the air"—he raised his arm in habitual demonstration—"and bang it against the crutches, trying to get at the leg, over and over again. He became adept at fending me off with his crutches. He'd hobble along on one crutch and fend with the other. But he'd always tire before I did, and down he'd go. Then he'd start to cry, and I'd stop."

"Then what?" the Hen asked, the catechist, when he had stopped talking.

Then nothing. Nothing had happened, except that eventually, when the boy's leg had healed and he was off the crutches, they had become just vague friends again, still in the same class at school.

"I don't know what became of him later."

The Hen questioned him again—how many times had he endured the same questions? —about his feelings toward the triptych.

Time was, he recalled, when he had not been able to

relate the three episodes coherently from start to finish,
when a cringing in his stomach would interrupt the narrative as soon as he saw his arm raising the leash, or when,
seeing the lunch box above his head, his own arm had raised
before his eyes in involuntary protection. He was identifying, he had supposed then, with his victims: with the dog,
with the boy on crutches, even with the ants, victims all of a
boy's omnipotence. He could still identify partially, if he
forced himself, but now he suspected his own reactions. He
was, he thought, to an increasing degree, merely recalling
old reactions and seeking to copy them for the Hen's benefit,
or for his own, as if to convince the two of them that once
he had been monstrous. Or to convince them that, in his reactions to the triptych, as in so many other areas of his memory which they studied and restudied in the sessions, circling
around them like two scouts, he had not changed at all.

In truth, he had long been able to complete the entire
triptych in a single narrative, with or without prompting. If
he didn't, if he faltered or paused for promptings, it was
because he was playing along with the Hen. The vignettes
had ceased to disturb him. He contemplated the dog, the
ants, the cripple, with virtual indifference. The acts of a boy
could not be relevant to a man who, allegedly, was "going to
live with his guilt."

Or were they?

For even as the Hen questioned and as he answered and
as the Hen noted his responses on paper, an old question,
extraneous to the catechism, was forming in his mind. It
lodged there and grew, despite his attempts to dismiss it, his
reluctance to acknowledge its presence. He hated to ask the
Hen questions, however trivial they might be. They would
build and build in his mind, antagonizing him, assuming
fantastic proportions, until he blurted them out at last.
Immediately upon hearing his own voice, he would recog-

nize how ridiculous he was being, whereupon, ashamed at his imbecility, he would not even want to hear the answer, if indeed an answer was forthcoming. His mind often tricked him that way. It worked and worked on him, obsessing him with its demands, until the demands mushroomed out of all shape and reality itself became twisted and distorted. But, too busy listening to the demands of his mind, he would not know what was happening until he heard his own voice.

He hated to appear ridiculous. He detested it, this image of himself displayed before the Hen in outlandish postures and shapes. To avoid it, he would wrestle with his mind, trying to master it, control it, to fight down its demands. Sometimes he succeeded. Thus he had never asked the Hen his real name, had never asked the blend of tobacco he smoked or his age or if he had children or what he wrote on the pads—even though irrelevancies of this sort continually plagued him. He could never sort out in advance what was trivial and what was important. His mind made all questions equally pressing.

He could not dismiss this particular question. The more he tried to fight it down, to concentrate on the Hen's words and his own in an effort to escape it, the more it sprouted in his consciousness.

He would have to ask it. His mind craved to ask it, demanded that it be asked.

When the Hen had stopped, when he had answered the last question and, in the ensuing lull, saw the bald head framed against the heavy damask drapes, the spectacles reflecting light, he blurted it out, immediately astonished by the timbre and inflection of his voice, as if it was not his own.

"Are the vignettes what you mean by my guilt?" And: "Is this the guilt I am going to live with?"

As soon as he heard the words, he cursed himself for his

idiocy. The question was patently unnecessary. He had considered it and answered it satisfactorily long ago, only now his mind had magnified it so, bloating it, surrounding it with such mystery and significance, that he had forgotten his answer. Hadn't every boy at one time or another crushed insects in just that way—willfully, methodically, efficiently? Hadn't every child a trace of the monster in him, of this need to inflict power, of this cruelty which exists in every creature which impels him to flog an animal or maim a friend? And wasn't this very cruelty part of and even indicative of his former innocence?

Guilt!

If the triptych was his guilt, if that was all his guilt was and what he was "going to live with," then all men were guilty, then all men ought to live in the Henhouse!

The Hen seemed to share his opinion. Laughing heartily, the creases of his ruddy skin dancing in the light and shadow of the room, he arose from his desk and stood with his hands in his pockets.

"Yes," the Hen said, still laughing. "Yes, if you like it, you might consider the vignettes as part of your guilt!"

Then the session was over. Ashamed of himself, of his predictably ridiculous posture, Y was eager to leave as quickly as possible. He got up. He reached the doorway, saw the functionary in a blurred glance and Z waiting his turn patiently in one of the anteroom chairs. But behind him, the Hen's voice was summoning him back.

"I almost neglected to tell you," the Hen was saying, smiling. "We have decided to move you. In fact, as you are just going to find out, you have been moved already."

7 The Runner

The starter called his commands. The racers poised in a pack. *Pock* went the starter's pistol, and off they ran to the cheers of the crowd, off on the First Daylong Run for the big brass pot which awaited the winner on the steps of the city hall. Off they ran, bunched in dozens, fresh and hardened from daylong running-hiking-running, training for the First Daylong Run. Off they ran, numbered placards flapping on their backs, up the steep first hill and down the other side, through the high grass and into the woods and out of the woods and into the first treacherous drifts of sand. Off they ran, zealots pumping for the lead, jostling, elbows flailing, for the lead, trailers easing into the slipstreams of front runners. Off they ran, to the squeals of town girls who had bicycled into the hills to cheer their favorites at the starting point, to the shouts of encouragement which burst from local sportsmen, to the calculating eyes of bookmakers, reporters, cameramen.

Near the foot of the first downslope, the lead runner tripped over an obstacle, plummeted in a headlong dive, and slashed open his leg on a rock. Two others, running on his heels, tumbled over him in a tangle of limbs, picked themselves up and ran off in the rear of the pack, but the early leader, disconsolate, blood streaming from his wound, limped from the course, the first casualty, to be surrounded by well-wishers and newspapermen in search of a statement.

At the sand dunes another cluster of runners fell. In their frantic efforts to extract themselves, to regain their footing, they became hopelessly ensnarled. Blinded by sand, they fought each other, one man seeking to climb on the shoulders of another, only to sink farther back. The more they struggled, the more difficult it became to escape the pull of the sliding sand. In the end they capitulated, slid in an angry mass of bodies to the bottom of the dunes, slowly untangled themselves, and withdrew from the competition.

When the leaders of the moment, running four abreast, scrambled from the last of the dunes onto the dirt road which the course followed for several miles, they had to pass a large flat rock on which posed the local Circe, the county beauty queen, eligible for higher levels of beauty contests, sunning herself in a bathing suit. As soon as she saw the approaching runners, she stood up on her rock to her full height, stretched her arms gracefully toward the sun, and with a few turns and twists of her body wriggled free of her suit. She laughed aloud and called to the four runners. Then she ran to the edge of the woods, beckoning behind her, and the four athletes followed the lure of her flowing black hair off the course into the woods. As the rest of the pack passed this point, which came to be known in local legend as Circe's Corner, they could hear, down to the last straggler, her husky laughter cartwheeling through the trees.

Halfway down the course's dirt road leg was a beer stand, erected as a publicity stunt by an enterprising local brewery,

which became a trap for unwary contestants. The first group
of runners to reach it, a cluster of three, paused to quench
their thirst. One of them, his sides heaving, drank too much
too quickly. Soon after he resumed running, his stomach
rose in rebellion and he stood by the side of the road,
vomiting. The second quickly passed him, but soon he felt
an irresistible swell in his genitals, and, unable to continue,
he stopped to urinate against a tree. The more he urinated,
the more he felt the need. Subsequently the third beer-
drinker joined him, and the two athletes stood by the tree,
urinating helplessly as the remnants of the pack jogged past.

So it went through the lengthening day, runners dropping
from the competition for one reason or another, some as
frivolous as those which disqualified the followers of Circe
and the beer-drinkers, some more serious. There were those
who, unable to take another step, dropped along the way
from sheer fatigue. Others sustained injuries of one kind or
another. By afternoon the length of the winding course was
strewn with also-rans. At the three-quarter mark only a small
percentage of the original dozens, of all those aspirants who
had started so confidently and hopefully in the morning,
remained in contention, and of these all but a handful
yielded to exhaustion in the next few miles. At last there
were but four, three of whom had been among the betting
favorites, careening down the hillside which led to the swift-
water hazard, a dangerous passage for a fresh, vigorous man,
not to say a daylong runner. The first three, the favorites,
plunged pellmell into the water, unable or unwilling to slow
themselves. All three lost their footing and were swept
downstream by the current. Only the fourth, who saw the
fate of his predecessors, braked in time and took the more
prudent course of trotting along the riverbank to the rocks.
Gingerly he picked his way across, concentrating to the ex-

clusion of all else on each slippery stepping-stone as it appeared before him.

And so it was that in the gathering dusk this last runner entered the outskirts of the town, trotted past the filling stations and the first houses, the first lawns and shade trees, to the scattered applause of the first spectators, who hurriedly scanned their programs in search of his number and name. As he ran through the streets, this inconspicuous contestant, neither a particularly fast nor a particularly slow runner, who throughout the day had neither led nor trailed very far behind, who had surely been overlooked in the prognostications of the bettors and bookmakers, who was just another male citizen of the region, looked over his shoulder in search of his competitors. He failed to see them. There were none.

Spurred by the anticipation of victory, he lengthened his stride and raised his head in reply to the growing acclaim of the spectators. He crossed the little bridge which spanned the railroad tracks and ran easily toward the end of the course, his arms swinging at his sides, his hair blown back by the early evening breeze, his number flapping against his back.

He was that man! He was that man!

As he turned the last corner onto the main street, the crowds of spectators on the sidewalks, ever denser, began to shout, and their chant spread rapidly along the sidewalks like fire along a fuse. He was unable to understand what they were chanting until suddenly he recognized his own name. They were chanting his name!

The crowd could not contain itself any longer. Breaking through the barricade of policemen, spectators poured into the street. He ran the last mile of the course through a narrowing gauntlet, flashbulbs popping in his face, the

sound of his own name ringing in his ears in mounting
crescendos. He virtually leapt in triumph as he sprinted the
last block, heart pounding, eyes dilated, while fireworks
exploded in the darkening sky and tickertape rained from
the upper windows and rooftops.

With a final lunge he broke the tape. Children from the
town danced in front of him, strewing his path with flowers.
A plump blond girl threw her arms around him and kissed
him. Someone placed a garland of laurel around his neck as
he trotted toward the steps of the city hall where the brass
pot awaited and the mayor of the town amid a cluster of
local dignitaries.

As he approached the group, the mayor broke away and
started down the steps, taking off his hat in homage to the
winner. Seeing him, the winner tried to turn away, but
before he could move the mayor extracted a small pistol
from an inside pocket and, firing at close range, shot him in
the center of his chest. His body jerked violently, like a
marionette whose strings have suddenly been yanked by its
master, and collapsed into the street.

The mayor ascended the steps of the city hall and, speaking through a microphone, announced the name of the
winner. The crowds of spectators cheered wildly, chanting
the name aloud. Only much later did they disperse, leaving
only a single pair of eyes to guard the corpse of the winner
through the night, the corpse which lay amid crushed
flowers and twisted masses of tickertape, a residue which
would be cleaned up the next morning.

He was soaked in his own perspiration. He was clutching
his chest. His heart thumped violently, shortlong, shortlong,
shortlong. He was exhausted, as if he had been awake for
several days.

The mayor was the Hen. He had known it as soon as he took off his hat.

"It is time for your meeting, Mr. _____." The functionary stood in the doorway. How long had he been there, watching him?

He threw off the covers, stumbled from his bed, disappeared from the functionary's view into the alcove at the rear of his room. A thought nagged at him. He reached for it, clutched at it, but it eluded him and raced free about his mind, a loose thought amok in his mind, a pig escaped from its sty. He grabbed for it again, lunged, missed. Empty-handed, he found himself staring at his face in the mirror. He opened the faucet, splashed his face with cold water. He stared at himself again. Something was different. The thought. The thought was still there to be grabbed. Its presence teased him. But when he reached once more, it fled once more.

While he was dressing, he tried to organize his mind, tried to still the pounding in his chest. Something had happened. What?

Only when he followed the functionary into the corridor did the thought alight once more. He grabbed at it, caught it, held it.

The Hen had moved him.

Yet absurdly, the Hen hadn't moved him at all. When he had left the Hen's office the previous afternoon after the Hen's belated announcement—was it deliberate, this last-minute afterthought?—he hadn't known what to expect. A change, any change, would have been welcome. Wasn't that what he was always telling himself? Yet his reflex had been one of anxiety. "You can't do this to me, just like that, without consulting me," he had wanted to shout, but already it was too late, already he was in the anteroom, already Z had taken his place in the office.

He and the functionary had taken just a few steps into the first corridor, no more than twenty in all, when the functionary stopped abruptly, inserted a key into the lock beside a door, turned it, then stood aside as the door opened to allow Y to enter. As he walked into the room, he had laughed aloud in astonishment. In every first impression it was identical to his own.

He had turned to protest, or at least to question, but there was the waiter already wheeling in the second meal of the day on his metal cart.

"Your meal is served, sir."

The usual words, uttered in the usual monotone. Then quickly, before he could speak, the waiter had gone, the functionary had gone, the door had slid shut, and he was alone in his new room.

He neglected his meal for a long time. Instead he examined the room thoroughly, searching carefully for differences. On the subject of his room, his old room, he was an expert. He had measured its dimensions countless times. He knew just how many tiles deep and how many tiles wide it was, knew just how far from the floor the striped counterpane hung on both sides of his bed, in just what order on his shelves he had arranged his books. He studied everything, like a detective investigating the scene of a crime: the placement of his papers on the writing table, of his clothes in the small closet in the alcove, of his toilet articles on the alcove shelf. The furniture was the same, but that meant nothing. One writing table was like another, one mass-produced mattress could not be distinguished from dozens of other mass-produced mattresses. But his personal possessions, the positioning and placement of the items which bore his personal stamp?

Nothing had been altered, not the slightest detail.

Yet he *had* been moved. The Hen had said so. Not only

had the Hen said so, but he was certain that, despite his state of excitement, his mind had not been playing tricks on him. They *had* stopped in the first corridor. Yes, they had. They had not passed through the other doors, the other corridors. Hadn't he almost bumped into the functionary when he stopped suddenly in the first corridor?

Then he began to bang on the door. He banged on it until it slid open and the functionary appeared.

"Some of my papers are missing!" he shouted, feigning outrage. "You've taken some of my papers!"

The functionary's face was utterly impassive.

"I'm sorry, Mr. _____. You have made a regrettable mistake," the functionary said, in the longest speech Y had ever heard him deliver. "Nothing has been touched. All has been left as it was."

They had stared at each other for several moments until the functionary turned his key again and the door closed.

Later the sound of his laughter filled this new room, *his* room, impelled beyond his control by the comedy of the Henhouse. Did the Hen have a means of switching entire corridors merely by pressing a button, so that all the inmates of Corridor 3 and all their possessions could be transferred in a flash to Corridor 1, and Corridor 1 transferred to God knew where? No, of course not. The answer was simply that every room, every last *cell*, in the Henhouse was identical to every other. Why should this strike him so funny? He did not know, only that he roared with laughter at the idea that the Hen's imagination had been exhausted by his own office, that it could not extend beyond the décor of his office exhausted as it was, that either the Hen, or some pedigreed interior decorator to whom he had entrusted the task, had contrived to design his version of the ideal modern cell—yes, *cell!*—and, newly exhausted by this transcendent achieve-

ment, had merely repeated the same cell on all three corridors, and on all the corridors beyond, dozens upon dozens of
cellular repetitions through all the corridors of the Henhouse. Furthermore, it was more economical that way! The
Hen could buy in bulk: mattresses by the carload, counterpanes by the gross! The image of the Hen negotiating with a
wholesaler over the purchase of counterpanes by the gross,
of the Hen poring over sample swatches, rubbing various
materials between his fingers and arguing about prices,
overwhelmed him with paroxysms of laughter. Sheets too!
He doubled over on his bed, shaking hysterically, recalling
capriciously the old punch line: it only hurts when you
laugh. And this punch line, even though he forgot what
preceded it, made him clutch his pillow for support and
started the tears rolling down his cheeks.

He had calmed then, though occasionally his sides still
shook involuntarily from the residue of hysterics. An old
hypothesis, one he had long ago investigated and discarded,
struck him with renewed plausibility. He was already dead,
the hypothesis said. He had died. This was what death was.
The Henhouse was the resting place of the dead. Surely, one
offshoot of the hypothesis insisted, the Henhouse was in-
fernal, the Henhouse was Hell itself, presided over by the
Devil, who was not, despite popular legends, a twin-horned
creature with a tail and pitchfork, but a rather kindly, bald
man, slightly paunchy, of ruddy complexion, who wore spectacles, smoked a pipe, dressed sedately—on balance a mild-
mannered man, whose mildness did not, however, conceal
the authority of his presence. Hell was a place of identical
cells and corridors, of white walls and red floors and fluorescent lighting, an eternal state of being where nothing ever
changed, where references to "guilt" and "progress" were
mere subterfuge, where inmates were shifted about from

time to time, from one identical cell to another identical cell, merely to divert them, to keep them guessing, and therefore docile.

Then there was the hypothetical branch which proposed that the Henhouse was Limbo, a clearinghouse, a way station, where the defunct were processed and measured for further disposition, where the dossier of a defunct's life was screened, studied, and evaluated, where there were constant arrivals and departures and the Hen, appointed chief executive by the hierarchy of the hereafter, decided, after due deliberation, who was to be sent here and who was to be sent there. The Henhouse, in this aspect of the hypothesis, had but a temporary function in a defunct's career and was therefore purely functional, without frills or sentiment. If it was ponderously slow in the fulfillment of said function, could not the same be said of any bureaucratic establishment? And in any case, was there any reason to hurry?

Finally there was the third prong of the hypothesis, the *pièce de résistance*. He always saved it for last, a special treat, for invariably it made him laugh, as it did now. The Henhouse was neither Hell nor Limbo but Paradise itself! What a lovely irony, what a joke on the earnest preachers of history, those somber men of the cloth who had wielded such power over countless unsuspecting flocks, to learn that Heaven was, after all, no Elysian paradise but merely another social institution no more and no less adequately managed than their own, that an eternity of boredom and, practically speaking, solitude constituted the heavenly state (such occasion for meditation, for contemplation, for study, in which the holy defunct could continue to expunge their sins in peace and quiet!), and that the beloved Host, that glorious, mysterious Trinity which had held men captive for two millennia, which had brought generations of supplicants to their knees, was embodied—lock, stock and barrel—in none other than this same rather kindly bald man, slightly paunchy!

All of which meant that God, the God men had imagined over two millennia and beyond, was, like the Wizard of Oz with his thunder machine, fraudulent. That the millions of human beings who had listened to their clerics had been duped. And that God, the real God, was neither omnipotent nor omniscient, but merely a pipesmoker, well-versed in Freudian technique, with a penchant for oracular pronouncements. And finally, that, unlike Oz, Paradise was a dream from which no one awoke.

In the end this train of thought drained the laughter from him. The joke was too bleak to be funny. It was not so much the possibility that the Henhouse was an eternal state which destroyed the comedy. He had survived the Henhouse thus far; he could continue to survive it. Rather it was the idea that humanity had been misled by its self-appointed charlatans, that the generations of mankind which had molded their lives according to the precepts of their religionists had been gulled, taken, swindled. The Henhouse was their reward. How many men had lost their lives in defense of this or that image of God? How many families had been impoverished so that the self-perpetuating societies of charlatans could live in comfort? How many of the unswindled had been hounded, enslaved, murdered, by the swindled and their swindlers?

And yet he was not dead. That much he knew. When, on that remote and terrifying day, he finally encountered death, he would recognize it, and in the event, however unlikely, that his conscious continued to exist afterward in some form, it would know that he was dead and how he had died. He was not yet dead. Therefore, his entire tree of hypotheses

about Hell and Limbo and Heaven was constituted on a
false premise, as in fact he had long ago decided, and was
nothing more than a fiction, an entertainment, although a
gruesome one, to help pass the time, like the various reli-
gious mythologies themselves.

Shortly thereafter, he had gone to sleep in the new bed,
which was just like his other bed, and dreamed the dream of
the daylong run.

The dream, he thought, mirrored his previous waking
state of mind, the horror of its denouement reinforced by the
ludicrous elements with which it began. The first parts of it
had been so comical—Circe on her rock, the beerstand
hazard. He had enjoyed them thoroughly. But as soon as he
recognized the lone runner as himself, the tone had shifted
abruptly. He had swelled so with pride at the image of that
inconspicuous runner, of himself as the inconspicuous
runner, that when he trotted through the last gauntlet of
spectators, he had been at once the runner and one of the
well-wishers who clapped him on the back in congratula-
tion. When the mayor descended the steps to greet him, he
had rejoiced—until the hat came off and he saw that the
mayor was bald and wore spectacles, that the mayor was the
Hen. Then, instantaneously, an alarm had sounded throughout his body, a revulsion, an impulse to turn away, to escape,
a sense that something had gone wrong, that he wasn't the
intended victor after all, that the prize for his victory was
not the brass pot but a bullet in the chest. The Hen had been
too quick for him. He had seen the gun, had tried to turn
away, but then he heard the shot and suddenly, as if he was
a spectator, witnessing the scene from the rooftops, he
watched his own body jerk and fall. He had come awake

almost instantly, to the pounding in his chest, to the sight of the functionary in the doorway.

He was getting even with the Hen, the loyal Freudian would say, by casting him in the role of murderer.

For the move had infuriated him: both the casual offhand manner in which he had been informed of it, almost as an afterthought, which falsely belittled its importance (surely the Hen had planned it that way, so that it would occur without explanation or debate, so that he would be thrown back on himself, on his spontaneous reactions); and the fact that his new room was identical to the old, which made the event absurd, meaningless. He had neither risen or fallen in status; he had been neither rewarded nor punished. He had merely been moved, and the only change, if it deserved to be called a change at all, was that he was now nearer to the Hen.

"Perhaps," he said to the Hen after he had related the dream and his interpretation of it, surprised that the tumult he had felt just a few moments before upon wakening could have been so quickly translated into an insipid joke, "the functionary has a touch of gout. Poor old man, perhaps he finds it too difficult to walk as far as the third corridor four times a day."

The Hen smiled, dutifully he supposed, and asked, "But what did you expect to happen?"

"I don't know," he replied. "Something. Something else. I don't think you know what it is like to live on my side of this desk, when you endure the same routines day after day after day, week after week, endless repetitions, without knowing why . . . Yes, without really knowing why, except for passing obscure references to guilt, progress, case, situation. You come to anticipate a change, any change, however small. To convince yourself you are not mad. Some signal of progress. Or even regress. Or neither but just a change, even the slightest variation. Haven't you ever wanted to cut yourself intentionally, just to see your own blood, just to know that you're alive?

"Then finally a change is announced. From the sound of it, it isn't petty. It is even important. Though you learn of it in the most offhand way, that doesn't minimize its importance. You are accustomed to nuances, to looking for nuances. You feed on nuances; you live on them. In the absence of anything more substantial, you live on nuances. But this is more than a nuance."

"And so?" the Hen asked him when he stopped.

"So it turns out to be nothing but a nuance after all. Or even less than a nuance. Nothing, nothing at all."

Which led you to try to trick the functionary, accusing him of taking your papers. Which then led you to hysterical laughter, it was so funny that your sides ached. Which finally made you see me as your arch antagonist in disguise, your murderer. Is it not so?

But despite his anticipation, the Hen said nothing.

Finally the Hen rose and began to pace the carpet behind his desk, back and forth like a plump and irregular metronome, revolving his spectacles in his hand, back and forth before the heavy drapes, as if he were rehearsing a speech.

"It didn't occur to you, we are to assume then," the Hen said, "that I might have informed you of the move in the offhand way you have described because I knew that if I attempted to convince you that it was unimportant, you would not believe me, and because I knew that, nonetheless, its apparent unimportance would be a shock to you?"

"No, it didn't," he answered. Was the Hen trying to appease him? No, he reflected wryly, whatever else he might be, the Hen was not an appeaser. Parenthetically, he could only admit that the Hen was right: there was no way the move could have been presented to him so that he would have accepted it with equanimity.

"And I didn't react," he continued, "as you would have had me react. I didn't take it in stride. I am not docile, not the way you would have me be docile. And, you know," he said calmly, watching the Hen, who had ceased pacing and now, his spectacles once more perched on his nose, his hands in his pockets, appeared to lean against the drapes as he listened, "I don't think I am ever going to be the docile member you have worked so hard to achieve. It is not to be. I am not an automaton. It is not possible for me to be an automaton. Maybe your techniques have worked with the others, with X and X^1 and Z and all the others, but they haven't with me. And do you know? I don't think they ever will. I'm sorry if I disappoint you. Really, I am sorry. I don't hold it against you for trying, but I really believe you are wasting your time. It may be that I am a bad risk for you, but I am what I am."

He uttered the words steadily, without emotion. Once he would have delivered the message with the obstinate defiance of an ultimatum, but now he merely stated the case as he saw it, describing the raw material, the evidence, as if from a distance.

"Do you think that is what we want? To make you an automaton?" the Hen said quietly, still standing against the drapes, his voice slow and friendly, his eyes watery orbs. "An automaton? Is that what you think we want?

"Haven't we always agreed that you had a will of your own, a mind of your own? You are absolutely right, it seems. Certainly, if we wanted to make an automaton of you, we could not have chosen a poorer specimen."

Once too he would have challenged the Hen immediately, would have demanded to know once and for all for what purpose he was being prepared. And why he was treated the way he was. Why he was always kept in ignorance, like a child to whom certain secrets cannot be revealed until he has attained a certain age, if, in the Hen's eyes, he had a mind of his own and a will of his own. This morning he felt the same impulse, the old reflex to defiance, to self-assertion, but quickly it evaporated. He would know in good time, if there was anything to know. He had waited this long, had he not? He could wait a little longer then, in this new room of his which was not a new room at all.

"As it happens," the Hen said, resuming his seat, "it was inaccurate of you to assume that the moving was entirely without significance. When you found that your new room was identical to your old, you were so quick to conclude that you were being deceived, that we were playing some sort of sadistic joke on you.

"To the contrary. Whatever interpretation you placed on it, the moving was not without significance. In fact, we *have* progressed." He paused and peered over the upper rims of his spectacles, like a lecturer underlining a point. "Yes. And I think you are already aware of it, no?"

Y nodded.

"If you were to consider the move as an insignia of our progress, you would not be deceiving yourself, even though in physical appearances your surroundings are no different from what they were. And in addition, you have no need to berate yourself for your newfound patience. It won't disappoint you, I think."

In that morning session he had displayed more signs of his transformation than he at first realized. He hesitated to call it progress, whether or not it justified the label in the Hen's design. For the moment, change would do.

The change came to be symbolized for him by the bizarre ending of the dream, which had occurred so quickly—almost instantly he had come awake—and had seemed of such little importance that he had omitted it from his account. He had identified the mayor as the Hen. He had seen the Hen smile and reach inside his coat for the pistol. At that very point, after realizing in an instant what was in store for him and realizing too that it was too late for him to do anything about it, he had fled his body and, like a director observing his creation, had watched the unfolding of the remainder of the action from a perch atop the city hall. He had *seen* his own body jerk from the impact of the bullet. He had *seen* it collapse at the foot of the steps. His had been the single pair of eyes which watched over it, guarding it, long after the crowd had disappeared, all during the night, until in the morning it was removed. He was at once the director and the actor, the dreamer and the subject of the dream.

It was just this sense of detachment from himself, as if all the deeds and reactions under consideration—the move, his sense of its absurdity, his hysterical hilarity, the dream itself—belonged to another man, which had kept him in that morning session from fighting the Hen. With one voice, the dead voice of the corpse, he narrated the events which he had experienced; with another, a voice astonishingly like the Hen's, he commented upon them. He anticipated the Hen's reactions, the Hen's very words. He applied them to the evidence without prompting or coaching.

That was why he had not challenged the Hen that morning! That was the source of his "newfound patience"! Had he become at last the Hen's co-investigator, probing and considering the . . . (What was the word the Hen had used?

. . . the specimen, that was it! . . . the specimen!) . . .
probing and considering the specimen before them? Had he
virtually become the Hen himself?

If this were so, then the Hen was superfluous. If this were
so, then it would have made no difference at all if the Hen,
standing against the heavy drapes, had suddenly melted into
the damask and disappeared. The session would have continued. For the space of at least one session, he would have
been the Hen!

He was both excited and unnerved by this sense of new-
ness, of transformation. The realization that progress in the
Henhouse, or at least change, was not only possible but that
it had happened, exhilarated him beyond measure. And yet,
he missed something too, he knew not what. With the ache
of longing with which throughout their lives most men
search in vain for their lost childhood, for the green world of
innocence, he missed . . . something. Perhaps it was just
his old self, when his actions and reactions were spontaneous, when, for better or worse, his mind and body, his whole
being, functioned as one, as one single unit. There had been
a time when, after experiencing the previous day and night,
the move and the dream, he would have stormed the citadel
of the Hen's office like a revolutionary. Now he could only
sit back, and watch, and contemplate, and sometimes be
amused by what he saw.

It was not that he had ceased to act and react, had ceased
to be. He was not dead. He was still capable of stimulation,
of response. He could experience the reflexes of his lifelong
patterns. But very quickly now, like the runner leaving his
own body at the sound of the shot, a part of him separated
from the rest, like the part of him which, that morning, had
stood in front of the drapes with the Hen and listened to the
voice from the armchair.

Something still held him back from pursuing the transformation to its unseen conclusion, from following this new and unfamiliar road, wherever it led. Some spark inside him, however dim and whatever its inspiration, told him to proceed with caution. If he was going to proceed at all. Perhaps it was better to accept the bullet in the chest, to endure the spasms of dying, to become a corpse in the street, than to fly to his rooftop perch like a crow and watch himself die with a crow's eyes.

And yet, part of him, part of him, had already flown to the rooftop. He had dreamed the dream. He couldn't take it back. Hesitate as he might, like the man in the square who revolved and beheld, he had no choice but to proceed. Maybe the spark of caution was only a reflex, a last gasp, from his former self, that part of him which was dying. Maybe it would go out, and maybe it should.

Of one thing at least he could be certain: he was changing. The change had begun in him and was likely to continue. And if there lingered any doubt in his mind, this doubt would be erased by the changes he began to detect in the Hen himself, in the sessions immediately ahead.

8   The Interruptions

The Hen was called the Hen just as the other members he had seen were X, X¹ and Z, just as he himself was Y: out of convenience and relevance. The Hen looked like a Hen; moreover, he acted like one. His eyes were not beady; he had neither rooster's ruff nor wattles, though certain portions of his jowl and neck skin, already flabby and drooped, suggested that in his old age wattles would yet develop. Still, from his plumpness, the heaviness of his hips, and most particularly from the counterpoint to these physical features of his quickness of gesture, his assured, self-confident mien, Y formed the impression that, somewhere along the line, in some previous or subsequent incarnation, the Hen would be found producing and hatching eggs.

Though the Hen led, though he presided, his managerial style was somehow maternal. He did not command. By his own devious devices he persuaded, he cajoled. He was sympathetic, habitually patient, at times almost apologetic. His authority over his flock was that of a headmistress.

The Henhouse was at once hatchery and incubator, metic-

ulously furnished and maintained. Even its lighting and
temperature were carefully regulated. Its members, once
hatched, were neither forcefed nor artificially fattened, but
nurtured slowly, constantly weighed and measured. Slow-
developers, such as Y, were not abandoned; at most they
were housed in separate incubator-corridors for special attention and processing. None of them knew for what market
they were being prepared, only that great care and time
were devoted to their maturation.

He had twisted the metaphor of the Hen and the Henhouse in various directions before under the dictates of
circumstance, but the events which followed his move to the
first corridor, notably the alteration of the Hen, himself,
which, he finally concluded, was an intrinsic development,
external to the shifts in his own point of view, forced him
either to renounce the metaphor entirely or stretch it beyond
its previous dimensions. He saw himself now as a fattened
chick, but there was more to it than that. It was as if the
Henhouse had suddenly been menaced from the outside, as
if its routine serenity had been disturbed by this new threat
which endangered the security not only of the Hen but of
his entire flock. Or alternately, as if the Hen, when his
charges reached a certain level of fattening, began to lose
interest in them, as the females of various species in nature
abandon their young at an early age.

At first, in those sessions which immediately followed the
move, the Hen seemed only distracted, his mind preoccu-
pied with other matters. Perhaps, Y thought, a new batch of
incubants had arrived. Perhaps the third corridor was newly
inhabited by fresh candidates, as bewildered and recalcitrant as he had once been. Or perhaps some inmate, cleverer
and bolder than he, had actually achieved the impossible,
had contrived to escape the Henhouse walls.

The Hen had always been prone to certain gestures which, while some of them could be called functional, were carried out in involuntary rituals or mannerisms. He would toy with his spectacles, wiping them, twirling them by an earpiece, arranging them and rearranging them in various symmetrical juxtapositions to the other objects on his desk top. Or he would play with the objects themselves: the tobacco jar and the pipes, the pencils and the pads. But recently, in an absentminded way, he had begun to fidget. There was no word for it other than fidget. He would rise and sit down, then rise again and pace back and forth behind his desk, then sit again and finger the various objects, one after the other, placing them here and there before returning them to their original positions. Several times Y caught him unscrewing the top of the tobacco jar and rescrewing it shut without filling the pipe he held in his other hand. The Hen was constantly lighting and relighting his pipe these days, as if in the interim he had forgotten to puff it.

Nor was it only a matter of fidgeting. Increasingly the Hen was distracted in the dialogues themselves. Y would have to repeat a statement or an answer, not, he realized, because the Hen wanted to emphasize or amplify a specific point, but simply because the Hen's attention had been diverted. The Hen hadn't been listening. More often than not, it was: "I would like you to repeat that please." Or: "It seems I have difficulty understanding that. Please to go over it once more"—like a piano teacher asking his pupil to repeat perfect scales.

For his scales were increasingly perfect. Had the pupil outstripped his mentor? he began to wonder. By the Hen's standards of judgment, which, implicit though they were, he had come to recognize and apply, separating for himself the inaccurate from the accurate, he was learning to live with

his guilt, which more and more he took to mean learning to
live with himself: with the fragmentary data of his memory
and with his situation in the Henhouse. These twin realities
—the Henhouse and his years before the Henhouse—had
themselves begun to separate in his mind, as if the latter,
like a photograph in which the details had become increasingly clear even as they faded, constituted some prior incarnation, the life of a man as dead as the corpse in the
street, and hence of dwindling interest. Parts of this former
life-before-birth he could remember with perfect clarity and
indifference, focusing squarely on them without qualm, just
because they had occurred in the life of another man. He
viewed them from afar, from a crow's perch. As for those
inchoate odds and ends which belonged neither to his conscious nor his subconscious, neither to his waking nor his
sleeping self nor to his past nor to his present, which nonetheless, at times, washed ashore on his conscious like flot-
sam, he had, like the Hen, ceased to regard them as note-
worthy. To be sure, he still experienced the mindrace—in
the middle of the night, in the early mornings—but quickly,
quicker than ever, he could detach himself from it and,
reorganizing, regain his equanimity.

He accepted the mystery of the Henhouse as a mystery.
His presence in it had not been explained to him. Therefore
he considered it temporarily inexplicable. Nor did it obsess
him that he had no recollection of the time and nature of his
arrival. After all, did a child remember the time and place of
its arrival on earth? Did it remember its rebirth, those last
moments in the womb when, always hungry, always devour-
ing, it slid slowly down the dark, slime-covered channel to
be ejected like a cork into its new life? And did it remember
its cry of terror when, still floundering, still helpless and
choking, it first glimpsed the sun?

He did not remember either how, frightened and be-

wildered, he had first awakened in the Henhouse, and the
memory was as unnecessary to him as the memory of his
rebirth to the child. Suffice it to say that he had come from
some other place to this place. Soon, he thought, it would be
possible for him to reject entirely the concept that he had
died and been reborn and accept instead the concept of
birth, as the child believes that it has been born, and not
reborn.

He might have continued to progress indefinitely in this
way, consolidating and reaffirming his beliefs, had it not
been for the changes he observed in the Hen, who had
always been a constant in his life. The Hen was disconcerted
these days. The Hen was fidgeting, impatient. The Hen was
in a rush. Had it not been for his mounting self-confidence,
the Hen's new manner would have shaken him severely. As
it was, the day might come when he would have to assume
the chair on the other side of the desk and see what could be
done for the Hen. Yes, he reflected with a smile, in a few
light years.

Early in one session, when he had finished reviewing his
triptych once more—without the need of catechetical assis-
tance, in perfect control of himself and his materials—and
was embarked upon another memory fragment of more
recent vintage, someone rapped at the office door. As surprising as was this phenomenon itself, even more surprising to Y
was the Hen's reaction. When the rapping was impatiently
repeated, the Hen arose, in the middle of Y's sentence, to
answer it. From his position, Y could neither see another
person at the door nor hear another voice, but the Hen
nodded, as if in response to the other person. Then, he
returned to his desk, closing the door by pressing the button
beside him, and said, "I am very sorry. It is regrettable, I
know, but we will have to interrupt you now and terminate

the session. We can discuss these matters again at our next
meeting . . ."

As Y rose to leave, the Hen continued, but in such an
obvious and unnecessary effort at reassurance, and so
absentmindedly, as if he were brushing a fleck of lint from
his sleeve, that Y could but doubt his sincerity: "And in any
case, we are doing very well these days, is it not so? Yes, our
case is progressing very nicely, would you not agree to
that?"

The interruption was to prove no isolated phenomenon. In
ensuing sessions, the rapping came more and more frequently, so that Y almost began to anticipate it when he sat
in the Hen's office. The Hen would pause, sometimes with an
apology, before opening the door and rising to listen for
varying lengths of time to the unseen, unheard voice. Sometimes, upon resuming his seat, he terminated the session
immediately. Or, on the other hand, they might continue.
But the Hen was never the same after an interruption. His
attention strayed more than ever. He fidgeted flagrantly, to
such an extent that he, himself, must surely be aware of it.
True to his style, however, he never commented on the
interruptions, save once. When the rapping began that particular occasion, he exclaimed irritably: "Will they never
learn to leave me alone?"

As if these interruptions were not enough—for though
they disconcerted him, Y could nonetheless endure them—
entire sessions began to be canceled. Under the normal
schedule, every so often, at five- to eight-day intervals, an
afternoon session was omitted. Now it happened that two
and even three afternoon sessions in succession would not
take place. He would be waiting in his room for the functionary to appear. He would wait and wait until, finally,

when the door opened and the waiter appeared with the second meal, he would know, to his chagrin, that yet another session had been deleted from the calendar. It was not just that his allotted time with the Hen had been taken away from him like candy snatched from a baby. It was that just now, when he *was* progressing, when everything he and the Hen had worked for *was actually happening*—just at this particularly crucial period in his evolution—the Hen had decided to ignore him!

"What's happened?" he asked the waiter once, when he appeared with the second meal.

"Sir?"

"What are you doing here? I haven't been to my meeting yet."

"I'm sorry, sir," the waiter said, wheeling the meal cart into the room and removing the metal covers from the dishes, "I know nothing of your meeting. It was time for your meal to be served, sir."

In spite of himself, he had grown irritated, even jealous. The Hen must have been devoting himself to other cases. He must have taken on an overload, must have been overly ambitious in gauging what one man, even a man of his diligence and caliber, could accomplish in the span of one working day. As much as he might sympathize with the Hen's problems, however, it was his own case that he had to be concerned with, his own progress. If he was selfish, he had a right to be selfish, hadn't he? Hadn't he done all the Hen had required of him? Hadn't he come to want his case to progress? And hadn't it progressed? On the balance of the record, he had been the good soldier, and if he had not been exemplary in every detail on every occasion, then who was? Yes, he believed in the Hen. Yes, he was obliged to the Hen for showing him the way to his road, for many things. But the Hen was also obliged to him, and neither one of them could renege on his commitment, not now, not at this stage.

He had refrained from expressing these feelings, not wanting to aggravate the Hen's harassment. He had regarded all the interruptions and cancellations as regrettable aberrations in the schedule. Then came the morning when he and the functionary sat in the Hen's anteroom. They had waited what seemed an unconscionably long time when the functionary arose and, timidly it seemed, as if he scarcely dared, knocked on the Hen's door. Receiving no answer, he waited a brief interval, then knocked again. Finally he opened the door with a key and peered inside.

Apparently the office was empty, for, closing the door again, the functionary turned to Y and said, "There will be no meeting, Mr. _____."

Y could contain himself no longer. When not even the functionary knew when the Hen would keep his appointments, the system had totally disintegrated. Where then was the Hen?

"I demand to be taken to him," he said tersely. "I am going to sit in this chair until either he arrives or you take me to him, wherever he is. I will not tolerate being treated this way. I tell you, it won't be tolerated!"

The functionary, as bland as ever, merely repeated himself: "There will be no meeting, Mr. _____. It is of no purpose to wait."

The functionary turned his key in the slot of the corridor door and waited like a sentinel until at last Y, with an exaggerated stamp of his feet, rose abruptly and followed him to his room.

That afternoon he let his feelings spill out, knowing as he released the controls that he was reverting to his old self, knowing too that, if that was what he was doing, it was not his fault. He had but one remaining method of retaliation.

Yes, there was a session that afternoon. Yes, His Highness the Hen deigned to receive him at the appointed hour. He stood before the desk—how long had it been since he had occupied the same position, shouting in similar indignation?—and slammed the desk top with his palm.

"I refuse to be treated like this," he cried, focusing on the top of the bald dome, his eyes almost shut, as once before he had focused upon it from this height. "I absolutely demand an explanation. It is a requisite for our going on. Otherwise there is no point to it, no point at all."

"Please," the Hen said wearily, "please to calm yourself and take a seat."

Yes, that was the Hen, even the words were the same. And the eyes. If anything, they were more tired, more harassed than ever, but they lodged large and watery in their orbs, these same sad brown eyes, sadder than ever without the cover of their spectacles.

He was not going to sit down this time. He made that clear. Nothing could induce him to sit down except an explanation. He was entitled to an explanation. There was no point trying to appease him with kind words, no point telling him he was being childish. He was fully aware of his childishness, but if he was anything more than a child, he need not be kept in the dark any longer, and if he was to be kept in the dark, he was justified in acting the child. He had committed himself to the Hen, *committed* himself.

The Hen was rubbing the corners of his eyes with thumb and forefinger. How tired he looked from this vantage point, Y thought, as if he had aged a decade, the chandelier light etching the lines and creases of his face in deep relief. Even his cheeks lacked their customary ruddiness, that usual red

glow which had now withdrawn from the surface, leaving a
waxen gloss.

"You are right. So right. I cannot blame you," the Hen said
at last. He ceased rubbing, donned his spectacles, and
studied the rigid figure before his desk. "Under these circumstances, I cannot blame you at all. Were I to occupy
your side of the desk, I would doubtless act the same way,
childish as it is, as we both know it is.

"Tell me," the Hen went on, raising his head so that their
eyes met, "if I were to give you my word that many of these
mysteries would be clarified for you very soon, that as soon
as possible you would have your explanations, sooner in fact
than you realize, would that make a difference? Would you
then sit down so that we could proceed?"

Y shook his head. The muscles of his eyelids squeezed
downward, almost shutting out the light, forcing him to
squint in order to see. His whole body tingled in its rigidity.

"No, I thought not," the Hen said. "And I cannot blame
you. In any case, I apologize for all these interruptions and
delays. They cannot be helped, but you are right, you are
fully entitled to your explanations. *And you will have them.*

"Meanwhile, I can only assure you that your status will
not be affected, not at all. Your case is to go on. It will not be
jeopardized. That much I can promise you."

Seeing that his words had no visible effect on Y's resolve,
the Hen rose.

"There is no point, then, as you say, in our proceeding any
further just now," he said.

The door had opened. The functionary waited in the
anteroom.

Y did not have long to wait. Later that same day, it must
have been in the evening, the functionary came for him. As

he followed him down the corridor, a tumult of contradictory feelings swept through him. Was he going to be punished? Had the Hen been baiting him, coaxing this new
exhibition of passive resistance from him so as to justify
punishment? He doubted it. The Hen did not function that
way. And even if the Hen had changed in this direction too,
even if he *was* going to be punished, it would make no
difference. He would hold to his convictions. He would
refuse to sit in the Hen's office. If the Hen and his hirelings
forced him to sit, he would not speak. Nothing could make
him speak. There was no device sufficiently clever or dia-
bolical to force him to speak. If there was to be a crisis, let it
come now, without further delays. The Hen had provoked it.
Let the Hen answer for it.

They did not pause as usual in the Hen's anteroom. The
functionary knocked on the Hen's door. Then the Hen, the
bald little man with the spectacles, slightly heavy in the
hips, was extending his hand, palm upward, like an usher.

Y entered.

The heavy damask drapes had been drawn aside. They
had concealed another room. The second room was the same
size as the Hen's office. It was identical to it in every respect,
except that in place of the desk was a semicircle of armchairs. All of the armchairs, save one, were occupied.

The only men he recognized in the semicircle of armchairs
were the inmates he called X^1 and Z.

9   Simon

✿

"I assume no one here knows any more than I do."

He was the first to speak. His words, his own voice sounded foreign to him. They had sat so long in awkward silence after the Hen left, the six of them, strangers to each other, six pairs of eyes studying each other with furtive curiosity, avoiding confrontation.

After Y had arrived and had taken the remaining vacant seat, the Hen perched on the edge of his desk facing the semicircle, a leader briefing his troops, a master of ceremonies. Like a man brought suddenly into bright light, Y was so startled by what had happened, so dazzled, that his mind could not begin to handle the questions which assailed it.

Who were they? But he couldn't think. He could only hear the Hen's voice, and that sporadically. All that he retained after the Hen had finished was his tone of friendliness, of joviality. The agitated, wearied air, so familiar and so characteristic of him in recent days, had disappeared as if mirac-

THE HEN'S HOUSE

ulously banished. His ruddiness had returned. His bald head glistened. He was almost debonair.

"Let me introduce you to each other," the Hen had said from his perch on the corner of the desk, one leg anchored to the floor, the other swinging freely. Thereupon he had proceeded around the semicircle from left to right, nodding to each man as he came to him, completing each introduction by the same ushering gesture. He used only first names. Y heard them all, but, hypnotized by the gesturing hand, the swinging leg, the timbre of the voice, he retained only two. There was a Leo. After the semicircle was completed, however, he could not match the name with the man. And there was his own name, which was Simon.

"You will have time to become acquainted with each other," the Hen continued when the introductions were concluded, "but I suggest you start at once. At some of your group's meetings, it may be that I shall be present, but this time I am afraid you will have to get along without me."

With that, without another word, he had risen from his perch, and smiling, nodding a tacit good-bye, he had left them alone.

In the silence which followed, while the six of them sat rigidly in their chairs, Simon sought to pull himself together, to consolidate, to reorganize as he always had to reorganize. Simon! It seemed so long since he had heard his first name! He scarcely recognized it, as if he needed to be introduced to himself. In the Henhouse his last name was always used— by the functionary, by . . . But no, the waiter and the valet never called him anything but "sir" whereas the Hen, he realized to his surprise, had rarely used any name whatsoever in addressing him. To himself, ever since he had identified the order of X, Y, and Z, he had been Y, or Member Y, or Inmate Y. But Simon!

X^1, the man he had once almost confided in, occupied the second chair from the left. What was his name? And Z, old Z, sitting right next to him, what was his? They were the two familiar faces. And who were the rest? Which was Leo?

He assumed they were all inmates, the six, even though he had never seen three of them before. They were to function as a group, weren't they? Hadn't the Hen as much as said so, with the reference to future meetings? If so, to what end? And if so, which of them could be trusted?

Surely the Hen would have planted at least one agent of his own among them, to inform on the rest, on their real progress as opposed to the progress reported face-to-face in the sessions.

But no. An absurd fantasy. A typical Y delusion. The Hen had no need of agents, not as such. An agent would be superfluous. He remembered X, the advanced inmate, how X had informed on him, how X had betrayed him on his own initiative, had then disappeared, doubtless having outlived his usefulness. No. No formal agent would be necessary. They would all inform on each other, naturally and easily, each of them on the other five, in their individual sessions, without any prompting whatsoever. They would all confide in "the person they were accustomed to confide in."

He would have to be cautious.

Yet what did he have to be so cautious about?

Were they all as advanced as he? Certainly. They must be. It would make no sense to include a newcomer, a recent arrival. Else why hadn't he been included in such a group long ago? Still, there was X^1, a relative newcomer. He had never seen X^1 before the disappearance of X.

How long had each of them been in the Henhouse?

He had to know it. But how would he, Simon, answer such a question were it put to him? He couldn't say. He had no idea. Doubtless none of them knew any more than he. How could any of them know if he didn't know?

Suddenly he had so much to ask, so many questions, a dossier of questions! Why wouldn't one of them speak out, anyone, just to break the silence? He glanced quickly at the semicircle, caught another pair of eyes staring at his. Was this the one called Leo? He couldn't be sure. Immediately he looked away, unable to hold the gaze.

Then the silence began to work on him. Why didn't one of them speak? What would happen if he, Simon, suddenly shouted?

But what could he shout? What could he say that would make any sense?

As if in response to him, the man two seats away, on the other side of Z, coughed. Though it was an innocuous dry cough, the kind heard in concert hall intervals, nonetheless the noise was so incongruous that all five heads turned, all five pairs of eyes stared at the hapless man who had coughed as if he had committed some intolerable outrage, then, catching the other eyes also staring, quickly looked away.

All such babies, Simon reflected, all five of them. No, all six. He was no better, he was included. The absurdity of it! Six grown men afraid of their shadows, six grown men unable to say a word to each other.

Simon! There it was again! Simon! His mind had said it again.

He had to struggle to muffle the laughter inside him. Simon! It was his name, to be sure. He had heard it all his life. No, it wasn't a bad name at all. Simon. He rather liked it, rather liked the sound of it, but then he had to squeeze his stomach muscles to fight away the laughter, and then he tensed the other muscles of his body to control his mounting impulse to fidget, to scratch himself, and still another: an urge to go to the bathroom, an urge which came out of nowhere to plague him.

He had to admit it: he was anxious. He was growing more anxious each minute. He had to stop being so anxious. Silences always made him anxious, didn't they? But hadn't he learned to handle silences? Yes. How? By talking, by filling the silences with words so that they would pass unnoticed.

To distract himself he began to study his surroundings. A closer look confirmed his initial impression. The second room was identical to the Hen's office save for the absence of the desk. Had the desk been removed for this occasion, or were the armchairs always there, in its place? The bookcases? No, there were no bookcases in the second half, now that he noticed it, but the carpeting and the wallpaper were the same. The chandeliers were twins.

But why the second half of the office, or the second office? Did a similar anteroom and a similar sequence of corridors lie outside this second door? If so, who used the second office? And why the damask drapes? As heavy as they were, they could not completely muffle sounds in one office from its neighbor. Could there have been people in the second office during his dialogues, observing him, listening to the interchanges, watching his self-display? Yet in all his sessions with the Hen he had never heard a sound behind the drapes, not the slightest sound. And even if their conversations had been overheard, what did he have to be afraid of? He need not be ashamed of anything he had done or said. He—Simon, Member Y—was what he was, wasn't he?

He sifted these and similar questions like an accomplished dealer shuffling a deck of cards, quickly exhausting their possibilities. He was not interested, not really, not for the moment. He wanted to hear what the others had to say. He was insatiably curious about them. Why didn't they speak? Why didn't one of them speak?

In the end, the silence had overwhelmed him. For some time his mind had urged him on, baiting him, prodding him to be the icebreaker, the initiator, however unfamiliar the role. He resisted the temptation, seeking to divert his mind with other subjects, but at last he too was quiet, his mind was quiet, like the shrieking quiet which filled the room. Or the two rooms.

He was unable to stand the silence another instant. He yielded. His mouth opened, closed, then opened again. He spoke.

The sound of his voice appeared to astonish the others as much as it did him. For several seconds the five pairs of eyes focused on him in amazement, as if dumbfounded that one of their number was actually capable of speech.

Then another voice piped up in a high pitch, a pitch apparently unnatural to it, for the speaker interrupted his first sentence to clear his throat.

"I don't think that I do," the voice said. It came from the third man from the opposite end of the semicircle, a slightly built young man, swarthy in complexion. He wore a white shirt open at the neck and a gray V-necked sweater. A Latin, Simon thought, staring at him.

"I've been here a long time," the voice went on. "I don't know how long. Is there anybody that does?"

The answers came rapidly but in turn, from left to right around the semicircle.

"No."

"No, I don't." That was X^1, the stocky blond member he had once almost trusted.

"No," accompanied by a shrug of the shoulders.

"I've been here a long time too"—this was Z, old Z who sat

next to him, the young man who contrived to look old—
"months perhaps, or perhaps even years, but I couldn't say
exactly."

Then it was Simon's turn. He shook his head. "No," he
said, "I've no idea either."

At last the barrier *was* broken. They began to talk to each
other, hesitantly at first, guardedly, as if unseen repercus-
sions awaited them if they proved too open, too frank, if
they let their tongues get away from them, then more and
more excitedly when the imagined pitfalls turned out to be
illusory and they began to realize that they were six men in
the identical predicament, with common stories to tell. By
some tacit election, perhaps only because he had spoken
first, they appointed Simon their leader. It was he who
initiated most of the questions, who turned their attention
to new subjects, then joining himself in the responses and
discussions.

They reintroduced themselves. In addition to Simon were
Martin, a tall bespectacled young man with light brown hair
and the serious look of a divinity student; Alexander, who
was X^1; Josef, the Latin who had spoken earlier and who
accented the second syllable of his name; Leo, who had
coughed; and Z, whose name—how, Simon smiled to himself, could a man like Z have a name like Keith? All of them,
Simon guessed, were younger than he, but, with the exception of this one detail, they appeared to have little in
common save their common experience. They were all sizes
and shapes. They spoke with different accents. He could not
tell about the social strata from which they might have
originated. With the exception of Z—he could not say Keith
to himself without having to fight off laughter—they could
have come from any of the social classes. Life in the Henhouse had blurred such distinctions, made them unimpor-

tant. Their conversation revolved on the present, on where they were, not where they had been, as if by common consent the origin and past of each of them were acknowledged to be private concerns.

What did they call the Hen, and not only the Hen but the various functionaries and the Henhouse itself? Though he had never been able to find out, though he had never, lest he appear ridiculous in the process, put a direct question on the subject to the Hen, Simon nevertheless wanted to know. He half expected to find that the others used the same nickname. Theoretically, wouldn't all men in their circumstances, confronted every day, twice every day, by the Hen, who was so obviously the Hen, inevitably arrive at the same invention?

"His name is Dr. Maartens."

Three of them spoke the words almost in unison. Three of them knew! But how?

"It was very simple," Josef said. "I only asked him. I wanted to know his name, so I asked. He told me I could call him Dr. Maartens. He spelled it for me."

Incredible! An incredible piece of news! The other two who knew had, like Josef, merely asked.

Dr. Maartens then. He was almost disappointed to learn that the Hen had a name. Dr. Maartens.

But Doctor of what? Of medicine? Or of what? In its European usage, Doctor could mean anything.

None of them knew. None of them except Simon seemed to care or have cared, once their curiosity over the name itself had been satisfied. The majority, evidently, saw their relationship with the Hen as that of student to professor. Three of them, he discovered, happened to have used "Professor" as a nickname. They had not questioned the relationship more closely and would not now. Hadn't any of them undergone fantasies similar to his own: that the Hen, or Dr. Maartens, was a psychiatrist or a warden or even the Devil, and the Henhouse in turn an asylum, a prison, or Hell itself?

But he refrained from putting the question. It was too direct, too demanding. Or perhaps, as strange as it seemed to him, he had begun to fear their answers. Instead he asked Josef if he knew the name of the place itself.

No, Josef did not, other than the society. That was what they all called it, the establishment or the society, which were only the Hen's habitual ways of referring to it.

"What do *you* call it, Simon?" It was Martin, the divinity student, who spoke, holding his head in such a way that Simon could not see his eyes but only the reflection of light on his spectacles.

As he started to answer, he was suddenly embarrassed. The Hen and the Henhouse were inappropriate, almost sacrilegious. He was tempted to lie, to invent anything, to say that he had no name for it or that he called it the society too. But he was what he was. For better or worse. Remembering this, insisting on it, he explained his metaphor of the Hen and the Henhouse.

A nervous titter spread among them. Obviously they didn't know whether he was joking or not. They looked at each other, looked back at him, for a clue as to his intent. Not seeing any, for the metaphor was no joke to him but his accurate representation of reality, they turned away from him, embarrassed too. He felt apart from them then, in that moment, different, a different species. He was not just another of the Hen's minions. Separate.

To bring them back, not for the purpose of reasserting his leadership—had he sought it in the first place?—but merely to be with them, to rejoin their number, to be one of the six, he started talking about the physical dimensions of the

Henhouse. Here too, however, their experience had varied from his own.

All of them had been moved to the first corridor within recent weeks, all except Leo, the most quiet of the group, who hardly spoke unless asked a direct question. Leo had just arrived on the corridor the previous day. But he, like Martin and Josef and Alexander, who was X^1, had lived in a different area of the Henhouse, and from their descriptions, the Henhouse now appeared much vaster than Simon had believed, corresponding more to his fantasies than to his observed reality in which corridors ended in doors and doors opened onto corridors. The Henhouse had a third dimension. They talked of elevators, of being escorted through corridors to elevators, of riding up and down in elevators to reach the Hen's office. Their accepted image of the Henhouse therefore differed greatly from his own. To them it was an institutional enterprise on a considerable scale. To them the Hen, Dr. Maartens, was not unique, was only one of a staff of professors. Increasingly alarmed, Simon questioned them closely on this point, learning to his relief that none of them had actually heard of another Hen or known of another member under the tutelage of a different Hen. The existence of multiple Hens was only their assumption, as the single Hen was his own. Nevertheless, the Hen appeared to have played a less significant role in their lives. Though they called him the Professor, though they referred to him deferentially, the Hen was not substantially different to them, despite his office, despite his function, from the other functionaries who served them. All of them—the Hen and the functionaries—formed part of a staff.

Whereas his first impulse had been to separate the group into halves: those he knew—the X^1, Y, Z sequence—and those he didn't—Martin, Josef and Leo—he now realized that the division was inaccurate, that X^1, who should be thought of as Alexander and not X^1, rightly belonged to the second trio, that only Z's experience truly approximated his own. As unlikely a companion as Z might be, he alone seemed to share Simon's attitudes toward their circumstances and toward the Hen. Only Z had lived on the third corridor. Only Z had endured the two-sessions-per-day schedule from the beginning. The others, even at the peak of their interrogations, had only seen the Hen once a day, save for Alexander, for whom a morning session had been added at the time of X's sudden disappearance.

Simon's original fantasy about X^1 had been wrong in at least one respect: Alexander was no newcomer. He appeared to have been in the Henhouse fully as long as any of them. At first, he had seen the Hen once daily, in the afternoons, just prior to X, who had immediately preceded Simon— which explained why Simon had never encountered Alexander until X's disappearance. Alexander had nothing to contribute to his speculations about X, and indeed the subject did not appear to have concerned him. Yet there was one factor in the mystery which fascinated Simon. In order to fill X's vacated slot in the Hen's afternoon schedule, either his second session would have been advanced or Alexander's delayed, and yet neither of them had been aware of any time change. Nor had any of the others, he quickly verified, any certain knowledge of Henhouse time, of the beginning or ending of any given day, of the hours of sessions and meals. They had only, like Simon, assumed time, with one significant and perplexing difference: none of them, save himself, had ever suffered from this lack of knowledge.

Of late their sessions had been irregular too, even more so than his own, and they too had noticed the Hen's increased agitation. For some of them, several days would pass without their visiting the Hen. The quiet man, the one called Leo, who had just arrived on the first corridor the previous day, had seen the Hen at the beginning of this evening meeting for the first time, he estimated, in almost two weeks. Yet this hiatus had not dismayed Leo, Simon learned, and not a one of them had objected to either the irregularities or the transfers. Not a one. Instead, when he broached the subject, their faces looked puzzled, as if they failed to understand what he meant, as if even the idea of objecting was foreign to them.

This question embodied a natural and obvious extension. He wanted to avoid it, half dreading what he might find out, and yet he could not. His mind started to nag him just as soon as the idea of avoidance occurred. Inevitably then, he asked if any of them had any experience with rebellion, if, for example, any one of them had tried to escape or, in other ways, major or minor, contrived to obstruct the functioning of the Henhouse.

Even as he spoke, he knew the answer. Not only had rebellion in any form not been tried, but the very concept was anathema, to all of them that is except, amazingly, to Z.

"Would you call it rebellion? I don't know that you would," Z began quietly, in his dignified, faintly English accent, "but once I assaulted the man who takes care of me . . . my functionary, as I believe you refer to him.

"I don't know why," he went on, his tone gradually becoming apologetic, halting. He looked around him, as if he too were ashamed at being so singled out from the group. "I had no reason. He was always perfectly decent to me, in his treatment of me. It was an impulse, an aberration, nothing more. Perhaps a momentary insanity. That is how I think of it. When he came for me one day, I swung on him. And I knocked him down."

"And then?" Simon asked, when Z hesitated.

"That was all there was to it," Z concluded.

"You mean it didn't occur to you to attempt to escape, or even to take his keys?"

"No. I only knocked him down."

"And what did you do then?"

"Then? I believe I helped him up, and then we went on to . . . to Dr. Maartens. Nothing more was ever said about it. He . . . the functionary . . . never referred to it, and neither did I."

That was Z's history of rebellion. All eyes focused then on Simon, as if, because he had initiated the subject, or because he had already shown himself to be in some ways different, they expected some monstrous confession from his lips.

Knowing this, he lied to them. He had done nothing, he said. Rebellious schemes had occasionally occurred to him, but he had never put them into practice. In his opinion, rebellion within the society was to no avail. There was nothing to be gained by it. One could only delay one's progress with it. In the end, he told them, he considered it self-destructive.

As he finished, he saw the look of dismay in Z's eyes, the trace of hurt, as if he had been slapped. Had his choice of words been too close to what the Hen would have said? Could Z tell that he was lying?

Suddenly he wanted to apologize. To Z. Suddenly it was terribly important. If Z, for reasons he did not yet fully understand, was to be his closest companion, he had already betrayed him. He wanted to draw Z aside and tell him the whole truth, leaving nothing out. He owed it to Z. He owed Z honesty. At least Z.

But not the others. He owed them nothing. That was the trouble. If the others knew the truth, they would turn him out, exclude him. They would not tolerate him in their midst.

They had asked him to be their leader, hadn't they? He had not sought it. They had turned to him for leadership, Z included. Then they would have to trust his judgment. He could not obstruct the Hen's training, could not contradict what the Hen had so laboriously taught them. In a similar situation, after all, what could the Hen have said? Wouldn't the Hen have altered the facts as he had for the communal good?

There remained Z. He would have to take care of Z separately, find some way to tell Z why he had done what he had done and thereby regain Z's confidence. He needed Z. Z was his potential ally. Not Alexander, even if the seeds of his distrust of Alexander had been planted by his own imagination. And not the others.

After his comments on rebellions, however, the conversation lagged. Despite his efforts, he could not get them to talk freely again, as if his lie, recognized or unrecognized, had cast a pall on the room. A direct question would be answered, but then only tersely, succeeded in turn by moments of silence in which each of them relapsed to his private thoughts.

Had they all known it? Was that why they had suddenly withdrawn, why the conversation had suddenly evaporated? No, only Z could have sensed it, only Z had looked right into his eyes.

Then why did six men in their common predicament have so little to talk about? He was amazed and disappointed, but the renewed silence gave proof to it. Understandably they had been reluctant at the beginning. None of them had talked freely to another man for months, save the Hen, save whatever paltry exchanges they might have had with the functionaries. Once he had uttered those first hesitant

words, however—"I assume no one here knows any more than
I do"—he had felt them start to pull together, drawn by
their common concerns. He knew he had felt it, the beginning of a bond. He was sure of it. But then, so quickly and
easily he could scarcely believe it, they had withdrawn into
themselves. Had they really exhausted all they had to discuss? Finally he gave up, allowing the silence to close in on
him like a shell.

They were frightened, he thought. Inevitably they would
be guarded, would harbor their secrets. Perhaps he was not
the only one who had lied, who had deliberately concealed
his past. Only the Hen would know. They did not yet trust
themselves.

No, it was that they did not yet trust him. Their appointed leader. He was the one who appeared most different
from the rest. That was precisely why they had chosen him
but the price he had to pay for their choice was that his
mere presence inhibited them. What would it have been like
if the Hen, himself, had stayed? Hadn't the Hen said he
would join them the next time . . . or some time? What
would it be like then? How freely would they talk then?

But why was he hiding so from himself, why did he persist
in lying? For his biggest disappointment quite clearly was
not their failure to communicate, but his own performance.
Here, in his first exposure to peers, to men who, however
different they might appear, shared his situation, he had
failed lamentably and utterly. No one else had lied. It would
not have occurred to them to lie. They were five simple men,
simple and direct. Yet Simon had lied. Simon had covered
up. And why? Because of their disclosures. Because not
everything turned out to be what he had expected it to be.
Because of this myth of leadership which he had concocted
for his own deception.

They had held no election, tacit or overt. There was no

leader. He was just one man among six. That he had spoken first was mere chance. It could just as well have been Z or Alexander or any of them. It signified nothing. The truth was that he too was frightened, as frightened of them as they of him, and more so, for he alone had felt compelled to parrot the Hen. The truth was that he had abandoned them. So there he was, circling again, back on the curve with the square in sight, and the fact that four of them were oblivious to it made no difference. One of them knew. Z knew. And even if he was wrong about Z, still Simon had lied. That was the fact, and try as he might, he could not deny it.

Right then he wanted to leave, to rise from his chair and walk out the door. Perhaps if he left, as the Hen had left, the air would be cleared for the rest of them, so that they could talk openly about who they were and what was to become of them, without his Henlike ear and his Henlike voice to impede them. That was just what he was going to do.

Before he could goad his body to respond, however, the door itself opened, and the Hen strode into their midst, ebullient, a wide smile creasing his cheeks.

"Well, then, is it that you have talked yourselves out so quickly?" he asked, rubbing his hands together. "I expect to find you in full-scale debate, or hatching a plot of some kind. No? Instead you are all so quiet, like six birds who have lost their voices. Or was it that you heard me coming?"

The Hen, his eyebrows raised in mock-question, looked from one face to the next.

"Well," he went on, still smiling, "there will be other times. You will have other times to be better acquainted. And it might be that one of your meetings I will stay and we will hatch the plot together. If, of course, you will allow me."

The words were a signal. The meeting was over. Without

further indication from the Hen, the six of them rose to leave, filing out one behind the other.

They really did all live on the first corridor. At least no one had lied about that. From what Simon could see as he walked past the opening doors, his eyes averted from the others, his suspicions about the Henhouse cells were verified: all of them were exactly alike.

10   The Leader

❦

"I lied to them," he confessed to the Hen.

He spoke dispassionately. In the intervening hours, through appraisals and reappraisals of what had happened, he had conquered his remorse. The confession remained to be made.

The meeting of the group had posed him a choice, he realized, and as so often happened, he had chosen intuitively, impulsively, without even knowing that he was choosing. Yet he had chosen: between the Hen and the group, between himself and his old self, between Simon and Y and the self before Y. Whether or not he had been elected, he had identified himself as leader, as the man apart. For the duration of the meeting, he had been in his own eyes at once participant and spectator, fellow member and inquisitor. In lying to them, he had chosen the second roles and their separate set of rules, the Hen rules, for he had betrayed not only their trust but his former self as well, his pre-Simon self, the self which had committed the acts of rebellion and which once, no matter how inaccurate they might have

been, had taken pride in these acts. In lying, he was killing Y
and the self before Y. In accepting the lying, he was burying
them. It remained for him to rewrite their history from the
crow's nest.

He had not reached his crow's nest without suffering, for
he had been attacked again by that inexplicable longing,
that sensation of seeing the corpse from a great height, that
powerful nostalgia for what had once been, for whatever
had once been. Yet the longing was absurd, unjustified,
absurd because it was inexplicable. He would not mourn. He
was not going back. He did not want to go back. If for Y the
act of lying would have been a sign of circling, of return to
himself, for Simon it was the unmistakable insignia of progress, and if the price of progress was a little absurd nostalgia,
he would pay it gladly.

"I had asked them about their rebellions," he continued,
sensing how easy it was to compound his betrayal with this
new one, to become the spy who was not a spy, "if any of
them had ever rebelled against you or the . . . the society.
I suppose it was important to me to find out if their histories
approximated my own. But none of them had, except . . ."
—there it came again, without prompting, furthering the
betrayal, the good parrot in action, even though the Hen
must already know about Z and what Z had done—"except
one who reported that he had once attacked his functionary.
When my turn came, when one of them asked me the same
question, I lied. I said I had never done anything like that,
that rebellion within the society was useless."

"Why did you lie?"

Why, the Hen wanted to know, the Hen, who expressed
neither surprise nor approval at his confession (though what
did he expect?), who was his old inscrutable and attentive
self again, twirling his spectacles in his most reflective pose,

as if all the harassment and interruption and cancellation of recent weeks had not occurred.

Once started, the betrayal had to be extended and completed. That is what he had decided. Thus, to explain the lying, he divulged the rest of the meeting: of how, he thought, they had selected him as their leader, of the degree to which their individual experiences in the Henhouse had differed from his own, of how, wanting only to be accepted and not set apart, he had concealed his own past. On this one point the Hen questioned him in detail, until finally he conceded that what he had really wanted was to belong and not to belong at the same time, to be set apart, if need be, but not to be excluded, to assume therefore the leader's posture. Throughout his description, and particularly in this one area, he was irritated by the Hen's suavity, his studied imperturbability, the effortless way he delved for the truth and found it. But his irritation was only a minor vexation, he realized, only Y, the anachronism, turning in his grave, and so he proceeded quickly to the end of his report.

"I have heard too," the Hen said when he had finished, the familiar Hen smile catching the light on his spreading cheeks, "that your name for me has been the Hen and for our society the Henhouse, is that not so?"

He felt a flush rising to his head; then quickly he was angry, furious at the man, whoever it was, who had revealed the secret. And just as quickly, he reflected that he had no cause to be angry, for who had divulged the most and who had been most betrayed?

Caught by the Hen's smile, he laughed and said, "Yes, I call you the Hen. I think of you as the Hen. I have for a long time, I always have. I didn't know your real name and, although admittedly for inaccurate reasons, I didn't feel I could ask. So I called you the Hen." He explained his

metaphor of the Henhouse, of the incubator-corridors and
the nurturing of chickens, and, laughing again, how the Hen
even resembled a hen, or so he thought when he considered
him in the light of the metaphor.

"I have heard, myself," he concluded, "that your actual
name is Dr. Maartens."

"Yes," the Hen said, "that is what you may call me, if you
like. But, do your know, it is not such a bad metaphor as
metaphors go, this Hen and Henhouse of yours. It is even, in
a sense, highly accurate, more than you realize, though
again, highly inaccurate. At any rate," he sighed, "I have
been called far worse names. And, though it may disappoint
you to learn it, I have even been called the Hen before, or
something close to it, the name of some bird—I can't recall
it—though not in your metaphorical sense, it is true."

"Is it a Dutch name?" Simon persisted. "Maartens?"

"Yes, I believe it is, in origin, though you would find it
today in many different countries, I would think."

That was that, then. He would get no more out of the Hen
about his name, and, were he to ask what "Doctor" represented, the answer would be similarly equivocal. The Hen
would divulge what he wanted to divulge, and no more.

But isn't that precisely what he had done in seeking to
manipulate the group: to tell only what he wanted to tell, to
lie, when necessary, to protect himself and his position? In
spite of himself, the subject haunted him. He could not
escape it, even though he—or the Hen—led the conversation
in new directions. How wrong it had been, he thought now,
to assume that he, and he alone, would describe the meeting
to the Hen, that he was the Hen's one and only agent!
Clearly the Hen had received a full report from each of
them. Since he knew about Simon's secret names, he would
know the rest. For if there was a truth to be ferreted out, a

secret, however large or small, and the Hen wanted it, the Hen would find it, in that admirably effortless technique of his, without even seeming to look. X, the only other "advanced" member he had encountered, had proven this long ago. He, himself, was proving it at this very session. Then why had he assumed that, if he had been compelled to describe the details of the meeting, the other five would not have been equally compelled, that Z, for instance, in the session immediately following, would not be led into his own version—without even seeming to be led?

Yet he had assumed this, just as he assumed that he had been elected leader, just as he had assumed that he was a man apart, not to be confused with the other five members, and these assumptions had formed the basis for his acceptance of the lying. But were they anything more than his mind's busy concoctions for purposes of its own? Had he done anything more than to work and rework the raw material of the meeting into a version which, if it was illusory, was nonetheless more palatable and flattering than the truth?

When he returned to the subject, however, the Hen was visibly annoyed.

"I am surprised at you, Simon," he said, rising impatiently behind his desk. "Obviously there are lies, and then there are lies, just as there are ideas and ideas. We are fully capable of distinguishing one from its neighbor, no? At least we have had adequate experience, would you not agree? Mendacity is not of itself bad or wrong or, as we would prefer to say, inaccurate. That much should be obvious to us. It is the motivations behind mendacity which allow us to separate into the categories of accuracy and inaccuracy."

Yes, Simon thought, that is what the Hen would have to

say about it. That is what he had said to himself, though in a form more tortuous and less pedagogic.

"We have already developed motivations for this one instance of lying," the Hen continued. "You identified yourself as the leader of the group. While you wanted to belong to them—a natural and predictable response, we might add, for one whose contacts have been so limited for such a period of time—you also saw that, needing someone to direct them, they chose you. As unexpected as it was, you rather like the idea. Why be so ashamed of liking it? You do not insist on it. They chose you freely and you accept it. Is that the way it happened?"

"Yes." He hesitated. "Yes, I think that's what happened."

"Then you worried—quite correctly we may assume—lest you appear too different to them, too much, as we have put it, a man apart. They might regard you only as dangerous rather than worthy of their trust. Accordingly you concealed a part of your past from them. Was this necessary? We cannot say, can we, though perhaps we will find out if it succeeded. But, we must note, you did not conceal it from yourself. Didn't you know what you were doing, and why?"

"Yes."

"Yes. Of course you did. We have already had your expression for it: you were paying a price. You were learning some of what leadership requires of the one who is chosen. It has perhaps been a little difficult to accept, this new knowledge of yours, but need that surprise us so?"

Simon nodded his agreement, reminded again of the two opposing arguments, both supportable by reason, and the choice which nonetheless had to be made. "No, not so surprising. I have trouble with changes, I always have. Putting the first foot into water or the first step out from dry land. I

want them and then I don't want them, and then they are
here, whether I like it or not."

"If your road doesn't curve by itself, you have trouble?"

"Yes, it is something like that. Sometimes I have to make it
curve myself, or so I think."

The Hen was right. Whenever he found himself on a road
he hadn't followed before and, by reasoned analysis, justified
his progress on it, the converse truth always came to his
mind, the antitruth, the argument which disproved what he
had proved and thereby caused the first arcing of the tangent. This sudden exposure to the group, together with the
requirements the group had made of him, constituted just
such a new road. It demanded a new stride of him who
walked it. If a part of him, a small part, still doubted,
arguing that he was only basking in the implied flattery of
the Hen's words, that was just Y, preaching caution, preaching tangents, curves and cycles, and he would banish him.
Weed out the flattery, and there were left behind his responsibilities. He would banish Y, and the Hen would help him.

"Or could we put the case this way?" the Hen said,
pausing in his pacing to stand against the drapes, his hands
linked behind his back. "In the past I have been your leader.
This was your choice, we must remember. I prefer to consider my function as that of an accomplice, a member. (I
was not, we might note, entirely jesting when I talked of
hatching a plot in conjunction with our new group.) You
even named me the Hen, mentally relegating yourself to the
role of the newly hatched chick. Like it or not, some of the
responsibilities of leadership fell on my shoulders.

"Let us take one such example," the Hen went on. "We
have seen recently any number of changes in our little
group. Let us suppose that they had occurred not when they
did, but long ago, when we were still new to each other,

when our analogy of the newly hatched chick was far more accurate than it is today. What would have happened?"

Simon did not reply.

"Let us suppose that all these unfortunate interruptions and cancellations and delays which have just plagued us had come much earlier, at a time when you were still under the spell of some of those old notions and delusions of yours which used to attract you so. Or let us suppose, a long time ago, you had suddenly been thrust together with five other men, all strangers, all as wary of you as you were of them. Can we imagine the result?

"We had our hands full as it was, did we not," the Hen, having paused, continued like a professor to elaborate points which required no further elaboration, "without the chaos these changes would have produced? No. As leader—a role you chose for me—I had to make certain decisions in your behalf. Everything had to come in its proper order. And, since we are sitting here today and can but point to the progress we have made, I was at least not wrong. That much we would have to say." He paused, as if debating his next words, then, with a sigh, proceeded: "We already know, Simon—it must be obvious—that I have not been able to tell you all these things which relate to the progress of your case. Certain things, certain measures . . . You could never have accepted in the past what you accept now. There still remain things you do not know, a not insubstantial number. That is part of my responsibility as well, the burden of our knowledge that I have to carry. You still share only a part of it. Yet we are making progress. Yes . . ."

The eyes had never looked so sad, Simon thought, now that the Hen's voice had trailed off, as if they alone bore the strain of responsibility. Seizing the opportunity, he asked the inevitable question:

"Why don't you tell me, then, what is in store for me?"

As if relieved, the eyes closed somewhat, the skin around them crinkling. The Hen was smiling.

"All in good time," the Hen said. "Everything in its proper order. We must be patient."

Later, when he was leaving, the Hen interrupted him with one of his afterthoughts, though this one lacked the usual oracular stamp.

"By the way, Simon, you should note," the Hen said, "lest you retain any doubts on the subject, that already they are acknowledging you as their leader. From the way they have described the meeting, it won't be long before actually they are using the word."

In the days which followed, Simon's sessions with the Hen were reduced in number to one each day, and in duration to a timespan which appeared shorter than ever. In counterbalance, however, the number of meetings of the group increased. Then, at certain hours of the day—in what he wryly called a further liberalization of Henhouse policy—the doors to all the rooms on the first corridor—the six occupied rooms, that is—were opened, so that the members could pass freely from one to the other. As Simon had sensed the night of the first meeting, Z became the one closest to him. He spent most of his free hours in Simon's company. The Hen encouraged their friendship, not by any overt statement but by his constant interest in Z, the way he always wanted to know what Simon thought about this or that aspect of Z's character.

In one detail of his interpretation Simon had been mistaken. Although he continued to neglect, in contradiction of his original impulse, to explain to Z the lie he had told at their first meeting, he realized that Z did not now suspect him of lying, and doubtless had not suspected him in the first place. The look he had seen in Z's eyes that night, the mixture of dismay and hurt, had not, however, been his own projection. According to the Hen, it had disturbed Z deeply to realize that he alone had acted in rebellion, in violence, just as Simon had sought to avoid beng set apart from the others. All of them wanted company, wanted to belong, even Z, who, in the Hen's opinion, was not only less capable of accepting his individuality than Simon but most zealous in considering Simon the leader of the six.

Evidently, in one small way, Z had lied himself, in his description of his assault on the functionary. "Nothing more was ever said about it," Z had said at the first meeting, whereas, from the way the Hen returned to the subject in Simon's own sessions, Simon gathered that it had been a constant topic of investigation in the progress of Z's case.

"But tell us," the Hen asked at one session, "how do you react to this act of violence of his?"

Seeing Simon's hesitant expression, the Hen extended his arms, palms up, as though to show he was concealing nothing, and said, "Please. Please not to trouble yourself with any more notions of betraying and betrayals. I have not asked you to be a spy. There are no spies in the society, just members. I am a member. You are a member. Furthermore, you must remember that I know everything there is to know about all six of you, everything you know yourselves and more." He paused, letting Simon consider the implications of this last remark, then continued, "But his act of violence. How do you react to it?"

"He has said very little about it," Simon answered truthfully, reassured more by his lack of knowledge than the Hen's plea of camaraderie, "only, really, that he attacked his functionary. He struck him, knocked him down, and that

was all there was to it. I gather it was an impulsive act. He
didn't say why he did it, only that he had done it, and that
was the end of it. That was that. 'An aberration' is what he
called it."

"Precisely," said the Hen. "That is precisely how he always talks of it. He acted on impulse. An aberration. When
the act was completed, it was completed. It satisfied him.
But does he impress you as the type of man given to such an
impulsive act? Or let us set aside unmotivated violence.
Would we expect violence of any variety from a member
such as he?"

"No," Simon said. From what he had seen of him, that
was not Z, at least not his "old Z," the Z of his imagination.
But his imagination had not led him astray in this instance.
From the very way Z talked, he could tell that any sort of
self-assertion was a source of embarrassment to him. His very
existence seemed to embarrass him; he seemed constantly
compelled to apologize for it. Doubtless he was bred that
way, for the embarrassment seemed so natural to him as to
have been inherited.

"Precisely," the Hen repeated, waving his arms from time
to time to punctuate the riddle of Z. "Now acts of rebellion
are not unknown in the society. We know that from our own
experience, do we not? Even, regrettably, violent acts have
occurred, though at distant intervals. In the example of your
own rebellions, however inaccurate they may have been,
you were always motivated, and it was your motivation
which was more conspicuous than the actions themselves.
You wanted your measure of control, or you wanted to
demonstrate the existence of your will, or you wanted to
avenge some imaginary injustice of mine. Regrettable
though the acts were, we could always examine your motivations, we could learn from them, we could make the
necessary adjustments.

"But not with him. With him, there is no such motivation. In all other respects—in every other respect, I assure you— he has proved himself an exemplary member. He is not unintelligent. He is cooperative. He is even . . . the word I am accustomed to using in such situations is: 'malleable.' He has learned to live with his own guilt in all respects except in this respect. He takes no responsibility for this act. He refuses responsibility. We have tried. How we have tried! I assure you, we have tried."

Simon could well imagine. Yet he did not know how to respond. The Hen's confidences puzzled him. The Hen seemed transported by his own voice, as if he were talking to himself, or trying Z's case before an imaginary judge. Perhaps even a man like the Hen, who spent his days in constant session with the members, needed a confidant, an accomplice. Simon could not but be flattered to be selected, yet this new role confused him. Apparently, however, the Hen anticipated his comment, for he sat now, lips parted, an expectant stare radiating behind his spectacles.

"Could you forget it?" Simon suggested tentatively. "Could you not consider it momentary madness, an aberration just as he says? If he has been as exemplary in all other respects as you say, could you not forgive this one aberration?"

"No!" The Hen awoke abruptly from the trance of his stare. "You do not understand. Of course. How could you understand? But it cannot be done. It is not that I could strike one entry from his record. It will come up. It is certain to come up. And it will hurt his case, I can tell you that now. Were his case to be concluded today, it would stand as the act of an innocent . . ."—again the Hen seemed transported, hypnotized by his own voice which now rose almost to a shout—". . . and that won't be tolerated!

"You see, Simon"—the voice had subsided, the eyes were

once more large brown pools—"I have cause to worry about his case. He gives cause."

Simon was astonished. Either the Hen, carried away by his concern for Z, had inadvertently revealed more than he intended or else, for reasons of his own, had chosen an oblique method of revelation. Simon could not know which was the truth—although he found it difficult to believe that the Hen ever would say more than he intended—but the implication of the Hen's words remained clear: They were, then, actually being prepared for some kind of conclusion. Simon had come to take the Hen's references to his "case" as an idiosyncratic manner of expression, equivalent in meaning to his "situation" or his "progress." But now there could be no doubt. He had been wrong. There was to be a conclusion of their cases after all, and therefore some kind of hearing or trial. Fleetingly, he pictured the Hen presiding, with all the pomp and mock formality of a judge, hearing the testimony of all concerned before disposing, with Henhouse justice, of the cases before the court. But why did he bother with a trial? More important, what was Henhouse justice? How did the Hen dispose of his cases? What would their sentences be?

The age-old questions remained. Though he posed them now in this new form, they were still unanswerable.

Strangely, he no longer found it difficult to accept his ignorance. Or perhaps it was not so strange. Did he have any choice? Had he ever had any real choice? And didn't he know, more surely now than he had ever known it, that his ignorance was temporary, that one day, sooner or later, there would be an end to it?

The Hen was worried about Z. Therefore he had to be concerned as well, although the Hen's terminology confused him, made it difficult for him to understand Z, to understand what was wrong with him, or why his case was in such jeopardy. He thought he knew now what the Hen meant by guilt, by living with his guilt. The concept involved learning to recognize, to acknowledge, and to accept everything that he was, the sum total of his existence, past and present, the good acts as well as the evil acts. He would have called it, as the psychologists called it, living with himself, but he supposed that it made no difference in the end. The learning process was accomplished by this detachment he had first recognized in his dream of the runner, by which one could continue to experience directly—receiving the bullet in the chest—but could also, simultaneously, evaluate experience from a detached and Henlike point of view. What he had at first taken to be a separation in his self, in which his old self, his Y-self, had to be killed, he gradually understood as an enrichment of his personality, a growth which included both selves operating as one. By this standard, his former self could be seen as innocent, as operating under the delusional lack of perspective which characterizes innocence. By this standard too, he could see why the Hen had labeled Z's attack on the functionary the act of an innocent, since Z had apparently been unable to attain the detachment, the distance, the height from which, like the proverbial sage, he could view below the terrain of his self. The Hen must feel he had failed with Z, and since, Simon knew, the Hen relished his accomplishments, his successes—as in the case of Simon himself—professional failure in the case of a Z would gnaw at him.

Still, at best, this was a peculiar use of the ideas of guilt and innocence. Perhaps it could be explained in terms of the Hen's general semantic peculiarities. And yet, as days passed, Simon continued to wonder. They were to stand trial, it seemed, a trial of some sort. But were they to be tried on the conventional basis of guilt and innocence, under the conventional meanings of the two terms? And if so, who were the guilty and who the innocent? And if so, were the guilty to be punished and the innocent rewarded?

One of the subsidiary results of their increasing concentration on Z in the sessions was that Simon's own focus enlarged. He could no longer concentrate solely on his own welfare, the progress of his own case. He had to include the others in his deliberations, or at least Z. If the Hen was worried about Z's case, that in itself sufficed to give Z a special place in his mind. In addition, he found that, despite the differences between them, he liked Z all the more as he came to know him.

As for the other four members, he could not help lumping them together in his mind, even as the Hen did. The Hen rarely referred to them by name. They were "the others" or "the other four," though whether the Hen did this for Simon's benefit—to segregate Z in his mind for special attention—or because he really did not distinguish between them, Simon did not know. He came to see the four as drudges, plodding workers, going about their tasks and errands like the ants he had once watched on the slates which led from the white house. Many of his first impressions about them had been incorrect, perhaps because the mere introduction of other members into his life had so excited him. Martin, the tall young man with spectacles, had resembled a divinity student with his serious, open countenance and his pinched, scholarly eyes, but Martin was no divinity student, unless one of the prerequisites for the study of theology was a total lack of imagination. He had admired the one called Josef, the Latin, because Josef had had the bravado to find out the Hen's name. Josef's free air, however, his frankness, his willingness to express whatever entered his mind, arose not from his having mastered his inhibitions but because inhibition itself was foreign to him. Likewise, Simon had anticipated a depth in Leo, the quiet man, convinced that one who kept his own counsel to such an extent must harbor an abundance of introspective wealth. Leo, however, was quiet only because he had little to say. When a response occurred to him, he spoke out readily enough, but his words never contained any special significance. As for Alexander, Simon learned that his fantasies about X^1 had been totally inaccurate. No one could be further from the imagined X^1 than this bland, clodlike man who, of them all, most justified the label of drudge.

It had never ceased to amaze Simon that men like the four others existed in the world. Yet he knew they existed. He had encountered them before. If his attitude toward them was callous, he justified it in terms of self-defense. For his four others were not social freaks. On the contrary, he suspected that they represented the majority and that he, Simon, belonged to the breed apart, the minority. They were the drudges, the ants, this majority, who, most of them, lived long, productive lives, who worked, ate, worshiped, reproduced themselves, and yet were never aware that they were alive. They were, like animals, like ants he supposed, totally without introspection. They did not know what introspection was. If asked what being alive meant, they would merely ogle the questioner in utter stupefaction. Confronted with the personal and social problems of life, they abdicated all responsibility. They could be led this way or that, it made no difference, as long as their time was occupied, as long as they could work, eat, and enjoy themselves. Perhaps once they had come mainly from the lower classes, though Simon was skeptical of it. For in the increasingly classless society into which men had evolved, the drudges continued to proliferate and flourish. They were everywhere, and they flourished.

Even in the Henhouse. What did the Hen do with them? he wondered. Were they possibly capable of that same process of detachment, of "living with their guilt"? True, they had undergone a less rigorous schedule, with fewer sessions, and it remained possible, since none of them had any certain knowledge of time, that they had actually arrived in the Henhouse much more recently then he and Z. Yet they too had called the Hen Professor. And the Hen had devoted time to them.

What were they doing in the Henhouse in the first place? With the kind of grim humor of which he was at times capable, Simon reflected that, after all, the Hen did not have a long roster of applicants and applications through which to pick and choose. They were there. Through some osmotic process, they had acknowledged him as leader, and he had no choice but to accept this, their latest abdication of responsibility. If they had to concern him at all, however, he would still, like the Hen, spend less time on their cases than on Z's and his own.

Despite the Hen's prodding, his approach toward Z was gingerly. In his diffident, self-effacing way, Z appeared to welcome Simon's special friendship. He sought Simon out. Yet for at least one reason Simon was wary of him, careful in his choice of words. Without any tangible justification for it, he felt at times that Z was a kind of conscience to him, that Z knew he had been lying that first night and had chosen, out of politeness or diffidence, not to mention the subject. Similarly Simon did not feel he could initiate the subject of Z's act of violence. The effect of Z's description had been to dampen further discussion. "Nothing more was ever said about it," had been Z's final statement. If Simon harped on it, Z would know that Simon and the Hen had been discussing his case, and the growing trust between them would be dissolved. Simon would be identified, once and for all, as the Hen's agent. As a result, he sought only to maneuver their conversations indirectly toward the subject, but as much as he tried, Z could not be led.

"What do you think is going to happen to us?" Simon had asked on one such occasion.

"I don't know," Z had replied characteristically. "I have never thought too much about it. I suppose I should have, as you have, but it has always struck me that there was little I could do about it. Nothing at all, for that matter. We will have to take what comes."

"And that is enough for you? And has always been enough?"

"Yes, it is enough. It is very fatalistic of me, I know, to be willing to accept whatever comes my way, but it is enough. I need nothing more."

"The trial? Do you think that when the trial comes you will have no control over your case?"

"No. I don't think so," Z had answered. "And do you, Simon?"

"Maybe. I think maybe that I will, and that you will too."

At this point the conversation had lagged, as if Simon's intentionally provocative last words had fallen on deaf ears. Was Z guarding his real thoughts because he suspected Simon, feared him? No, he decided not. This aura of resignation was too constant to Z's style. Z would accept whatever came to him, not blindly, as would the others, but out of resignation. In his own eyes, Z did not count for much in this world, or any other world. It was his destiny to follow the ebb and flow of forces greater than himself. If all the details of his destiny were not already known, they would be decided eventually by other men, without his collaboration.

And yet there was the one aberrational act, the assault. In a way, Simon thought he was beginning to see what so troubled the Hen about it.

On other subjects, however, Z was much more communicative. He talked at length about his life before the Henhouse, and for once, upon hearing Z's story, Simon found that his first impressions had been in the main accurate.

Z was the scion of a moderately wealthy family of moderate social reputation, the only child. He had attended the best schools, to which the position of his family easily entitled him, and while he had not excelled in school, he had not failed either. Throughout he was a member of the rank and file, the kind of student of whom, at subsequent reunions, his classmates would say, if their memories were joggled, "Yes, I remember old Z. I wonder what became of him," before proceeding to more amusing reminiscence. Immediately upon graduation—again Simon's guess had been accurate—Z had entered the family business, a venerable yet financially successful enterprise which, in the course of time, Z would likely have inherited. He had married early—a girl from a background quite similar to his own. He had known her most of his life. They had had one child, a son, who, Simon thought with a smile, had doubtless been christened Keith III, if Z himself were not already Keith III. And then, while still a young man, Z was in the Henhouse, like Simon, like the rest.

Unlike Simon, Z remembered his life in terms of its facts, its factual outline. About dates and places he was unfailingly precise. Whereas Simon saw vignettes, which in the main contained some emotional relevance, from Z's account, his life had been totally devoid of strong emotional responses.

Perhaps, Simon realized, Z's account was nonetheless complete, perhaps there had been no strong emotional responses, perhaps that was Z. In any event, Z seemed somehow relieved to be finished with it, this earlier life, to welcome the rupture his coming to the Henhouse had wrought, be it temporary or permanent—as if any change in the meticulously drawn blueprint of his life were welcome.

Did Z love his wife and son? All Simon knew with certainty was that Z had the wife and son because, or so it seemed, that was all Z knew. Once he had asked Z if he missed his son, to which Z replied, "Yes, I do miss him," but in a tone so dry and unemotional that Simon regarded the statement as nothing more than a stock social response.

Yet whether Z knew it or not, his life in the Henhouse was no different in its quality than his life before. To a much greater extent than he apparently realized, Z regulated the tone of his own existence. Even in a vacuum, Simon thought, Z would have found a means of self-effacement. But the same could be said of all of them, Simon included. Perhaps all men regulated the tones of their lives, if not the circumstances, to a much greater extent than they realized. For Z, the Henhouse was evidently another social system to which, no matter how much it differed from its predecessor, he had to resign himself. He would find out what was expected of him sooner or later, as he always had, and he would go along with it, as he always had. Whereas he, Simon, victimized by his own anticipations and delusions in the Henhouse as before, had manufactured his own issues when they failed to exist in reality. He had fought for his own imaginary rights mainly in the confines of his own mind, though from time to time he externalized the struggle, as when he made the Hen his enemy. Surely Z's had been an easier case for the Hen than Simon's—easier to handle and yet, paradoxically, far more difficult to resolve. For with Z there was still the incident of violence—that innocent act—which remained unresolved, while Simon had obtained the sense of detachment, that expanding growth, which to him, as to the Hen, signified progress and presaged conclusion.

The Hen continued to ask him about Z, but he had little to report. More and more he liked the man. Perhaps this was only because Z obviously liked him and sought his company, but he also admired certain of Z's qualities: this very fatalism, this ability Z had to resign himself, to flow this way and that with the currents of his life. Z had the effortless serenity of the believer. For Simon, that serenity, though ultimately attainable, required a constant effort, a struggle of will.

Despite his increased contact with Z, however, he failed to add anything to the Hen's knowledge, failed to win Z's total confidence as the Hen himself had failed. Perhaps Z himself lacked that acute sense of self which is the requisite of self-exposure, although it seemed to Simon that there remained in Z a certain reserve cache, like a strongbox, the location of which Z alone knew.

11 The Fallacy of the Metaphor

Wherever the walls of the Henhouse ended, Simon's world ended, as long ago the sky had formed the ceiling of the earth to those who beheld it. The Henhouse and the Hen, they were his constants, and the Hen, having delegated to him a small portion of authority, related to him as master to apprentice.

This vision of the two constants had become sufficiently axiomatic to him, and therefore so taken for granted, that he had little knowledge of how crucial and how necessary it was to his equilibrium. Once, briefly, he had been exhilarated by the notion that he and the Hen were interchangeable, that indeed the Hen was superfluous to him, but now he was to pay for this momentary hubris, as at the time he had been suspicious of it. For when half of his vision of the constants was suddenly proven inaccurate, when what he had conceived and accepted as fact turned out to be misconception, the resulting shock was almost greater than he could bear.

The realization of his error struck him acutely, suddenly,

but, as he later reflected, he should have recognized the signs much earlier. He had experienced, had he not, the first series of disruptions in the Hen's schedule? Now they came again, and with them strain returned to the Hen's manner. Finally, but not least suggestive, had been the disclosures made by the other members at their first group meeting.

If, however, the truth had occurred to him, and if he had encountered ample evidence for it, it had nonetheless failed to penetrate. He would not, before, believe it. He had believed what he wanted to believe.

As before, the disruptions began inconspicuously. The individual sessions which, for Simon and Z and Alexander had been reduced to one a day, were further reduced. Sometimes he would not see the Hen for several days. He would wait in his room in the mornings, but the functionary would not come.

At first this signified to him only that the Hen was delegating further responsibilities, as a new step in the program under which he was being tested and trained. But then the interruptions started again. In the midst of a session, they would hear the rapping at the door. The Hen would respond. Seeing the unknown, silent figure in the anteroom, he would return to his desk and manufacture some apology for Simon's benefit, whereupon the session would be curtailed. It happened again that Simon and the functionary arrived in the anteroom only to find the Hen absent. Increasingly he was summoned to the Hen at odd times. Soon, in fact, all semblance of schedule had ceased.

The pallor and the look of strain returned to the Hen's face. His skin lost its luster. It sagged into pouches and sacs. His mind lost much of its ability to concentrate; it had to struggle to maintain focus. As a result, the Hen was often irritable, distracted, impatient.

The Hen began to press Simon about Z. He wanted to

hear about Z. What was Z saying? Hadn't Z referred, how-ever obliquely, to the act of violence? No? Was he sure? Was he absolutely certain? Had he tried? He wasn't conceal-ing information, was he, because of his foolish old notions about loyalty and betrayal?

The more Simon's reports thwarted the Hen, the more he seemed obsessed by Z, by the whole subject of Z's case, like a man with an insurmountable itch in the small of his back. Simon had to recreate conversations with Z word for word, and more than once, as if the Hen were determined to trap him into inconsistencies and errors.

In the midst of one paticularly trying interrogation, when the Hen's irritation had begun to rub off on Simon so that Simon's voice impatiently snapped out its answers, the by now familiar rapping came at the door.

The Hen sprang from his desk in a burst of anger. His face reddening, he rushed to the doorway.

"Tell them I'm not coming!" he shouted at the invisible messenger in the anteroom, the man Simon had never seen, whose voice he had never heard until now. "Tell them to wait!"

"I'm sorry, Dr. Maartens," the voice said loudly, using the even, undismayed monotone Simon associated with Hen-house functionaries. "They're calling for you now. 'Right now,' they said, if you please. 'Tell him we want to see him right now.'"

The Hen's face was almost purple. His whole body seemed to vibrate, as if fighting to control his welling rage.

"I don't care *who's* calling for me!" he shouted in answer. "Tell them I'm not coming! You just go right back and tell them I'm not coming! Tell them Dr. Maartens will make his reports when Dr. Maartens decides that he is ready to make his reports!"

"Yes, Dr. Maartens. I will tell them that."

For once, Simon thought irrelevantly, the Hen looked as if
he wished he had a door to slam. Instead he retreated to his
desk. The door slid shut on its noiseless rollers. The Hen
wiped his florid face with a handkerchief.

The incident had lasted but a few seconds.

The two men sat across from each other in silence.

The noise was excruciating. He couldn't tolerate it. Subsequent to that first irrelevant thought, his mind, failing to
grasp immediately the implications of what he had heard,
flailed wildly in the din for an explanation.

They're calling for you now!

Tell them I'm not coming!

Dr. Maartens will make his reports!

He flitted from one fragment to another, trying to brush
the din from his ears with swipes of his arms. He rummaged.
He darted here and there, careening. Where was the exit?
Where was it now? Too much noise. Please stop shouting!
Here. No, here! No there, over there, way over there! Why
was it so quiet? So very quiet he could hear his own
breathing? Why was he in this empty hall, this rambling
shambling empty hall? He of all people? Looking this way
and that, that and this, scurrying and hurrying, starting and
darting and stopping, and full stop, bang, against this door,
against that door, against the other door, and the other, and
the other. Tell them I'm not coming! Backtrack, track back,
back the other way. No, the other way. This way and that,
that and this. Flitting, twittering, skidding, stuttering, stopping, smattering, stuttering, stopping, stuttering, stopping,
stop. Stop. *Stop!*

He had control of himself again. He mastered the mindrace, pushed it into unseen corridors. He knew what he had
heard.

He repeated the words to himself, flinched from them,

grasped them. Too sudden. That was the trouble. It had come too suddenly. He had had no time to prepare.

His mind was numb. Right now it was numb. Right this minute!

And the Hen was speaking.

"They're ruining me, Simon," the Hen was saying, his voice ticking quietly as if in an empty room. "Too much rush. They're ruining me. With all this constant rushing. They demand more of my time every day, and still they rush me. Well. They'll have to pay for the result. We won't be held responsible. Not when they rush us this way."

Then he saw Simon, but he went on as if he hadn't noticed him.

"They won't be responsible. That's the trouble. Never. They'll listen. Yes, they'll listen. That's all they'll do. They'll listen. They'll sit and they'll listen and they'll deliberate. And it's Dr. Maartens who will pay. Dr. Maartens. And Simon. And the others. All of us will pay."

He saw Simon again.

"Do you know what they want, Simon?" he asked. "I do. They want to abbreviate our schedule again. That's what they want. To tell me I've taken too much time as it is. My time is up. Our time is up. They want to abbreviate the schedule again. They demand more of my time, and still they want to abbreviate the schedule. Do you know that, Simon? What do you make of it? But they will do it. I don't even have to leave this office to know what they want, and they will do it."

He paused, his eyes closing, as if he were hearing voices and answering them inside his head.

Finally, however, it was Simon who spoke, fighting to keep his voice steady.

"Who are they?" he asked.

"They?" The Hen shook his head, awakening. "Yes, they. They will ruin us, Simon, with these schedules of theirs and these orders."

Then the Hen sat forward in his chair, his eyes opening wide, his gaze suddenly intense. But as quickly, the intensity faded from his eyes, and when he began to speak, from the tone of his voice, from his look, it was as if nothing had happened, as if, through force of will, he had become once more the old Hen.

"You see, Simon," he said, "it is too soon, but they leave me no choice. Had they let me alone, I would have explained everything to you at the proper time, in the correct order, when you were ready. But now, I see, I am going to have to tell you, ahead of schedule.

"Simon," he went on, leaning even further forward, "and you must believe it—when I didn't tell you these things before, when I didn't explain, when I kept you ignorant, I did it with your own interest in my mind. For no other reason.

"You have, you see, developed a number of misconceptions, a certain number of inaccurate ideas, about the nature of our society. I did not put these inaccuracies into your mind, you created them yourself, and developed them. But I did nothing to stop you, to correct you, when I saw the way your mind was working, when the delusions were springing to life, when they took hold of you. It was better temporarily for you to be deluded. Your progress was more sure, more quick, than if you had been corrected too soon.

"You smile," the Hen said, for, despite the mixed dread and anticipation with which Simon listened, this numbness which allowed his mind to concentrate in one direction only, the reference to his progress had not escaped him, "but I assure you, your progress would have been slower if I had

corrected these inaccuracies of yours. Much slower. It has
been tried, the other way. It is, you might say, the more
usual technique. In my opinion, the results have been a
disaster.

"Well. Let us take your own metaphor, this picture of
yours, this Henhouse. It is inaccurate, you see, in several
important details. You made me as an Almighty Hen, presiding over our society, hatching the eggs, such as yourself,
nurturing them, developing them, maturing them for some
fate of which you were unaware but which I, the Supreme
Hen, would decide. I, and I alone, would decide this fate for
you, at the proper time. I think, Simon, that our society, this
Henhouse of ours, is much vaster than you imagined. You
see, I am not the only Hen. There are many of us, many
people in my role, who, if you will, nurture and develop the
chickens, and there are many more chickens too, and many
more incubators than the ones you have seen and heard
about from your friends."

Then the Hen himself was smiling, perhaps in enjoyment
of the metaphor, perhaps in sympathy with Simon, who was
struggling in his confusion, struggling to keep the edifice he
had built with his own mind from toppling.

"It is even inaccurate," the Hen continued, "for you to call
me a Hen. I have, in my way, tried to tell you this, but you
would not believe me. How could you? I do not preside, you
see. I am not even a member of a presiding committee of
Hens. Some of my fellow Hens are known to me, but there
are others I have never seen, and perhaps even others
beyond these of whose existence I am ignorant. We—we
Hens—are much closer to the chickens, to you and your
friends, than to Hens. We are here to help you, to aid you in
your progress, to speak in your behalf when the time comes,
but we have no control over your fate, none whatsoever.

"You ask about the 'they.' Who are 'they,' you wanted to know, the 'they' I report to, the 'they' who are rushing us, who are going to abbreviate our schedule again, as they have before. Perhaps you would do better to call them the Hens, and yet I am not so sure. They may be Hens to you and me, surely they will decide your case and the cases of your friends, but just as you have learned today that a hierarchy exists in this society above and beyond our immediate group of members, so do I believe that there are hierarchies above the hierarchy I know, hierarchies upon hierarchies. If there is a Supreme Hen for you, Simon, I don't know who he is, or where you will find him."

The Hen stopped then, seeing that Simon, if he was not crying, for no tears were visible in his eyes, was yet as close to it as a man can come and still restrain himself. Simon's emotional progression, while the Hen spoke, had passed from his initial numbness when he had banished the fragment of mindrace, toward a tension which mounted to an unbearable point, at which something must give, something must snap, followed by this oppressive, all-enveloping sadness, this familiar sense of longing so intense he could not sustain it, like that which he had once felt for his dead self, like that which every man feels, at times, for his past. What did he long for? He did not know, not really, nor did he yet grasp why the Hen's disclosures should have unnerved him so completely. He had heard and understood every word the Hen said, but the image with which the words left him was one of his own, an old one, irrelevant to the disclosures but which he could never confront without the same evolution toward this overwhelming sadness. It was the image of the toppling building, the huge structure of glass and steel which towered into the sky, soaring proudly above its neighbors which swam in a sea of buildings below it, which suddenly, because of some awful architectural flaw, began to tilt crazily toward one corner. Its support columns could not stand the strain, the terrible strain. With a snap, the gigantic structure doubled over at the waist. Its upper half broke off and free-fell upon the vast sea beneath it. Its lower half keeled over, like a man dying in slow motion.

Normally, when Simon experienced the image, when he saw the elevator shafts twist in pain, he watched from afar, an observer on a far shore, an angel floating through the heavens. This time, however, when the Hen spoke, he was himself in the building. When the terrible snap came, he fell with it, fell and fell in a gradual, agonizing free fall.

"I think," the Hen was saying softly to him, "there is no point in our continuing just now. We will talk again of these things, and other things as well."

12 The Hierarchies

He dreamed of the swamp.

Half the night he tossed and thrashed, frantic to free himself from its suction. When at last the tendrils had leaked around his legs, forming a thousand links from which he could not escape, and when they began to reach upward for his arms, slowly slithering and coiling in deadly grace to pinion his arms, he awoke, flailing and gasping. Violently he kicked away the sheets which twisted around him, until he lay free, uncovered, panting in the dark. Then he waited, rested, until the mindrace arrived and seized his brain in its giant leather glove, forcing him back to swamps and colors, to the horrible lisps of suction, to the fetid, rotten smell, to the raucous cries of unseen birds and the slither of underwater creatures.

In the end he had to turn on his light and get away from the bed. To calm himself, he picked up a deck of cards and dealt a Canfield layout, snapping the cards from habit as he placed them. But it was no good. He couldn't concentrate. He pushed the cards away and, resting his elbows on the table, leaned his head on his hands.

He had come full circle. If the circle he had described was larger than its predecessors, it was nonetheless a circle. He was back at the beginning. All his life, he thought, he had been looking for his . . . what was the word the Hen had used? . . . his hierarchy? . . . no, his hierarch. It would be his hierarch. He existed, this hierarch, he was there in the world, he had to be, but Simon had never found him. In his place—perhaps some of them operating as his agents—were the masses of human beings who shared with Simon his human failings—his anxieties, his remorse, his doubt, his guilt, as the Hen might say—and yet were indifferent to him. Without his hierarch he swam in the swamp of humanity, unable to free himself from it yet unable to join it, to lose his identity in it, for he was Simon, and therefore he belonged, and therefore he was separate. He belonged to the human race, and yet he did not belong. He was a clump of putty, a raw material, in search of its form.

In the Henhouse, however, he had come face to face with his hierarch, he had found him finally, disguised as he might have been at first glance, in the personage of the Hen, the bald bespectacled guru who had shown him the way from the swamp, so that he might at last be free of it, apart from it, gathering his strength for his leap into a new life among the hierarchs.

That was not to be, that leap. Not now. His hierarch, divested of his trappings, with which, in some cases, Simon had endowed him, was in reality no hierarch at all, but the little man with a thunder machine, the mock-wizard, a man like himself, a grain in the same human swamp. His true hierarch was as far away as ever, hovering beyond the horizons, permitting intimations of himself in this way and that but always unseen, always intangible. And he, Simon, had not leapt from the swamp at all. He was anchored in it still.

He bore the Hen no grudge. The Hen had done what he had to do. Simon believed him when he said he had acted in Simon's best interests. If the Hen was not omnipotent, neither was he malevolent, though once Simon had attributed both qualities to him. The Hen was only a man, like other men, and that was the trouble.

In a way, Simon thought in the middle of that night, the whole process, all that had happened to him in the Henhouse from the beginning through the Hen's disclosures, resembled his cycles of birth, of death and rebirth, of the road which curved upon itself. Once again, without having any choice in his destiny, he had died and been reborn, and the point of trauma had occurred at the convergence of death and rebirth, when his edifice toppled and crumbled, when, having perceived the square, he simultaneously regained it and revolved in its center. For long months, like a fetus nestled in its warm sea, alive as a water plant is alive, a sponge sopping glucose, he had allowed himself to be nurtured. No, he had not *allowed* himself. Powerless to act in his own behalf, he had been nurtured. Finally, under the Hen's impetus, like the fetus in its ninth month, he had begun to assume a life of his own. The equilibrium of underwater life, the feeding and eating, had been upset. Then the nourishing sea, exhausted, swollen, had ejected the fetus like a cork from a bottle, as the Hen had ejected him from his illusions. And like the child who, once he has escaped the womb, cannot return to its now-lethal environment, so did Simon, no matter how much he might long for the nourishing safety of the Hen and the Henhouse as he had once perceived them, have no alternative but to seek his fate in the new no-man's-land which confronted him, this new, untraveled avenue where, perhaps, the hierarch he at once searched and dreaded awaited him at any turn, bestriding

the way like a Goliath, or where, perhaps, there was no road
and no hierarch at all.

This was not the first time it had occurred to him that, like
Z, like the others, he was in the Henhouse because he
wanted to be there. The child seeks to regain its womb,
knowing all the time that, were it to succeed, it would
suffocate. So he, Simon, sought hierarchy, order, an escape
from swamp, and found them, only to discover that, once
found, they were not what he had originally thought, that
they were only the swamp itself, in another of its myriad
guises. It was his lot and pattern to look, to find, to be
deceived, and to be turned back once more to his own
resources, which was what the parallel ideas of the curving
roads and the square, of death and rebirth, represented. He
was—he remembered having thought it before—as much a
pattern man as Z. He had sought the Henhouse, only to
make of it his prison. For a time the impulse to escape it had
attacked him continually. Then it had become for him not a
prison, but a hierarchy, a framework within which he could
function and perhaps flourish. And finally—now—his hierarchy, his framework, had disintegrated, abandoning him to
the uncertain prospect before him, the new and unknown
cycle ahead.

It could be too that the child of his analogy was not as
innocent as he had imagined. Was the child the helpless
victim of the environment and its processes, the innocent
projectile catapulted into life? Or did the child, in some
way, make of its environment what it wanted to make of it?
Did the pattern already exist before birth, was it already
formed, irrevocably, in that first prelife state, or was it
grafted onto the raw material of the child as language and
knowledge were later to be grafted onto it? Was the new-
born child properly called it or he? And were there men

alive whose lives, unlike his, unlike Z's, were not grooved into repetitions of patterns?

As crucial as these questions were to him, he could not answer them, for he was as much the victim of his own analogies as their creator. They both explained and confused the issues which inspired them. For one, the birth analogy disturbed him. Something about it did not ring true. Or did it? Using the Hen's phraseology, he put the case this way: the Hen, or the society which the Hen represented, would have him accept his guilt, by which he understood accepting himself, all that he was, through a learning process which included, at least for those members under the Hen's supervision, a detailed, analytical investigation and reinvestigation of the past.

(Yes, there were the other members! Yes, and the other Hens! He *admitted* it. But he had to block them from his mind, he could not be concerned with them. Didn't they understand? He could only follow one road at one time!)

This was the society's attitude toward his case then, or the Hen's version of this attitude, and its implications were several. One was that this self he was to accept was precisely definable and unchanging, that he was already formed, complete, that he was incapable of original action, incapable of breaking his patterns, his cycles, that any apparent change which might take place in his character was only an illusion created by the discovery of a new area or aspect of these patterns. There is nothing new under the sun, the Henhouse seemed to tell him; you are what you are; Simon; you have always been that way, you will always be.

Another implication, which seemed self-evident to him, was that *all* men, not just he, Z, Leo, Alexander, Martin, Josef—but *all* men, were similarly guilty, were already formed, were what they were, would be what they were. For he was not a special case. If he had not arrived in the Henhouse by pure chance, still he had not been selected for special qualities. He was a random sample, one member among many, and if the Henhouse was saying it to him, it was saying it to all of them: that no man could be reborn, that no man, from his cradle to his grave, was capable of innocence, of that inchoate state of which not even the child was truly capable at the instant of birth. Innocence was a human myth, no more valid on the evidence than countless other human myths.

Were there no exceptions? he asked. Were there not individual cases . . .?

No. There were no exceptions, no individual cases.

Not even the Hen. For hadn't the Hen insisted that he was one of them, that he was a man like them? Simon understood his meaning now and believed him. No, not even the Hen was an exception, not even the Hen who was not a Hen at all. Was it then that there were only systems and guilty men, hierarchies without hierarchs?

Simon could not say if, contrary to the Henhouse's dictum, he believed in the possibility of his own innocence, or if he had ever believed in it. He could not remember ever putting the question in this form. He only knew that, soon enough— from what the Hen had said it could not be far off—he would stand trial, and that not the Hen but others he had never seen would decide his future. His case would be heard. Even he, perhaps, would be given the chance to speak for himself. And the members of his group as well, their cases would come up, to be heard and considered and judged by whatever criteria the Henhouse applied.

Before he knew it, then, day had come, its arrival signaled by the appearance of his functionary in the doorway. To his surprise, as he walked behind the little man in the gray suit,

walked the length of the familiar corridor to the Hen's
anteroom, he realized that he was much calmer than he had
been at any time in the hours since the Hen's disclosures,
that in effect he had thought himself out of the anguish and
the longing. For better or worse another session was at hand,
and he was ready for the new series of disclosures which, he
sensed, awaited him this morning in the Hen's office.

The Hen was pleased to see him, as if they were two old
friends at a convention. He was businesslike, busy, hos-
pitable.

"I see that you have survived," he said, smiling, arranging
and rearranging the objects on his desk. "I was concerned
about you, you looked so desperate. But, you see, we human
beings are much more durable than we think, is it not so?
Much more resilient, would you not agree?"

Simon was disappointed by the Hen's clubby ebullience.
Not that he should be surprised, for wasn't the Hen full of
surprises? But he had expected sympathy, he guessed, an
aura of mourning and seriousness. He had wanted sympathy,
the sense of commiseration over their common plight. The
Hen sympathized, to be sure, but in such a way as to
minimize the importance of what had happened. Yes, you
have undergone a shock, haven't you, you poor Simon, the
Hen seemed to say callously, but we have business to trans-
act, let us proceed with our business. Doubtless that was the
Hen's remedy: a dose of callousness, of toughness, sympa-
thetically but firmly administered.

"You will have a number of questions to ask," the Hen
said, working with his pipe: reaming, stuffing, tamping,
fumbling with matches, "and I will give you the answers to
my best ability. There can be no more secrets between us,
can there? No. But first allow me to put a question to you.
Did you tell the others?"

Simon waited, in order to allow the Hen to light his pipe, but the Hen prodded him, speaking over his puffs: "Did you tell them what you learned at our last session?"

"No," Simon answered. No, he had not told them. He had retreated into himself after the Hen's disclosures, had avoided contact with the others. When the doors had opened for their freedom hours, as they were jokingly known, he had remained in his room instead of visiting them, as was his habit. Little by little they had sought him out, but, seeing that he had little to say to them, they had left him alone. Only Z had not appeared, Z, who would never intrude, who was doubtless suffering from the conviction that he had committed some offense and was therefore, temporarily, excommunicated. No, he had told them nothing.

"Well," the Hen said. "It is of little importance. You will be able to tell them later. Or, since you will have another meeting shortly, perhaps I will tell them myself. I believe I must join the six of you this next time. Let us proceed, then," he concluded. "Your questions. I am at your disposal, Simon."

Once more Simon was disconcerted, wary. He knew the Hen's Byzantine ways, knew how he relished mystery, yet here he was pleading his openness, insisting on his availability, almost to the point of extending his arms to show that his sleeves concealed nothing. Could it all be a deliberate subterfuge, he wondered briefly, the content of the disclosures and/or the manner in which they had been revealed? He had noticed the Hen's pattern in critical moments, how he would build toward a critical point in a state of mounting agitation, as if to emphasize the imminence of crisis, and then, like a mime changing his mask, would become jovial, ebullient, a man with nothing to hide. Magically, at such times, his ruddy countenance would return, as it had this morning, suggesting that somehow the Hen could age or grow youthful at the click of an interior switch. Had the Hen planned everything then: even to the point of planting the loudmouthed functionary to rap on the door at a certain hour, to deliver certain passages of dialogue— *They're calling for you now; Yes, Dr. Maartens, I will tell them that*—at this certain hour? Was the Hen such an accomplished actor that he could dissemble rage, fatigue, harassment, sympathy, detachment, joviality—all with the clicks of switches? If so, which was the real Hen? If so, for what audience, for what purpose, had the performance been given?

But the Hen was shaking his head, puffing at his pipe and shaking his head in gentle disapproval.

"Simon, Simon," he intoned in mock despair, extending his palms. "What are we going to do with you? I am not trying to deceive you. As much as it may disappoint you, you must remember that I am no longer your wizard, your Hen, I have no magical powers." Then he actually did hold his arms out at full length, like a magician preparing a card trick. "I am a man like you, nothing more, nothing less. We have business to accomplish, you and I. Our time, I think, is short now. If you are wondering why I am the way I am today, perhaps you would realize that you are not the only member of our society with that capacity of detachment we have talked so much about.

"But enough. There is no magic here. I am no more magical than these draperies behind me, to which, we will remember, you once ascribed such magical properties. Please now, can we not commence? You will have questions, and I am once more at your disposal."

That was that, then. He accepted it, marveling as always at the Hen's power of perception, which bordered on clairvoyance, at how the Hen always seemed able to read his mind. Or was that—just that—the answer to his debate with himself about patterns? To the objective observer, were his patterns so definite, so unmistakably visible, that his reactions were predictable without error?

The Hen's words had, in any case, operated on his mind like a key. A stream of old questions, pent up in some hidden mental vault for so long that he had virtually forgotten their existence, now poured forth into his consciousness. Yet the one which his mind insisted on, intruding it into the foreground like a candidate in a beauty contest, was so incongruous, comparatively so unimportant, that he could not ask it without laughing apologetically.

"Do you ever see the light of day?"

The Hen laughed too.

"It is not, though, a bad question at that," he observed, reflecting, pausing to strike a match which he then brought to the bowl of his pipe. "No. The answer is no. It will surely surprise you to hear it, but I can only wonder, as you have wondered, if there are windows in the society. I should like to see the light of day also. It is not important to me, not crucial, but nonetheless I would like to see it, as I assume you would. Though windows may well exist, however, if they do I have never seen one. Possibly the offices of some of my superiors have windows, or my superiors' superiors, if they exist, but you must realize that I do not have complete freedom of access here. None of the members has complete freedom of access. There are thus parts of the society I have never seen."

"Your superiors," Simon said. "These superiors you talk about—"

"The wrong word," the Hen interrupted quickly. "It is the wrong word, an error on my part. Like you, I also have some

old habits that sometimes get the better of me. No, they are
not 'superiors,' not in the usual meaning of the word. It is
that each member of the society has his own specific tasks to
perform, and there are many such tasks, as you will imagine.
It is mine to assist new members in the preparation of their
cases. It is yours, for the moment, to concentrate on your
own case until its successful conclusion. It is others'—those I
erroneously call my superiors—to supervise the preparation
of cases, to hear them, to decide them according to the rules
of the society.

"You have seen, for example, the notes which I sometimes
take in the sessions." He waited for Simon to nod. "It is for
reports. There are endless reports, an endless paper work, all
for the Committee. They abbreviate our schedule and demand more of my time, both together. They watch me
carefully, me more than the others of my function, for I am
known in the society as an experimenter. For an example,
your group is one of my experiments: the meetings of your
group, and the opening of the doors of your corridor, among
other things. It is right and proper for me to experiment, but
they watch me closely, and they are always rushing, always
such a rush. Yet my results are good. As good as any other's.
Though not better, it is true."

"The rules of the society," Simon said. "What are these
rules?"

The Hen paused, as if the question had interrupted his
private argument with the Committee. Then he answered,
"Well, Simon. Now that you are learning about us, you are
going to be surprised so many times that you will reach such
a point when nothing surprises you. You ask about the rules.
I am afraid I can be of no help to you. They exist. That I
know, but no more—not precisely. Rules exist, and we have
to abide by them, but if they have been codified, if they are

written down, no one to whom I have talked has ever admitted seeing them, and I have not myself. But they exist. Make no mistake. They exist. Any one case can be reopened at any time. My own, for an example. Tomorrow, or the day after tomorrow, I could be informed that my case was going to be reconsidered. I would leave this office and be placed in a situation just like your own. Not that it happens often, but it has happened. It has been known to happen. Do you remember the member you called X, who at one time preceded you at these sessions?"

"Yes."

"His was just such a case," the Hen said, "a reopened case."

"What happened to him?"

The Hen looked away, as if he wished Simon had not raised the question. Then he said, "Again, Simon, I am afraid I cannot help you. I don't know myself."

"You don't know?" Simon exclaimed. "But how can that be?"

"We never know what happens to the failures," the Hen said, his eyes suddenly mournful, "simply that they are never seen again. The others I sometimes do see, from time to time, fulfilling various functions in the society. Indeed one of the members of the Committee itself once sat in the chair which you are occupying today. But the failures? I cannot tell you. I don't know myself."

"And can't you ask?"

The Hen chuckled softly, amused by the incredulous tone of Simon's voice.

"You don't understand," he said, "but then, how could you understand?"

He chuckled again before continuing: "No, Simon, you can't ask. Or yes, you can ask. Would there be anyone in my function who has not asked at one time or another? All of us care about certain of our cases, as I care about yours. But it is no good. You are told, most politely, that it does not concern you, that it is not in your province to know. And in the long run, I think we are better not to worry too much about such particular cases, those of us who work on them. After all, they are not so frequent, the failures, though they do happen, to all of us. And in addition, there is plenty to occupy us, there is always new business at hand."

"But these failures," Simon persisted, for he could not believe the Hen's attitude, his apparent disinterest. "Can't you find out what happens to them? What becomes of them?"

"For all I know, Simon, and all we will ever know, they are chopped into little pieces and fed into a furnace to keep us warm."

Immediately after he had said it, the Hen apologized:

"No, I am sorry, you see, I don't mean to frighten you, or to be frivolous. It is a serious question and deserves to be answered seriously. And as you yourself must know, from your own experience, force and violence are not characteristic techniques of the society. But I have nothing else to tell you. I do not know what becomes of our failures, and no, I have no way of finding out, none at all, and still I am sure they are treated humanely, however the Committee disposes of them, if indeed that is one of the Committee's functions. There is a great deal that I do not know. I have found, as you will find, that it is better for us not to spend too much energy on what we don't know. This is something all of us must accept, every member, that there is much we don't know."

The Hen's tone was at once so gentle and so sincere that

Simon could not doubt his explanation. If what he had
learned upset or outraged him, he could not attack the Hen
for it. It was dawning on him finally, emphatically—it had
taken him forever to be finally convinced—that the Hen
meant precisely what he said: that he was just one member
among many members of the society, of which Simon himself, if he was not already, would soon be a member. He
realized too that much of what the Hen had revealed to him
in months past, through terms of reference which he had
taken as symbols, oracular metaphors which veiled the
truth, had been literally intended. There *was* in reality a
case, his case, and the Hen's job *was* to help him in its
preparation. Still: was the Hen nothing more than his defense counsel? He could not believe, in spite of what the
Hen said, that the Hen would not in some way judge him as
well, that this Committee he referred to, however it was
constituted, would not include the Hen as one of its members, if not its guiding force.

"So there is to be a trial after all," Simon said.

"Yes, there is to be a trial."

"When will it take place?"

"We never know precisely," the Hen replied, "but I can
tell you that we have entered the period when it could come
at any time. They could summon us tomorrow. Or again,
they might not for some time."

"Will all of us be tried together, the six of us?"

"No. Each will be heard in his turn. Once the Committee
commences its hearings, however, they will receive the pre-
sentations of all six cases, and some others as well, before we
learn the results."

"Is it a real trial?" Simon asked. "Is it conducted like a
regular trial in a court of law?"

"Well, you will see this for yourself. It has a certain ceremony, yes, a certain formality, but it is not so formal, I think, despite the appearances. There is no prosecutor. I will present your case alone. The Committee is free to ask any questions they choose, at any time. They have been known to ask some which are called very peculiar, which are said to be petty or stupid or unnecessary, but they are clever men. I think there is a point to everything they ask, though it is not always so apparent. Then again," the Hen poked at the dead ash in his pipe with the end of a pencil, "there are times when they ask no questions at all."

There remained the major unknowns which loomed in his mind, but he could not bring himself to confront them. It was almost as if he didn't want to know the answers: the charges which might be brought against him, the criteria of judgment, the results of the Committee's deliberations. Or rather, he did want to know, he wanted to know desperately, but having survived so long in a state of ignorance, he found himself reluctant now to leave it, to leave its solid ground for what might be solid ground again and yet might be something else. He could only advance gingerly, consolidating his gains as he went. He could not jump. Nor would the Hen help him jump, give him the push so that he would have no alternative but to jump. The Hen was there to answer his questions. The Hen was at his disposal.

"Will I have to speak?" Simon asked then.

"Perhaps," the Hen said. "Or perhaps not. You will certainly have the opportunity if you want it. They always allow for that. It is not my practice to call my cases as witnesses, however, though some of the others do. Probably the Committee will want to put some questions to you. But you must not be surprised at anything. Even I will say some

things which may strike you as peculiar. Much of it will
seem foreign. You won't understand everything. But, I can
assure you, there is a logic to the procedure, to every aspect
of it. And in addition, I will be there with you, acting in your
behalf."

"The successes? The successful cases, then? What becomes of them?"

The Hen smiled slowly, his ruddy cheeks rising, his mouth
gently widening.

"Simon, if you are worrying about losing your case, well,
yes, you have a right to worry. It would be inaccurate for me
to promise you anything, and I will make no promise. At
times cases are lost on the most capricious grounds. Or
rather, I should say: sometimes the Committee will reject a
case for reasons of its own, reasons too obscure or compli-
cated for us to grasp—which is why we call these decisions
capricious. But my average is high, as high as any member
in my function. All of us lose cases from time to time,
sometimes when we least expect it. That is the frustrating
part of our work. But you, Simon, you . . ." The Hen spread
his hands. "If necessary, I would wager on your case."

"And if—"

"Though there is one among you," the Hen interrupted,
"who frankly gives me cause for worry, one case among the
six which is not certain at all, and you know which one I
refer to."

Simon nodded, but he insisted on the question he had
begun: "And if I win?"

"If you win? You mean the outcome if your case is decided
in your favor?"

"Yes."

"Well then, you are accepted into the society, you be-

come one of us, what you might want to call a *bona fide*
member, although in fact, in the eyes of the society, you are
already a member."

"Then there is no chance of my ever leaving?"

"Leaving?" The Hen paused, as if the question itself had
been too incongruous, too unexpected, to be immediately
understood. "Simon, I did not realize you were still so
plagued with old preoccupations, old and inaccurate ideas."
He stopped again, then, measuring his words: "The idea of
leaving the society is one of them. Do you remember all your
escape schemes? And your fantasy about some kind of train
station and your ticket? Well, I think you must try to forget
about leaving, as you have forgotten your schemes and
fantasies, just as you have already stopped concerning yourself about how you came to the society in the beginning."

That much was true, he had to admit. He now considered
the subject of his origins in the Henhouse unanswerable and
therefore, as the Hen pointed out, he had ceased to pose it.

"For those of us who are here," the Hen went on, "for the
members, the society *is* the world. I cannot emphasize that
too strongly. I mean it quite literally. To conceive of leaving
it is as absurd as the fear seamen once felt that they might
one day sail off the end of the earth. You see, the society is
enormous, Simon, to such an extent that—for practical purposes—it must be considered without dimension, infinite. I
doubt that even your most extravagant imaginings pictured
its size, its capacity, accurately. Not that any of us could be
more accurate. Just as I have never seen daylight through a
window, so have I never seen a wall of which I could say,
with certainty: *this is the end of it,* here is where it ends,
beyond this wall lies something else, some different place. It
may well exist, this wall, just as, in contemplating the
universe, we can always postulate an end, a specific point in

time and space where everything stops and beyond is nothing, or something else—and who is there who can disprove
the postulation? But I ask you, Simon, is it easier to conceive
of an end to infinity or of infinity itself?"

"Then by that logic you would have me consider my past,
all that occurred before I arrived in the society, as nothing
more than an illusion, as something I made up in my mind,
which never really happened?"

"I am a poor philosopher, Simon. I am just one member
among members, you see, and a poor philosopher in addition. I am afraid that is the kind of problem you will have to
solve for yourself, as each member has had to solve it for
himself."

Doubting the Hen's protestation (for he had never encountered a mind more sinuously philosophical), Simon
nonetheless was more reassured by the Hen's last statement
and thereby more convinced of his sincerity than by all the
direct answers he had received. As he had foreseen, the Hen
and the Henhouse once more turned him back on himself.
More than that: in the end, all members were turned back
on themselves. The mysteries remained, and were to remain,
mysteries, for the Hen and the others as well as for himself.
The Hen had not been devious: incredible as it was for
Simon to think it, he had merely been ignorant. Perhaps one
day some new member of the society, more intrepid and
curious than he or the Hen, would seek to explore beyond
the immediate confines of his knowledge and thus explain a
part of the mystery. But for Simon it was enough that neither
he nor the Hen knew, and it pleased him to believe that the
greater part of the mysteries would remain unsolved, even by
his hypothetical explorer, just as the universe itself had frustrated the efforts of generations to perceive it wholly and
thus understand it. If he had failed once more to find his

hierarch, he took solace in the company of ignorants and in this new awareness that the Henhouse was like some infinite organism, hopelessly complex and mysterious, with its committees, its hierarchies upon hierarchies, its walls beyond walls, its infinity of levels and directions.

"Assuming," he said at last, "we win my case, and I am accepted into the society. What then? What will become of me?"

"I expect that you will be assigned a new function," the Hen exclaimed, in mock astonishment that Simon did not already know. "Every member has such a function—if you liked, you could call it a job or a contribution—and as you might imagine, there are many different functions or positions in a society such as ours—indeed an infinity of functions."

"And mine?" Simon said. "What will it be?"

"We can never be certain until the Committee determines. The Committee will sometimes appear as capricious in making assignments to individual members as they are, at times, in their basic decisions. So we never know . . . But come, Simon," the Hen said, his eyes suddenly clear, transparent, "don't we know, the two of us, for what function you are intended?"

Simon did not answer.

"Of course we do. And isn't that what you want?"

"Yes." He had blurted out the word spontaneously, surprised as always when his voice seemed to speak without his direction, as if his mind were reacting independently. "Yes," he repeated, "that is what I want."

"Good," said the Hen.

As if on cue, Simon rose, anticipating the Hen's closing remarks, the usual ritual which would end the session.

"Well then," the Hen said, "as you see, it is time for us to

stop. If you have more questions, we will have time for
them. Actually I doubt that they will be calling us for a little
while, though it remains a possibility that they will.

"But please to stay," the Hen went on, suddenly rising, "I
want you to stay this time. Your friend Z is coming, as you
know, and this one session I would like you here to talk to
him with me."

Before Simon had a chance to speak, the Hen was rearranging the chairs, placing one of the two armchairs to the
left of his desk and, with a gesture, offering it to Simon.
Then, resuming his place behind the desk, he opened the
door, and, ushered in as usual by his functionary, Z appeared.

13 The Functionary

If Simon was destined to be a hen, then Z's future role in the society became increasingly evident to him as he observed Z's session. From the extra chair beside the Hen's desk, he listened and observed, venturing no comment, doubting that his presence in the office had any material effect on the two participants. The Hen offered no explanation, nor did Z seek one, and if Z had been at all surprised to see Simon, he had concealed it behind his characteristic mask.

To a man like Z, self-effacing and imperturbable, what counted were not the external events of life but the attitude, the style, in which he endured them. Z had no control over hierarchies and frameworks. He found himself in their midst, identified their power, abided by their regulations and decisions. Although the Henhouse had constituted an unforeseen hierarchy, he did not, in reacting to it, differentiate between it and those other predictable hierarchies which had formed the skeletal structure of his blueprint. Z accepted. Z endured. That was his lot, Simon thought, the legacy of his background, for the trademark of all old families, old societies, of age itself, was just this emphasis of style over content.

Put a Z into the jungle and see how long he would last.

Yet that was not necessarily the case, not at least with this one specimen, this Exhibit Z, so impeccable in his clothes, in his countenance. Perhaps—the memory of this old fantasy never failed to amuse him—Z would only say "I'm terribly sorry" if the total stranger shouted obscenities in his ear, but his stoical acceptance of whatever befell him, his equanimity, his reliability, were assets in the jungle. Z might be no explorer, but he would survive where others straggled and perished.

Z was the perfect functionary.

The realization forced Simon to reappraise the sad little man in the gray suit with the lightly oiled hair, whom he had seen every day for countless days. He had always regarded his functionary as an automaton. Push the right button, pull the right switch—(did not the Hen control the buttons and switches?)—and the automatic functionary would walk certain corridors, open certain doors with certain keys, deliver certain simple messages, and return for reassignment and rewinding. How wrong he had been, wrong all the time! For if you struck an automaton, the automaton would strike back. Stimulus and response, that was the mechanism of human reflex, and the truly automatic human being would be the one with the most average reactions and reflexes, the Martin, the Alexander, the Leo, the Josef. They would strike back. They were not functionaries. Doubtless the Henhouse was large enough to find employment for them in other echelons, but the functionary could not strike back. That was the point. He could not even wince. At most he could say, "I'm terribly sorry, sir, but it is time for your meeting." He could but receive and endure, without blinking.

The remorse he now felt toward his functionary was, he thought, a cheap emotion. It would not pay back the debt he owed the man, for he had tried him severely, disparaging him all the while, and yet the functionary had never failed him. Z, imperturbable Z, inspired some of the same feeling in him. He detested the element of condescension in it, its underlying assumption that he was somehow better than the two men, that he, as erratic as he had been, would outperform them in any hierarchy, just because he was Simon.

The irony was that, of the six of them, only Z's case was in jeopardy. The Hen knew it. Therefore he knew it. Doubtless Z knew it as well. The other four were going to win their cases easily, and it was this that he held against them: not that they were drudges, for there were always drudges in the world, there always had been, there always would be, in any society, but just that they would win—and win easily. They, who were the true automata, would cross unchallenged, as every day men of their kind passed through the turnstiles and checkpoints of the world, unnoticed and unchallenged just because they were indistinguishable from each other, while a man of undoubted worth, a Z, was going to have trouble. Z had committed an act of violence: capricious, gratuitous, innocent. Therefore, Z was in jeopardy. Not only was such an act a poor recommendation for a potential functionary, but undoubtedly, from the society's point of view, it would be considered antisocial behavior on the part of any member.

Strangely, the subject was not mentioned in this particular session, as if it were some malady or handicap which, in the judgment of the presiding physician, was better localized and isolated than exposed to additional treatments of ques-

tionable value. Given the imminence of their appearance
before the Committee, the Hen must have abandoned the
idea of probing any further into Z's aberration. Z would
stand trial as is. Perhaps the Hen thought the act of violence
would not come up. Perhaps the Committee would ask no
questions in Z's case—which, as the Hen had said, was
always a possibility. Or if the questions did arise, then the
Hen would seek to explain and integrate the aberration into
Z's overall personality, in the hope that the balance of his
record would weigh more heavily in the Committee's deliberations. The trouble, Simon foresaw, would come only if
Z had to speak in his own behalf.

It was ridiculous to think that Z was in jeopardy! Surely
the members of the Committee could be neither sufficiently
stupid nor sufficiently idealistic to expect that every case
brought before them be lily-white in its every detail. Hadn't
the Hen implied that their numbers were increasing, that
the society was expanding constantly? Wasn't it obvious
then that, given the society's system of processing new
members, men of Z's particular nature and caliber were
invaluable? There had to be exceptions.

But there were no exceptions, he remembered thinking,
none at all.

During most of Z's session, the Hen repeated for Z's
benefit what he had just told Simon, about the Committee
system, about the Committee's hearings and deliberations.
Predictably Z heard these revelations with apparent aplomb.
His questions were fewer in number. He expressed interest
only in details. If he had not known the man, Simon would
have guessed that Z's placidity was a cover maintained only
through the most rigid control.

When would the trials begin, Z wanted to know, and in
what order would they be heard?

To the former, the Hen's reply was the same as to Simon: they did not know; the Committee could call them at any moment, or then again, not for some time. As for the latter, the Hen predicted that they would follow the same sequence in which they sat in their group meetings: beginning with Martin, ending with Simon.

How would the Committee disclose its findings to them?

In person, the Hen said. With the seven of them present, the six new members plus the Hen.

And when would this take place?

That too was uncertain. It depended in part on how many cases the Committee was hearing in this one cycle. The Hen did not know the actual number. It also depended on how long the Committee deliberated after the conclusion of the hearings themselves. Usually, in the Hen's past experience, the verdicts were delivered several days after the conclusion of his last case. Once they had come immediately after his last case. But again, longer intervals sometimes prevailed.

Then Z asked about the terminology in which the verdicts would be delivered.

"What precisely will they say to us?" he wanted to know.

"It is one of the anachronisms of the society," the Hen replied, "—or if one chooses to regard it this way, as some of us do, an intentional irony—that the terms 'guilty' and 'innocent' are still used in the Committee's verdicts. Anachronistic because the meanings of origin of these words are now outmoded, are they not? Ironic because, in the terminology of the society, they signify almost the very opposites of their meanings of origin."

Quickly Simon looked at Z. Had it struck him too, this fleeting suggestion that the Committee's intention in the use of the words and the Hen's interpretation of these intentions might be at considerable variance? But Z, if the idea had occurred to him, did not reveal it and, as if anticipating the objection which had arisen in Simon's mind, the Hen continued:

"There has been some agitation within the society that the terms be abandoned and substitutes found. You see, we too have our radical and reactionary elements. I believe one or more of my colleagues, those who share my function, has actually put the suggestion to the Committee, on the basis that the terms cause confusion in the minds of newer members, who still, regrettably, expect innocence to be rewarded and guilt punished. To this date, however, the Committee has taken no action on the idea. Their ways are peculiar at times, which to some is a most charitable explanation. They may indeed seem resistant to change. But it occurs to me that their position is"—here the Hen smiled—"that it is incumbent upon the newer members to adjust to the society, not to the society to adjust to its newer members.

"A verdict of guilty," the Hen went on, "strange as it may seem to newer members not yet accustomed to the society's ways, is nonetheless what we seek. A verdict of guilty is our route to permanent membership, and I think that, at least in the case of the three of us here today, we have come to understand what is meant by the word 'guilty.' At times all we are given is the simple verdict itself, nothing more, but occasionally—more frequently in the unfortunate event of an adverse judgment—the verdict will be accompanied by an explanation. Though I must say"—here again the Hen smiled and sighed, like an attorney explaining the mysteries of law courts to his clients—"sometimes the language of these explanations is so abstruse, esoteric you might say, that they offer little consolation, even to those of us who regularly appear before the Committee."

Then the Hen asked, turning to include Simon, "Are there any more questions?"

Simon did not feel it his place to speak, and Z was silent.

The Hen then told them that a meeting of the group would be held shortly so that the rest could be informed of the trials and their questions answered. As he finished, Simon felt a faint flutter in his stomach. Was this all: his session and Z's session? (Though why he should have been included in the latter he did not know, unless the Hen too enjoyed variations in his habitual procedures.) What had he expected? He did not know, but further preparation of some kind, even specific rehearsals in which they would seek to prophesy the Committee's questions and try out their own answers. Their cases had been prepared interminably, but was this it, was there nothing more?

No, apparently not. The Hen was already ushering them from his office. What it came down to, Simon thought, was that if, like candidates for a degree confronting their final examinations, or a team before its last championship match, they had not been adequately prepared in all the sessions upon sessions behind them, nothing profitable could be accomplished at this last minute. They had rehearsed and rehearsed, all of them. They had no need of a dress rehearsal.

This must be the Hen's attitude, and in the end they could only trust the Hen. He was the sponsor of their candidacy, their counsel before the Committee. Despite the Hen's evident and self-confessed eccentricity, his experimentation, Simon knew that he would rather have to rely on the bald little man with spectacles, his Hen who was not a Hen, than on any other Henhouse lawyer, whoever he might be and whatever his qualifications. The Hen had prepared them according to his own judgment. That would have to do.

At the promised meeting of the group, the Hen divulged

little additional information, other than that, during this
period when the Committee heard and deliberated their
cases, the rules of the society were to be rigidly applied and
respected. There could be no more visiting between rooms.
The doors on their corridor would remain closed, except for
the normal routines of meals and other services, Furthermore, this would be the last meeting of the group until all of
them were brought together to hear the Committee's verdicts. The Hen then assigned them the numbers by which
their cases were referred to and by which, it appeared, the
individual members of the Committee might address them,
if direct questions were asked.

All of them, the Hen included, himself included, seemed
to Simon more formal than usual, as if unconsciously they
understood that the end of one period in their lives was at
hand, and that their appearance before the Committee,
which would terminate the old and inaugurate the new, the
point of junction on his cycle of death and rebirth, would
itself constitute a formal, ceremonial occasion. It amused
Simon to realize that he was experiencing a certain nostalgia, a false sense to be sure, as a prisoner on the eve of his
release feels an inexplicable nostalgia for his turnkeys, his
warden, his prison itself, but a sense nonetheless that, whatever the Committee's verdicts, their future would differ
markedly from their past and their present, and that this of
itself was sad. He felt real camaraderie only for the Hen and
for Z. He would miss them, assuming his future career in the
society led him away from them, though not, to be sure, with
his familiar pangs of longing. He was done with such pangs.
And the others too, in spite of himself, he would miss them,
for all of them had existed as a group. They had existed
together, for a time. That alone had sufficed to form a kind
of bond, which was now to be broken.

Then the Hen was telling them that, if time permitted,

individual sessions would still be held at which they might review their separate cases once more—which sessions were not, however, to take place—and he asked if they had any questions. The questions were few in number. Then the Hen was bidding them good-bye. Stiffly they arose and stiffly shook hands with each other. With awkward, embarrassed reticence they wished each other good luck. Then they were on their way back to their separate rooms on the corridor to await the Committee's summons.

14 The Visit

His trial had been a common fictional theme. In the long days of waiting, when one routine day followed another and, seeking diversion, he concocted fictions, the idea of a trial had popped up many times. Habitually it was an elaborate ceremony, one man's judgment day, held in a huge courtroom, attended by throngs. He spent hours describing the hall to himself, and the throngs and their costumes and speech. The case itself was interminable. It never reached the moment of judgment. Parades of witnesses spoke for the prosecution, all the personages of his past, those he could remember and those he couldn't. His relatives testified, the boy on crutches testified, his teachers and schoolmates, his friends, his enemies, stray acquaintances, even people he had never seen before—all contributed to the body of evidence against him. If the time for his defense ever arrived, he would be his only witness. But the prosecutor, sometimes the Hen and sometimes an anonymous figure, was tireless. He wove a tapestry of crime. He never stopped. And if he did stop, what could Simon say in his own behalf? That he

was innocent of *all* these crimes? That he was not the man
they described? That he was the wrong man, a victim of
mistaken identity?

His appearance before the Committee, however, would
bear little resemblance to the fictions. There would be no
parade of witnesses, only Simon and the Hen; no tapestry of
crime, only Simon and what he was. The criminal acts
which, under the pressure of the Hen's obscure references to
guilt, he once thought might lay hidden in his past, had not
taken place. He was no criminal, except in the sense that
every man is criminal. The Committee, he thought, would
be no more interested in his past than he, for this past had
become like the events of a novel read long ago and dimly
recalled. He had conquered it, mastered it, so that he could
resume the open road. Once that had happened, his preparation was complete. His case had a number, a place on
the Committee's calendar. He was ready to be summoned.

The first day passed without a summons of any kind. So
did the second. Through all the waiting and the anticipation, Simon grew increasingly calm. For the first time since
the kaleidoscope of changes and revelations in the days
behind, he had breathing space: to think, to digest, to
consolidate, to reorganize. The kaleidoscope dissolved; its
colors reassembled into wholes. He would win his case. Even
the remote possibility of losing did not preoccupy him. He
simply could not believe that catastrophe awaited those who
lost. Like an ultraconservative lawyer preparing his clients
for any eventuality, the Hen had stressed the possibility of
losing, of the bizarre, capricious verdict. So? If he lost his
case, he lost his case.

This too, he realized, expressed his progress, this attitude
of acceptance. He had been wrong in telling himself that Z
would make a better functionary than he. He too would

accept and willingly endure whatever role the Committee decided upon, and flourish in the process. He trusted the Committee, as he had come to trust the Hen. And if, as he and the Hen expected, he was to be trained to be a hen, he knew that he would bring to the function the leavening of his own personality.

So he waited, undismayed by this period of waiting, of anticipating at every moment the summons which still did not come. He took the delay as a sign that the trials had actually begun, that the Hen was already presenting Martin and Alexander to the Committee, with Leo and Josef to follow. His own turn could not be far off. He read, he even played solitaire, amused to recall the intensity with which he had once attacked Canfield and doubledeck, when his gambling fantasies loomed larger than the realities of the Henhouse. The Henhouse system, he thought, tested a man. It worked on him constantly, forced him inexorably back on himself, on the cycles which led to the self, until in the end the individual, the new member, could only yield to the pressure and open his eyes. Then, very quickly it seemed, once the process was begun, once that first glimmering acceptance was achieved, the new member recognized his self and, just as quickly, renounced it, spreading his wings for that first crow's flight.

Once, in the days of Canfield and doubledeck, he would have called it a taming process, a system of domestication, and he would have rebelled accordingly, protesting his inno-cence with his eyes shut tight. Now, however, he saw it for what it was: a process of liberation in which, by accepting the framework, the hierarchy which was not a hierarchy, he could soar and expand—yes, leap—into full-fledged mem-bership. A slow process, admittedly, but, by its very slow-ness, efficacious and sure.

He was a believer then. At long last he was a believer. So be it.

Late on the second day, long after the second meal, so late that he was on the verge of going to bed, the door to his room slid open. Startled, he looked up from his book. What did the functionary think he was doing? The idea of such a late summons, when he was tired, when he was not at his best, made him momentarily angry, until he saw that the man who paused in the doorway, as if asking permission to enter, was not the functionary at all.

It was Z.

"I think we can talk without interruption if we are reasonably quiet," Z said in a low voice. "They've shut up for the night. All the other doors are closed. There is no one around."

Simon glanced behind Z, half expecting to see the figure of a functionary silhouetted against the white background of the corridor walls. But there was none. Only Z.

"There's no point in your asking me how I did it," Z said, "for I'm not going to tell you. I devised a method a long time ago, and I've saved it for now. It's safe, I think, and anyway it's the last time I'll use it." He paused. Then: "I have to talk to you, Simon."

Z's appearance amazed him. Z had always been a faceless man. You would pass that face on a street and never notice it, you would see it in a photograph and fail to retain it. But this evening, with his close-cropped hair clinging tight to his skull, Z's face seemed abnormally long and gaunt, elongated, as if it had been stretched. He was unshaven. Shadows had formed in the hollows of his cheeks. He wore no tie, no jacket. The cuffs of his shirt sleeves were unbuttoned.

He refused the chair Simon offered him, remained standing at first, then perched stiffly on the edge of Simon's table like a man unused to sitting. He stared resolutely at Simon, as if making certain it was Simon. Then, finally, dropping his head, he spoke again, his voice still low:

"When do you think they'll be coming for us?"

"I don't know," Simon answered. "Soon. Soon enough."

"Tomorrow?"

"Perhaps."

"It's going to be tomorrow. I think they've already started, with the others. They'll be ready for us tomorrow."

Simon was silent, waiting for Z to ease, to lapse into the easy strides their conversations usually took. But Z did not ease. The note of tension, almost of belligerence, remained in his voice.

"What do you think is going to happen to us?"

He thought then, to his astonishment, that Z must be frightened. Why hadn't it struck him before? Simply because Z was always so imperturbable, Z never flinched, never grew excited, Z accepted what befell him with that bland, resigned equanimity. Yet here he was in shirt sleeves! How long had it been since he had slept?

"You know as much as I do," Simon began gently. "Our cases are going to be heard. The Committee will hear us, or Dr. Maartens in our behalf. Then they will deliberate, hand down their verdicts, and—"

"And then?" Z interrupted.

"And then? . . . We don't know. No one knows with any certainty what the verdicts will be, not even Dr. Maartens himself. But I assume each of us, every one of the six of us, is going to win his case and be integrated into the society."

Z suddenly stared at him, accusing, his dark eyes seeming to glitter. "Is that what you believe? What you really believe? You are talking only to me, you know. He isn't here,

Simon. And no one else is listening. Is that really what you believe?"

The challenge in Z's question, the implication that Simon had a public and a private voice, made him bristle, but immediately he was angry at himself for his own insensitivity. The man was frightened. And he had lied to him. But he could not lie to Z, not any longer. He knew him too well not to be truthful. Z's case was in jeopardy. Z knew it, and all too obviously the strain of the situation had worked on him, eroding his civilized exterior, burning the glitter into his normally placid eyes. Z also had had two days to think, to live with his mounting uncertainty.

"No," Simon said then, noting, as he spoke, how Z seemed to hang on his words, how Z's eyes followed the physical movements of his mouth. "That is not really what I believe. I am sorry. The truth is that I am afraid for you, afraid for your case. Dr. Maartens is too, as you probably know. I think they may well, as Dr. Maartens puts it, declare you innocent. But it is never certain, you know, there is always—"

"Because I attacked the functionary?" Z interrupted again. It was the first time Z had mentioned the subject since the night of their first meeting. "And you need not pretend you don't know about it, that he has harped on it continually in my sessions. I know you do. He told me."

"What do you mean?"

"He told me you knew all about it, that if I wouldn't discuss it with him, perhaps I would with you."

Why? Simon wondered. Why had the Hen done this without telling him?

"Because I attacked the functionary?" Z persisted.

"Yes."

"And suppose that I am declared innocent? What can I expect?"

"No one knows, I no more than you, Dr. Maartens no more than either one of us. No one knows what the opposite of acceptance is. But I've thought about it—obviously you have too, we all have—and I think the only reason it frightens us is just because we don't know, the way people are always frightened of the unknown just because it is unknown. If you're frightened of it, of the consequences, still I don't think you need be. I don't believe the society means us any harm."

"In other words, you accept everything he says?"

"Yes," Simon said. It was true. ("You must accept, Simon, that the society means you no harm," the Hen had once said to him.) He did accept the Hen's word on faith, even, he realized again, to the point of parroting his phrases. "And you don't?"

Z gestured with his hand, as if to wave the question out of the air.

"Do you want to hear about this act of violence?" Z asked.

Simon nodded. Somewhere in his mind the shreds of an idea had begun to cluster, to formulate, vaguely disturbing him. But they were not yet words, did not yet form a picture, he couldn't grasp them, and now Z was rushing on, speaking faster, the words tumbling from his mouth, as if he had rehearsed this part of the conversation many times, harboring it for the proper moment.

"I did it only because it was necessary," Z began, "I had no reason, none at all, at least none that could be put into words. But you will understand it. You know me, you know all about me. I did it only because I had never done anything like that. If that can be called a reason, that was my reason. I had always done what was expected of me, down to every detail. All the details of my life I had filled in according to plan, every last detail, from niche to niche to niche. Do you understand that?"

Simon nodded. Of course he did. It was the pattern, the Z pattern, which had been the first aspect of Z that had impressed him.

"Sooner or later I was going to break the plan, the overall picture, just to break it, just for the sake of breaking it, to commit some crime, if need be, just for the sake of breaking it."

Z paused. Then, as if inserting a question into his prepared speech, he asked, "Do you know what I think I would have done?"

Without waiting for a response he hurried on, gesticulating with both hands: "If I hadn't come here, I would have killed them, killed my family!"

Confronted with Z's seriousness, his evident sincerity, Simon had to suppress the impulse to laugh out loud. Not only did he not believe it, but the idea was so unlikely, so incongruous. To Z, however, it was evidently not a joke.

"Don't you see?" Z went on, excitedly. "For a man like me, the pressure to act can become unbearable. An irrational act, you would call it. An irrational act! Of course! That's exactly what it was. Irrational! That was the whole point! He calls it my aberration, as if it were something horrible and impossible, and for the first part he is right on the target, exactly right. An aberration was *exactly* what I wanted. I had to do it! For a man like me an irrational act is inevitable." Z was almost shouting but, glancing at the open doorway, he lowered his voice again. "There was no reason for it, I tell you, no rational reason. I have nothing against the functionary. He has served me well enough. But once I had the impulse, I couldn't resist it. And you know, Simon? Once I had knocked him down, once he fell to the floor, it did occur to me to try to escape. But that was an afterthought, not a motivation. And as soon as it occurred to me, I didn't want to. It made no sense. I didn't care anymore. I helped him up, and if he had retaliated in any way, if he had struck back, I would have taken it. I wouldn't have said a word."

The banality of Z's explanation disappointed him. Z was so overwrought, and all because of the simplest act of self-assertion, however senseless, an act no different in quality, Simon reflected, than that of a little boy killing ants on a slate path. That was what he had meant by the Henhouse testing a man. Z's mind had been playing tricks on him, inflating his obsessions out of all proportion. He believed Z, he could not doubt his sincerity, but somehow he had expected more of him.

As if he had detected Simon's disappointment, Z said resignedly, "I know, it is not so much, is it? A better man than I would have gone on, a man like you, for instance . . ." Suddenly he looked straight into Simon's eyes again, and Simon saw the glitter, the excitement which Z could scarcely contain. Then his intensity subsided. "I should have tried to escape, I should not have been satisfied by such a petty defiance, an inaccurate little act. But I was satisfied. For a man like me, it was enough."

"Why didn't you tell all this to Dr. Maartens?"

"Him?" Z said. "Only because he would have killed it. He would have explained it away. He would have made me feel guilty for it, and then he would have found some way to work it into my pattern, so that it didn't even exist anymore for itself."

Simon knew that reaction as well. He had experienced it himself so many times, this power the Hen had to remove the dignity from ideas and acts like the sting from a bee, to destroy any dignity they might have, but for him Z's attitude was so remote, so obsolete, that it amazed him to hear it still expressed. Z was no new arrival in the Henhouse, yet the

attitude was pure childishness, a reflection of childish pride
which the Hen, despite all his skill, hadn't been able to
dispel. More than ever, Simon thought, Z's case was a problem. It was as good as lost, unless they were lucky, and,
insofar as the deliberations of the Committee were concerned, he had little confidence in luck. Yet what could he
do to help him, at this late hour? Z had accepted nothing.
His eyes were still shut tight.

"Besides," Z said. "I don't trust your Dr. Maartens. I don't
like the way he uses us against each other. And no, I don't
believe a great deal of what he has told us."

"And me?" Simon said. "Why are you telling me all this?
Why do you trust me?"

"I don't know," Z answered quietly. "I don't know why I
should. But something does make me trust you, even though
the others don't."

"The others?"

"Yes. Alexander and the rest. Perhaps they are not entirely
what you think they are. You don't know them so very well.
They haven't talked much to you, because they don't trust
you. They think you are Dr. Maartens' stooge. He told them
as much, Dr. Maartens did. He said that, in his absence, they
were to look on you as his substitute."

"Dr. Maartens told them that?"

"Yes. He said it to me as well."

The revelation surprised him. Why had the Hen done this
without telling him? Maybe, he thought, the Hen didn't
believe in trusting to luck either, the chance that he would
be identified as leader. But the Hen was preparing them, just
as he was preparing Simon! That was the point they had
failed to understand. The Hen was not trying to turn them
against each other. Just the opposite! To his dismay, he
realized then that the five of them, Z included, had totally

misinterpreted the Hen's aims. No, perhaps not Z, or not completely at any rate. For here was Z, at least, talking to him.

"They are not so special, the others," Z said. "It is just that I know them better than you do. It doesn't matter. They are misfits like me. They don't belong anywhere else but here, and you needn't worry about them anymore. Let me re-assure you: we are docile men, all five of us. No matter what we think, we will go along, we will make good members, you can be sure of that. Because, you see, I disagree with you. They are going to take me in tomorrow, me as well as the others, whatever you and he think.

"But that is not why I am here," Z went on. "I didn't come to talk about myself or the others. We're not that important. We are misfits, all of us, and docile men, whatever we think, and we will make good members. We will be members. Don't worry about us.

"It is you. Whatever the others think—and they wouldn't have let me come here if they had known—I came to talk to you about yourself."

What could he say? He had scarcely realized the extent to which Z was misguided, the extent to which the five of them had talked without him, playing unwitting tricks on each other just as, in times past, his own mind had played tricks upon itself. Did the Hen know their state of mind? Or had they succeeded in fooling him as well?

"Go on then," Simon said tersely, for Z had paused, as if awaiting a reaction.

"All right," Z said. "But I want you to hear me out. I don't want you to interrupt until I have finished, even if you don't agree with everything I say."

Simon nodded, unable to resist an inward smile. It was so incongruous of Z to make a demand of any kind. Again, the fragments of the extraneous idea tickled his mind, as if warning him, but he still could not catch it.

"You're a fool, Simon," Z said, "and more of a fool for not realizing you're a fool. Of all the men . . . Oh, I don't know. Maybe I'm mistaken, maybe he has been too successful with you . . ."

Z stopped, breathed deeply, then started again.

"That first night, at that first meeting, I thought right then that you were someone special, a man who had no business with the rest of us. I couldn't understand why you were there. Did you know that the others thought at first that you were one of *them,* one of the society? They still think so, in a way. But I don't. I never did, not even then . . ."

He stopped again, then continued: "You shocked me so when you said you had never tried to escape. Shocked? No, more than shocked. I simply couldn't believe it. I thought if any one of us would have had a chance at it, it would have been you, a man like you, who was different from the rest of us. And you could have done it, you could have gotten away, if anyone could have. When you said you'd never even tried it, I thought you had to be lying for some reason of your own. Maybe you didn't trust us, I thought. Who did, that first night? None of us really trusted the rest at the beginning. None of us really does now, not all the way to the bottom, not the way he has us twisted around.

"Do you know? For a long time I told myself you were lying. You had tried it and they had caught you, I told myself, and for some reason of your own you had to lie about it. Maybe you were too embarrassed to admit it.

"But now it makes no difference, not when you have swallowed everything he has told us, all his lies and omissions. Not so long ago you said it seemed to you that your life had almost not happened, it seemed so remote. You saw it from such a distance, you said to me, as through the wrong end of a telescope. Right then I knew it made no difference whether you were lying or not. I knew you weren't lying. He had convinced you, had won you over. Or maybe it did make a difference. I don't know . . ."

Z's voice trickled away, then returned: "Listen. Simon, listen to me. Dr. Maartens wants us to believe that the society is infinitely vast, is that right? All his talk of walls. Hasn't he used those very words to you? That it has no end, that it is some kind of eternal state, like life itself, that our other lives, whatever they were, don't matter now, that they virtually never happened. Is that right?" Z smiled. "Tell me, is that accurate?"

"Yes. That is accurate enough."

"Yes. We have both heard him say it, in one way or another. Suppose, then, I told you that he was lying, that this place, your beloved Henhouse, is nothing more than a building like any other building, that it is huge, to be sure, but that it has walls and roofs like all buildings, that outside these walls is the world as we knew it, still going on. Would you believe me?"

"No," Simon answered promptly, thinking then that, at least in the case of Z, the Hen had failed utterly. This too was an old notion, that the mystery could be solved, the walls found. He had discarded it, long ago. "No, I would not."

"Of course not," Z said, his voice tinged with bitterness. "How could you? I am not Dr. Maartens, am I? But suppose I were to tell you that I had *seen* these end walls myself, that there were windows in them, that I had looked through these windows with my own eyes, that I had seen the world outside with my own eyes?"

Z paused, but Simon said nothing.

"No," Z said, "that would still not be enough for you, would it? No, you wouldn't believe me even then, you'd say I was lying, or playing a joke, a bad joke at that, blasphemous too. Again, how could you believe me after all you've been told, after all his conditioning, all the facts he's pumped into your head day after day?

"But listen, Simon. Suppose I asked you to come with me now—*right this minute*—to look out these windows?"

Z stopped, allowing his words to hang in the air.

"Would you believe me then? Would you come with me?"

Simon had had enough. It had cost him too much to rid himself of delusions such as this one, which had long haunted him, to be plagued with them again. Not now, not when he was at peace with himself and his future. He was not going to let his confidence be shaken.

Yet Z had shaken him, he could only admit it. He steadied himself, sought control, found it, and only then did he say quietly, coldly, fighting down his anger, "If you have anything to show me, let us go now and have done with it."

Z shook his head sadly. He looked at Simon, looked away, then shook his head again. "That's what it's come to, then, that's all you can say: 'have done with it.'

"No, Simon, I've nothing to show you. I don't know where the walls end. All I know is that they end, they do end, somewhere. But it doesn't matter, does it? You don't want to believe it. Even if you saw it with your own eyes, you wouldn't trust your vision, you'd think someone was playing a trick on you. He's done his job, then, hasn't he? He's won you over all the way. Well—"

But Simon, losing patience, interrupted him. "I've heard enough, as it is. If, as you say—and as a matter of fact I think you're right—our own trials will come tomorrow, I don't want to talk anymore tonight. If you've anything more to say to me, aside from these suppositions, say it and be done."

"Stop," Z said angrily. "You agreed to hear me out and you're going to whether you want to or not. I haven't much more to say. Even though it doesn't make any difference to you whether I say it or not, at least I want my own conscience clear. Whatever becomes of you, I'm going to have to live with myself inside these walls."

"Very well," Simon said. "Go on, then."

"I want you to know what I think, for what it's worth—and the other four as well. What we think about the whole process we've gone through. All the talk about guilt and innocence, all the learning to live with your guilt, all this self-investigation, all this about the verdict of guilty being the verdict we are all to seek because it admits us to the society—all of it—*all of it, I tell you*—is a sham. *A sham!*

"I don't even know whether he and the functionaries are aware of it. Sometimes I think they are part of the game, sometimes not. Maybe they've been deceived just as you have. Maybe they really believe it. Or maybe they don't. But it is a sham anyway, a *sham*, Simon, a huge, invisible smoke screen. Do you know what I think—and the others? That this place is a prison. Nothing more, nothing less. A prison just like any other prison, except that it has devised or adapted techniques of manipulating its prisoners such as none of us ever conceived of. Whoever designed it was a genius—an absolute genius. Can you imagine a prison which handles its prisoners so skillfully that it not only convinces them of their guilt but makes them want to be guilty? Well, if you can't imagine it, Simon, neither could we, but let me tell you: *you are in it!* And you will rejoice in your verdict of guilty just as they want you to, and you will even go to work for them to convince others of the same thing, for that is what you and he have in mind, isn't it, that you are to be a new Dr. Maartens?

"Can you imagine a prison which needs no one other than the prisoners to run it? Well, *you are in it,* Simon! A beautiful idea, this prison of ours, it works like a clock. It is not even unpleasant to be here. Not at all. None of us is mistreated. It is run like a good hotel—by the prisoners themselves! But it is a *prison,* Simon, make no mistake. It is not paradise. It is not even the whole world. It is a *prison!*"

Z shook his head again. "But no, you won't see it—or you can't, although if you could, if I could convince you, you might still find your way out, if any of us could, if they do give us a chance to speak at the trial, if that too isn't another one of your Dr. Maartens' prescriptions to make us docile. My God, Simon! You have no business here, a man like you . . . You are not like the rest of us. It makes no difference to us, we can be inside as well as outside, and, God knows, maybe we're better off here. But you . . . a man like you . . ."

Then Z fell into silence, and Simon, thinking he had finished, began to rise. But Z had not finished.

"One more thing, Simon. I want you to know too, just that someone will have told you, whether it matters or not . . . and I suppose it doesn't . . . but I want you to know what I think the verdicts mean. I think they mean just what the words say. Nothing more, nothing less. Just what the words have always meant. A verdict of guilty means conviction, whether the prisoner has committed crimes or not, and sentences him to the 'society.' Where he can pass his life helping perpetuate the system. A verdict of innocent means very simply that the prisoner is set free, that he returns to the world we have all known, all of us, which still exists, no matter how near or far away it may seem to you or any of us.

I know it exists, that we are a part of it, that even this society is part of it. Don't ask me how I know. No, I cannot prove it to you. I know. That is all.

"But how we obtain the verdict of innocent I don't know. Maybe it doesn't even happen that way. Maybe he lied to us about that too, as part of this experimental technique he is so fond of. Maybe we are all declared guilty, and that is the end of it. But if not, if the verdict of innocent is used, maybe you, if anyone could, could decipher it, maybe you could figure out how it is done at the trial itself, and maybe you at least could escape. Or you could try, Simon. If only you would try.

"Well," Z concluded, "at least someone has told you, whether it matters or not."

This time Z really was finished. He sat on the edge of the table, his eyes staring at Simon's, a beseeching expression on his face. Then the expression went away. He shook his head again, as if to acknowledge that the conversation, one-sided as it had been, had ended, that Simon and he had nothing more to say to each other. He rose then and walked toward the doorway.

"Wait. Wait a minute." Simon too had stood up and called after him. "Maybe now that I have heard everything you wanted to say, you would allow me to put one question to you."

He smiled then, in spite of everything, and Z returned his smile.

"Let us say that all of it is true, all you've said—and I must tell you I think you are wrong, that everything you said is wrong, though I cannot prove it to you any more than you can prove it to me—but let us suppose what you say is true. Why then are you here, in prison, you and the rest?"

"Because we want to be," Z replied.

"Because you want to be," Simon repeated. "Hasn't it occurred to you, then, that I might want to be also—and that it is my right to want it, as much as it is yours?"

"Yes," said Z, looking back at him, "and that is the saddest part about it."

Then Z crossed the threshold and the door slid shut on his back.

15 The Last Night

He slept little after Z left. Every time sleep began to lick at
his body, every time the tingling sensation which signaled its
approach spread in his limbs, he became conscious of the
tingling, whereupon it stopped. Then he was fully awake
again, the kaleidoscope of colors and word fragments opening and closing in his mind like the pleats of an accordion.
He had described still another circle. He was home again
with the mindrace.

Finally he gave up. He could not fool his mind, could not
lull it to sleep with the usual fantasies which, like lullabies
or pills, sometimes eased it past the mindrace. His mind
posed too many questions. It insisted on them. Amazingly at
this late hour, with his trial imminent and the interminable
period of preparation behind him, he was suddenly beset
with questions, questions which surrounded him like an
army of guerrillas suddenly sprung from nowhere. Not that
he was alarmed. Part of him watched from above, smiling
down on his remainder which thrashed and struggled with
the mindrace, and this duality, this separating ability, this

second awareness, reassured him. But he could not sleep. As usual, he could not support the mindrace. So, in the end, he arose and sat at his table, organizing the questions into piles which he could then examine, sift, and answer.

Z's attitude did not threaten him. One believed what one chose to believe. And Z had been wrong. The Hen had not "won him over," not in Z's sense. He had not been brainwashed. The Hen had not obliterated his abilities to perceive, to understand, to deduce, had not substituted in their place a new system of perception and logic. Instead, through his association with the Hen, his innate abilities had been sharpened.

But it had astonished him—yes, astonished, he had to admit it—to learn that Z of all people still secretly espoused the reactionary viewpoint, which supposed that the world was as it had always been and that the Henhouse, or Simon's and the Hen's vision of it, was an illusion. Though he had long since renounced it, Simon himself had never entirely lost sight of that reactionary view, or so he believed in retrospect. They had come, at a particular point in time, to a fork in the corridors, where one truth lay in one direction and its converse in another. Z had followed one corridor, whereas he, of his own free will, had chosen the truth of the Henhouse, knowing only that he would never know with certainty which of them had been right and which wrong. He had embraced his truth, like a convert championing his new credos, knowing that someone, sometime, could—and would—call him a fool for it. Z could not prove to him that the walls existed. He, in turn, had not even sought to convince Z that they did not exist. For how could a believer convince a non-believer? Z's notion of the meaning of the innocent verdict—of being set free, of "returning to life"— was as naïve to him as the superstition that the dead return

from death to haunt the living. Hadn't the Hen said: "I think
you must try to forget about leaving?"

Yet how could he dissuade Z, any more than he could
convince the believer that ghosts did not exist? Maybe they
did exist! That was the point! He knew that they did not, but
maybe they did.

So the Hen, the accomplished, skillful Hen, had failed
with Z. Even though the Hen had feared all along for Z's
case, had complained constantly of the Committee's pressure, the abbreviation of the schedule, still Simon was unnerved by the realization of his failure. He had thought, he
supposed, that the Hen's complaints were those of a perfec-
tionist, who, he tells himself, is never quite ready for con-
frontations and tests. Perhaps the Hen had been wrong to
harp so on the act of violence, but Simon's approach had also
failed to win Z's confidence. The act of violence was obviously the key to Z's inner self, the route by which one had to
enter, the outer manifestation. Z had just demonstrated this.
Once he had described the act, together with his motivation
or lack of motivation, his banal rationale for it, his delusions
had crowded forward, as if demanding their release. What if
the Committee had relaxed its pressure? Would more time
have made any difference? Yes, it might have. In his own
experience, radical changes had always been preceded by
periods of extreme obstinacy, when the old misguided self,
in its death throes, demanded one last strident hearing
before capitulating to the transforming processes of rebirth.
But if the Z who had just expressed himself so forcefully,
this secret Z, was indeed a man on the brink of change, it
was too late. The trials were upon them. Z's case would be
heard in its present form.

So the Hen had failed. And the discovery had raised new
apprehensions in him, though he was not confronting it for

THE HEN'S HOUSE   216

the first time. The old reflex, the fear to which he had
succumbed when first he had realized that the Hen was not
infallible, had seized him again. He had put all his trust in
the Hen. If the Hen were not infallible, where did that leave
him?

The conversation with Z had raised other questions, left
other indications that the Hen was not what he had thought
him to be, other disquieting facts. Unless Z had been lying—
which Simon discounted as utterly incredible—the Hen had
deliberately undermined his position with his fellow members, had deliberately created a gulf between them. Why?
Was it simply an error on the Hen's part, a miscalculation,
an excess of loquacity? No. Surely not the latter. The Hen
was loquacious only when he wanted to be loquacious. He
said only what he wanted to say. His words were calculated,
intended. Could he be jealous of Simon? A preposterous
notion, but still . . . the Hen was not a young man, his
place in the society would eventually be taken over by men
like Simon. No, the idea of jealousy motivating the Hen was
self-evidently preposterous. But why then?

He saw the Hen's face, the large brown eyes in their
characteristically candid expression, and unconsciously he
began to pace his room, striding from the cubicle to the
doorway and back again, back and back again, back and
forth. There remained one explanation which he had rejected before he had fully perceived it. He had worked too
hard, too long. He could not acknowledge such a reversal,
not now, not at the last minute. But it intruded nonetheless,
this explanation. He had to open his eyes to it, to look at it.

If the Hen saw *his own case* as precarious, *his case*,
Simon's? Suppose that was true. Impossible? Preposterous?
Yes, but wait, suppose for just one minute that it was true.
Would the Hen have deliberately created a distance be-

tween him and the others for his own benefit, meanwhile preserving the illusion that Simon was their natural leader, that this distance between them was the normal price of leadership? Was his leadership the Hen's carrot, an illusion to bring him docilely before the Committee? He remembered his old doubts: that his leadership over the others might be nothing more than his own projection, an egotistical invention. If this were so, hadn't the Hen merely reinforced his invention in his sessions and, not trusting to chance, reinforced it further by identifying him to the others as the man apart?

Wasn't that at best a dangerous maneuver? Why hadn't the Hen kept them isolated from each other to begin with?

But it had worked! It had succeeded until now, it would have succeeded all the way, all the way through the trials, had it not been for Z.

And Z's visit? What about it?

That was the subject he had put in the low priority pile because he had wanted to ignore it, but which he now seized angrily!

How had Z managed it? Z would not tell him. *There's no point in your asking me how I did it*, Z had said. But how had he managed it? Conceivably he could have found a way to jam his own door so that it could be pried open by hand, but how had he managed Simon's, how had he opened it without a key, or if he had a key, who had given it to him? And how had he *closed* it? The door was now closed. Who else could have closed it, had it not been Z?

Had Z's visit been contrived? Had the Hen planned the whole conversation, using Z as an unwitting stooge? Or was Z the Hen's spy, who had deceived him all along, from the very beginning? And why? Why would the Hen want to throw him into a turmoil at this late date? For he was in a turmoil, make no mistake about that, yes, he was in a turmoil!

Why had the Hen done it? He had been the good soldier, hadn't he? He had done what was asked of him, hadn't he? He had made his appointments, he had followed instructions meticulously, diligently, he was trustworthy, competent in carrying out tasks, he had listened, he had listened well, he had believed. He had believed the Hen's orders and authority and the Committee's behind the Hen and whoever they were behind the Committee. He had believed in all of them. *He had believed!* Now he believed. Even now. Right now. *Right this second!*

"Simon! Simon! Stop it now! Stop it!"

The words reverberated in the empty room.

"Stop it! Stop it!"

"Stop it! Simon! Stop it!"

He was yelling at all of them, at Z, at the Hen and the other members, the functionaries, all of them, all of them dancing around him, watching him.

"Stop it! Stop it!"

Then, by the force of his own will, he did stop it, stopped the dancing and the watching, stopped the shouting, the questions, the pacing. He sat down. He was silent. He reassembled the questions into their proper piles. He put his elbows on the table, rested his head on his hands. He had to reassess, to reevaluate, to reanalyze. So little time. But calmly, calmly. Whatever time it was, he didn't have much left, no time for pacing, for shouting or flailing. There would be no more sessions with the Hen. He was on his own. He had to ask the questions and answer them himself. He had to put them in order, one by one, and answer them in turn. Reassess and reevaluate. But calmly, calmly.

He started.

Yes, he was different from the others.

But he put that question aside, to be answered in its proper order.

The other members. He began with them, the other four, Martin, Alexander, Leo, Josef: the drudges. Yes, they were still the drudges, the sheep. He had no doubt of it, not even after what Z had said. They had not trusted him from the beginning, according to Z. So like drudges, they had looked elsewhere for leadership, to Z, as incongruous a choice as Z might seem. That was the way of drudges, to seek out the voice of leadership wherever they could find it, and once they had found it, to believe it, until they were told by a leader of greater authority to disbelieve it. If Z had filled their minds with seditious ideas, these ideas would in turn evaporate before the Committee. Z, in his own way, recognized this. Hadn't he said that they were docile, that they would go along with the Committee and the society? Yes, but it was more than docility. Once the Committee took hold of them, they would go along all the way, whole-heartedly, with all the zeal, the fanatic, inviolable belief of converts. If they remembered Z's ideas at all, they would regard them as bizarre preachings, the flights of a madman who once had duped them. And they would pass, these drudges, walk right through the turnstiles, they would win their cases and become good, useful members of the society. He was sure of it, surer than ever. The Henhouse needed its drudges, as much as the drudges needed the Henhouse.

And Z? He had been mistaken. Z was simply not the man he had thought him to be. That was what had given him so much trouble. Whatever Z thought of himself, he was no drudge, he was also a man apart from the others. He had just proved it. Simon now rejected the suspicion that Z's visit had been contrived. His mind had merely been playing tricks on him, pushing old suspicions to the foreground. If he could not prove his trust in Z, he still had no reason not to trust him. However Z had managed to open the doors, he had done it himself, without help. He had acted out of good will, and he had acted courageously. Z had believed every word he had said. Whether or not he was misguided, he had not been prompted. He had wanted to speak.

He despised himself for not having tried to help Z. He had had many chances. Even this night he had had a chance; perhaps there still would have been time this very night. But he had been too concerned with himself, with his own case, his own progress, his own development. And now the door was closed. He had pleaded helplessness. Suspicious, he had tiptoed around Z, never confronting him with what he believed to be the truth, and why he believed it.

Perhaps, if Z's visit was an indication of crisis, and if by some miracle Z managed to survive his trial, he might one day succeed in breaking his patterns by himself, the master plan which, he mistakenly thought, he had disrupted merely by entering the Henhouse. Or perhaps not. Perhaps Z was incapable of change. By his own admission he had acted out of character once, only once, in committing the act of violence. That once, Z said, had been enough, sufficed unto itself, an isolated aberration, as if Z had had to prove to himself that he was alive, and, having done so a single time, would be satisfied for the rest of his life.

Well, it was too late for remorse. And perhaps it would have done no good. According to the Henhouse system, or at least the Hen's version of this system, it was useless to try to tell a man the truth. He had to find it himself, in his own way, in his own time.

Then there was the Hen. The more he thought about it, the more Simon became convinced that the Hen *had* deceived him, had in fact presented him to the others as their Hen-appointed leader, had in fact told Z that Simon knew all there was to know about his act of violence. Why? He could not, despite what Z had said, impart malicious motives to the Hen. Why then?

This was one question for which he could not find a conclusive answer. He could only speculate that the Hen did regard his case as precarious and had chosen to isolate him from the others: so as to protect him, so as to lull him along, to nurse him toward his trial, fostering in him the illusions of growth, of progress, of leadership.

And again why?

If this were accurate, why did the Hen consider his case in jeopardy? He did not think so himself. More than that: he *knew* that the Hen was wrong, at least this once, and his knowledge of the Hen's fallibility in the case of Z encouraged and reinforced his attitude. But wrong as he was, why did the Hen think it? What had convinced him that Simon required special treatment, this special, Byzantine deception?

He was back to where he had started, back to himself, turned back on himself by the Hen once more, for this final time.

He was different from the others, the man apart. Even physically he was different. There was not a member in the Henhouse, not one he had seen, whose physical stature approximated his own. He was older too, older than the other members of his group, even though of late, through his rebirth, he had discovered in himself a resurgence of youthfulness, of youthful energy, which made a member like Z seem much more advanced in years.

Yet of what importance were such petty distinctions: a man's size, a man's age?

He was the man apart in other, much more important ways. Whether or not he still took pride in his Y and pre-Y selves, he had rebelled against the Henhouse, whereas the others, save Z, had consistently acquiesced. (How he wished he had not lied to Z. Why had he? Only out of embarrassment, out of that childish wish to belong. For no other reason, really, no matter what rationalizations he had concocted for himself. He wished he could tell Z the truth right now, so that at least Z could know that one who had chosen a different corridor of truth had yet started from the same point, from the same attitudes.) Yes, he had rebelled, though long ago. To him, the converted rebel made the likeliest of candidates. Could it be that the Henhouse disagreed?

And he was destined for henship. He knew it and the Hen knew it. Whereas the others, Z included, assuming they won their cases, faced careers in the society which, necessary as they might be, were nonetheless less demanding and responsible. (Even at this late date, he continued to think of the Hen as a hen, and not as Dr. Maartens. He still would, he told himself with a smile, even when he himself had reached that noble and exalted position. Would he then call himself the Hen?) Wouldn't a prospective hen, given the importance of his future function, be subjected to a much closer scrutiny, a much more detailed examination? It stood to reason. Perhaps that explained why, just as the apprentice psychoanalyst is himself psychoanalyzed, the Hen had spent so much time with him, why they had examined the data of his memory over and over, sifting and hefting his past until, as through a catechism, the data had been drained dry and he could view them without emotion, could analyze them from his objective crow's perch. The Hen had had ample reason to be concerned about his case to the point of deceiving him, to coddle him like a prize exhibit at a fair.

But the Hen need not have worried. He had done his work well. Simon was ready. He knew it with a confidence which evidently outstripped the Hen's. If his trial came tomorrow, then tomorrow he would be himself, Simon, he would show the Committee his true self, as it was, in every last detail, and leave it to the Committee to decide. He had nothing to be ashamed of, no secrets to withhold. He was what he was: Simon. He had done what was expected of him. He would gladly stand trial. He would welcome their questions, answer them fully. He would accept their decision, would abide by it.

By this methodical process, by studying the questions before him, analyzing them with calm detachment, explaining what he could explain and accepting as unanswerable, as mysteries, those which eluded him, Simon succeeded finally in reassuring himself. Late—though how late he did not know—he was ready for sleep. He went to bed.

Still he did not sleep.

Far in the background of his mind, like Z himself standing unnoticed in the folds of a distant curtain, lurked the biggest question of all. He had put it in a special category, had segregated it, isolated it, abandoned it—because it was unanswerable. But now that his table had been swept clean, Z intruded again upon his vision. He could not be ignored.

What if Z was right?

Simon did not respond. He held his breath. If he was perfectly silent, perfectly still, Z might go away of his own accord.

You see, Z said, borrowing phrasings from the Hen, you can't deny it. Perhaps my walls do exist. You know they really do, is it not so?

No, Simon answered.

Do you want to see them?

Can you take me there?

Do you want to see them?

Impassive, Z waited.

When Z had put the question face-to-face, he had avoided answering, sidestepping skillfully, but now Z was not so easily diverted.

Do you want to see them?

Do you want to see them?

The words like a metronome in his mind.

No.

The word plummeted through him, spreading little ripples, to sink slowly at last to the bottom, to lie silent like a stone at the bottom of a pond. Wait! Stop! He wanted to call to Z, to summon him back, to explain. But Z had disappeared, fading further into the curtains. If he yet remained, he could not be seen. Simon was left alone with his own body stretched out on its bed.

The last question had been answered. He did not want to see the walls, even if they existed. He had said it to Z: he was in the Henhouse because he wanted to be in the Henhouse. Whatever the secret of its mysteries, even if Z's version were correct, he wanted to be there. To Z this might be indescribably sad, but Simon had learned what every prisoner must know: that his cell was infinite, that his prison was infinite, and that reality stopped at the prison gates. His own room, this room around him, however small its dimensions, was infinite. He had survived its confines, had entered into relationships with them, had flourished within them. He could expand his walls at will, by act of will, spreading them and spreading them until they were distant enough to encompass all the possibilities of his mind, and the possibilities beyond the possibilities. If, in the aftermath of his trial, he was to leave this room, to renounce his isolation, to enter the life of the society in a newly active role, he would nonetheless remain confined, as the Hen was confined, as all its members must be confined. But he would only have to identify the new boundaries of this new confinement—its physical limits, its hierarchical levels—to enter into new relationships, to flourish in the new framework, in order to regain the infinite potential he had known.

The alternative Z had posed—to be liberated, to be innocent—was an illusion, a carrot men had always sought but never eaten. To be truly free, to transcend the limits and the hierarchies, was beyond the capabilities of humans, a state, if not identical, than similar to death. Humans had always aspired to it, and this very aspiration was what had set the pendulum in motion, the pendulum of history which swung slowly back and forth between confinement and freedom. Never having accepted confinement nor understood its possibilities, men had yearned for freedom, had fought for it, killed for it, only to realize, those who survived and came close to it, that it was an illusion, a state attainable perhaps for some future evolutionary form, but impossible for creatures of their kind. One could admire men's attempts. Men were never daunted by what they learned, if they learned at all. They never gave up, never for good. Someone would come along to try again. And one could argue that, without the aspirations and the attempts, without the goal, illusory as it was, the race would not have survived as long as it had, that the pendulum would have stopped, that time itself would have stood still. But the attempts were nonetheless doomed to failure. The goal was a carrot which did not exist, which could not exist given those who sought it.

And yet. And yet.

Somewhere in Simon a spark still flickered. It had gone out, to be rekindled, to go out again. Now it flickered still. Then it went out. Then it flickered again.

He yielded at last to the kaleidoscope, to the mindrace, and this one time he did not seek to break its spell. Its fragments mounted in number, its din reverberated in his skull, its flashes of words and images darted and clashed, colliding at lightning speed to break away again in new fragmentary combinations, fleetingly perceived. His mind could not take it, could not sustain the roar and the pain. He reeled dizzily from the motion, the cyclotronic whirl. But he forced himself to linger, to linger and still to linger, his senses straining to grasp the fragments, to pinion them.

At last . . . at long last . . . the fragments began to collect, to slow down from the high-pitched shriek and collect, to cluster at first into stationary pairs and trios, then into groups of recognizable words and sounds, images which he could see, sounds he could hear and understand . . . and he found himself suddenly walking in the city, walking in the last scene of his life, the last picture of the world he had lived in before the Henhouse.

It was afternoon, and all afternoon he had strolled the city streets, dazzled by glass, glass towers reflecting glass, shadow glass on sunstruck glass. All afternoon he had walked, idly watching the slow, gaping bites of steam shovels, the quiet cranes nibbling tops of towers like huge metal giraffes. All afternoon he had wandered in the city, the watcher, studying the blur of traffic, the patterns of pedestrians, the tides of bodies, glass, vehicles, steel, sucked endlessly by space. What he saw was a city quietly eating itself, its excavating machines pawing its earth, its computers eating rolls of statistics in steady swallows, its tunnels gulping trains and cars whole in insatiable intake. He saw the

yawning mouths of empty ferry slips, the coin-biting machines, the vast electronic systems bloated with connections,
the buildings themselves pierced by digestive columns, and
he saw the cranes everywhere, the huge cranes, nibbling,
masticating slowly, like giraffes or peaceful dinosaurs, their
necks arching in the sky, reflecting gracefully in the glass of
their towers.

The picture was silent. He heard no sound save the quiet
rhythmic bites of the city, of huge metallic jaws closing
gently on each other, and opening and closing again, of
metallic teeth chewing steadily, indifferently.

Then it was dusk. His circuits were completed, but he was
walking still, heading in a southerly direction. Dusk and
silence. Giant dark towers stretched into the night, flexing
their antennae. Not a crunch of gears, not a siren's wail, not
a neon sputter. He walked on, sucked by the night, welcom-
ing the suction, following the white stripe of an empty
avenue, walked south, past dead dark towers and the cranes
now sleeping, past immobile bubbles of subway kiosks, past
deserted parks, empty, silent bridges.

Quiet. Not a voice, not a ragpicker, not a policeman, not a
streetcleaner, not a bird or a cat or a car, not a wisp of
newspaper wafted on the air. Only the regular click of
corner lights from red to green to red to green to red, only
the regular click of his own footsteps on the white stripe of
the avenue, and the regular sigh of a huge stomach, of jaws
gently closing, of teeth gently chewing.

He had walked on. He had kept on walking.

He saw this again, the city slowly eating itself. He walked
the white stripe again. And he stopped walking.

At last the spark had gone out. He fell into a deep and
dreamless sleep.

16 The Trial

❧

All morning he watched the door. Every time he heard a
sound or thought he heard a sound, he tensed, a runner
anticipating the starter's gunshot. He estimated seconds,
marked the passage of minutes in his mind. He paced the
room, relieved himself in the rear cubicle, resumed his chair,
and estimated seconds again.

Once his door opened, and he stood up, his whole body
rigid. But it was only the waiter and the first meal. He ate
little. He couldn't concentrate on food, on swallowing. He
couldn't even concentrate on the events of the previous
night. He should have felt tired, drowsy. He had, he
thought, slept no more than two or three hours. But he was
wide awake, hyper-alert, as if sleep had ceased to be necessary.

Then the functionary was standing in his doorway.

"It is time, Mr. _____," the familiar voice said, impassive and monotonous as usual, as if this were a day like
any other.

He rose. The tendrils clutched for his stomach. He always

felt them, every time the functionary summoned him he felt
them, but this day, this morning, they tightened like the
fingers of a fist.

"Are we going to the Committee now?"

The functionary said nothing.

Quickly he surveyed his room, struck by the premonition
that he was seeing it for the last time. He patted his pockets,
but what did he need? He was suddenly reluctant to leave,
suddenly flailed for delays. But the functionary was waiting.

Then they were in the corridor.

When the functionary turned in the usual direction, toward the Hen's office, the tension drained from him like
water. He exhaled, deflating, disappointed. He had worked
himself up for nothing. He felt like laughing. He and Z had
been wrong. The time had not yet come, he was only going
to the Hen, as usual. The tendrils, as if themselves disappointed by his reprieve, relaxed their grip.

Then they were in the anteroom, and Z's functionary was
sitting against the wall. What was he doing there? Z always
followed him at the Hen's, never preceded him. But Simon
relaxed again. These were extra sessions, worked into the
Hen's schedule as time permitted. The regular schedule no
longer prevailed. The Hen had devoted his first available
period to his most difficult case, and after all, what did he
and the Hen have to talk about at this late date?

Was Z telling the Hen right then about the night before?
No, he guessed not. Z would keep it a secret, would remain
in character. He resolved to do the same. For once, the Hen
would get nothing out of him. For once, he would play the
Hen's game, would withhold information on the strength of
his own judgment.

He did not have long to wait. Presently the Hen's door
opened. Z walked into the anteroom. He looked more than

ever the Z of old, dressed like a stockbroker, his countenance as imperturbable as ever, as if this were a day like the days before the changes, when X preceded Y and Y preceded Z.

Z smiled, and he returned the smile. As they passed each other, Z spoke:

"Good luck, Simon."

He had no time to consider what Z meant. The Hen was waiting for him on the other side of the doorway. His face was solemn, more solemn than Simon had ever seen it. His cheeks had sagged into his jaws.

Simon entered. The drapes behind the desk had been pulled back. In the second half of the office was a long table of highly polished wood. It was covered with neat stacks of papers, stacks of file folders. Behind it sat five men. One, two, three, four, five. He had never seen them before. To their right, at one end, sat a sixth. At his side, on a small table of its own, was a machine which was too small to be a typewriter.

"Please to take a seat, Simon."

The Hen was talking to him. He could scarcely hear the words. Suddenly afraid, he wanted to leave, he had to leave, to return to the anteroom, to his own room, to reconsider, to reorganize. He wanted to start again. The Hen was talking to him but he couldn't hear him. His ears were roaring. What had he expected? Anything. Anything but this. Not this office. Not these five men who were replicas of each other.

"Please, Simon, please to take a seat."

This time the meaning of the words penetrated. He crossed the room. He sat in one of the two armchairs in front of the table. He felt so out of place. He knew this office as well as his own room, yet he felt out of place. The chandelier light. The way the chandelier light struck the table and bounced back. He wanted suddenly to move the table, to change the reflection.

The Hen sat next to him. The Hen was speaking. Simon hardly recognized his tone, it was at once so solemn and obsequious. The Hen before his hierarchs.

So this was the Committee. These five replicas were the exalted Committee which even the Hen feared. Yes, whatever the Hen said, he feared the Committee. His voice betrayed him. However much the Hen railed against them, when they summoned, he snapped to like a second lieutenant.

What had he expected? His vast hall? A dais of judges in wigs and robes? A throng of lawyers, witnesses, spectators?

No, but not this. Where was the ceremony the Hen had talked about, the formality? In these five replicas who sat like minor bureaucrats on an obscure government commission? In the sixth, who was already typing away at his machine while the Hen spoke? It was X. He could only see the back of his head, but he was sure that it was X. He became obsessed with the idea that it was X, this clerk who typed while the Hen spoke.

"Gentlemen," the Hen said. "You have before you now the case numbered 24M06." Yes, that was Simon, that was Simon's number. "I believe each of you has the documents relevant to the case before him on the table."

The Hen leaned forward, indicating the five piles of papers on the table. The gesture was apparently superfluous. None of the five men looked down.

Then the man in the middle of the table spoke. He, at least, was not a replica, his face became a face when he spoke. He wore tinted spectacles. His hair, receding from his

temples, was close-cropped yet curly. His lips, when he
spoke, thickened as they turned outward. His voice was
stentorian, his words meticulously enunciated.

"How do you wish to plead the case?"

He was looking right at Simon, his eyes unblinking behind
the tinted spectacles. Was he supposed to answer? He
glanced at the Hen, but the Hen was already speaking.

"We plead the case guilty," the Hen said.

This was one of the formalities. Simon had been prepared
for it. But his body, already rigid, stiffened further.

"Please proceed," the man with the tinted spectacles said,
folding his hands on the table.

Then, relaxing in his chair, almost as if he were conversing
with a group of friends, the Hen began to describe Simon to
the Committee. He must have prepared his presentation
carefully. At great length, without the benefit of notes,
without interruption, he narrated Simon's history since his
earliest days in the Henhouse, incorporating details which
Simon himself had forgotten, so that Simon too became part
of the audience, as if he were hearing the story of a man he
knew only imperfectly. The clerk turned his head while he
typed so as to hear better, and Simon saw that he was not X
after all. Then, calmed by the familiar surroundings, lulled
by the familiar sound of the Hen's voice, he too, slowly,
began to relax and listen attentively.

There was nothing to be afraid of, he told himself. His
mind had only been playing tricks on him again, as it always
did when the unexpected happened. What really had he
expected? He didn't know, no, not really. He had thought
the functionary would lead him in the other direction, he
had thought they would take the elevators to a different
level, he had thought . . . He didn't know what he had

thought. Wasn't it better this way, all things considered? A certain degree of formality, but not the empty ceremony he had anticipated. Who needed empty ceremony? Why not be heard in the privacy of the Hen's office, by men who, now that he could study them soberly, were not replicas of each other at all but individuals with individual traits, men like himself? In a way, he smiled to himself, he was being judged by his peers. It was only that his mind had deceived him as usual, with its inaccurate notions, its quick assumptions about hierarchs and hierarchies.

It had deceived him too about the Hen. The Hen was not afraid. He could see that. On the contrary, his delivery was confident. The Hen had only been more formal in the beginning than usual. His rituals in confronting the Committee were different from those with which he greeted Simon, more solemn, more formal, and shouldn't they be?

Some of the Hen's speech, some of its phraseology and some of its contents as well, disconcerted him. He could not get it out of his head that the Hen, having betrayed him before, might betray him again. First there was the plea. Whatever the forms the Committee demanded, he did not appreciate the label of guilty. Why, after all, did they have to traffic with meaningless forms like pleas of guilt and innocence, if they were meaningless? But his objection arose only from his own preconception, didn't it, doubtless reinforced in its inaccuracy by what Z had said to him and by his ambivalence toward the Hen?

He did not like, either, being referred to by number rather than by name. The number disembodied him, as if he were nothing more than a dossier, as if the Hen was delineating some obscure case history, the subject of which was dead. And yet, he told himself, he had to allow the Committee a certain bureaucratic license, given the number of cases it heard. Using names would bring chaos. They had to use numbers, like 24M06, and 01 and 02 and 03 and 04 and 05.

But he was most concerned not by trappings but by the degree to which, in telling his story, the Hen harped on the acts of rebellion, as if these were the only significant facts of his Henhouse life, exploring them with frequent repetitions, almost like a prosecutor constructing a criminal portrait. Why was the Hen doing it? They had occurred so long ago. Like the chronic and inevitable rebellions of youth, they could scarcely be taken for serious crimes. He had not spent all his early days plotting escape, violence, rebellion. His life before the Henhouse, that earlier period which had become for him the deadweight of history, was not even mentioned. Apparently the Committee too thought it deadweight and could not be bothered with it. Then why spend so much time on what was also ancient history and could only be detrimental to his record?

As the Hen continued, however, gradually he began to understand and, understanding, to admire the Hen's technique all over again. He could only admire it. Like a debater manipulating his audience, the Hen had painstakingly constructed the image of recalcitrance only to annihilate it completely when he came in his account to Simon's later evolution and development. Here he went into as much, if not greater, detail. Simon had accepted his inaccurate ideas as inaccurate, had transcended them, had learned to accept his guilt. (Again, that damnable Henhouse terminology!) To Simon's momentary embarrassment, the Hen even incorporated the dream of the runner, dwelling on its conclusion as evidence of Simon's progress, his detachment from his past. By implication, though carefully avoiding direct statement (the Committee did not, Simon was sure, want its preroga-

tives usurped by those who appeared before it), the Hen
suggested Simon's future function, discussing at length his
relationship with the group, the purposes of the group, the
success, in the Hen's eyes, of the group experiment. Simon
had been their natural leader. They had adapted to him, he
too them. (Was the Hen lying in this appraisal, or oblivious
to what the others thought of Simon? Or had Z in fact
exaggerated the situation, projecting attitudes of his own
onto the others?)

As finally the Hen began to sum up, Simon marveled at
the coherent picture he had presented, at how he had
managed to organize the disparate elements of such a timespan, so many sessions, into a concise yet detailed discourse.
The speech had contained nothing new—Simon knew it
all—and still he marveled. Everything in its place. Everything at the proper time. He could not have done it himself,
though the time would come when he would have to do it
for others. But could he ever match the Hen's mastery, his
expert presentation?

He could not guess the Committee's reaction. Throughout
they had resembled men who were accustomed to listening.
They had sat quietly, apparently attentive, scarcely moving
during the entire speech. Still, men could sit in the most
attentive of poses and hear nothing, particularly those with
practice in the art. Since the Hen's style was not new to
them, they had doubtless not been as impressed by it as
Simon.

But when it came down to it, the facts spoke for themselves, did they not? The Hen had not shied from the truth,
had not slurred the record in any of its details. And the
record was Simon.

In conclusion the Hen said, "I believe there is no aspect of
this case which is not adequately covered in the documents

before you. However, as always, we will seek to answer any questions you may wish to put to us."

"Thank you, Dr. Maartens," said the man with the tinted spectacles. Again Simon was struck by the clarity of his voice, his overly precise enunciation. Evidently he functioned as the Committee's chairman, for he looked to his right, then to his left, as if soliciting questions from the other members. There were none. Then, looking directly at Simon again, his voice unnaturally loud, he said: "I have some questions to ask you."

Simon steeled himself. Here they came. Now it was his turn. He wished he could see the eyes behind the spectacles, but he could not, only the reflected light of the chandelier. He was conscious too of the Hen's eyes upon him.

"Why do you consider that you are here?"

"Do you mean: here in this room? Or here in the society?"

"Yes," the man with the tinted spectacles said. "Either one."

"Because I want to be."

"Yes. Thank you." The clerk's machine was clicking again. "Then will you tell us please what function you envisage for yourself, if your plea is accepted?"

"I will do whatever I am asked to do."

"Yes, but you must have a function in mind, have you not?"

Simon hesitated, then answered: "I would prefer Dr. Maartens' function."

"Do you consider yourself qualified?"

"Yes, I do."

"Thank you." Again the voice was louder than necessary, as if it were more accustomed to the lecture hall. "There being no further questions, the Committee—"

"Excuse me, please." The high-pitched voice which inter-

rupted came from the left end of the table, from the member
of the Committee Simon had least noticed. "I would like to
ask one last question."

The Committee Chairman nodded, and the high-pitched
voice piped: "Would you tell us, please: do you consider
yourself guilty of your crimes?"

What was he supposed to answer?

He didn't know what to answer. The five men were watching him expectantly, awaiting his reply. All he could see
were their eyes staring at him. But what was he to say? Even
the Hen was watching him, his watery brown eyes suddenly
inscrutable. Why didn't the Hen intervene? He was confused. What was he supposed to say?

Then his mental reflexes took over, interceding, putting
the words onto his tongue.

"No," he said, "I don't."

It was over then. Amazingly, it was over. That was all
there was to it. The man in the tinted spectacles said, "The
Committee can then consider this case closed."

The clicking of the machine ceased.

Simon remained seated. He could not believe he was
finished. The last question still hovered in the air like a
balloon, his answer beside it, too heavy to rise, too light to
sink to the floor.

"That is all," the Hen was saying to him. "You are to leave
us now."

Why didn't the Hen say what he thought? He looked at
him for some reaction, but the Hen's face was a mask of
solemnity, his eyes opaque. Why did he have to look so
solemn? It was over, wasn't it? All over? Why didn't the Hen
give him some indication? Had he answered correctly, or
hadn't he?

He had so much he could tell them, so much he could

explain, if they would only give him the chance. Why not? One more chance, that was all he needed. He would explain all about the guilt. Yes, he was guilty of his crimes, if that was what they required of him, if they wanted him to be guilty! He had committed them, most assuredly he had. Yes, he had! Hadn't he pleaded guilty to them in the beginning? Then what did they want of him?

And yes, he was innocent of them, if that was the required answer! He was no longer the man who had committed them, and even then they had been committed in moments of folly. He was innocent! Purged and cleansed! He had learned to live with his guilt. Yes, yes. Whatever they wanted. They had only to ask!

Then the awful impact of the word "innocence" struck him. He had said he was innocent! He had as much as told them that he considered himself innocent! But wait, that wasn't what he had meant, they hadn't understood. And why hadn't the Hen intervened? Why had the Hen allowed him to wreck the whole case with a single misunderstood answer?

As if propelled by a motor force other than his own legs, he found himself in the anteroom. He turned back to the door. It was already closed, sealing him off from the Hen and the Committee. He wanted to bang on it, to demand that his case be reopened, that he be heard, at long last that he be heard! He had so much to tell them. They hadn't listened. They hadn't listened at all! He knew it. To them he was just another case, a sequence of digits to be processed. And the Hen! The Hen *had* betrayed him!

Afterthought, he thought bitterly. He was a master of afterthought. He mastered all the crises of his life with afterthought. That was his pattern. That was Simon: the King of Afterthought.

And there was the functionary, waiting to escort him. How he hated the man! He loathed the mere sight of him! For once, he wanted to get him, just this once to get him good, to pulverize him until he cried out. He had to cry out, this goddamned functionary!

Already he was in the corridor, walking down the red tiles. Already he was in his room, which he thought he had seen for the last time. Already that door too was closed behind him. Already he was sitting in the familiar chair by the familiar table, which was his place, which was where he always found himself.

And why was he so upset?

No reason. No reason at all. That was only his way, Simon's way, when the unexpected happened. That was Simon for you.

His mind produced four statements for his inspection:

His trial had not gone badly.

The Hen had performed a virtual masterpiece of consolidation and presentation.

He, himself, had at least answered forthrightly.

He was not going to be judged on the basis of one answer to one question.

All true. He could not deny them. Quickly he began to organize corroborative material, and, as he sat at the table, the evidence poured forth, one item after the next. The allegedly key question had come not from the Committee Chairman but the obscure member at the end of the table. He had answered it, had he not, honestly, forthrightly, according to his own best judgment which, for better or worse, he had decided beforehand to trust? Yes. The Hen had said nothing, had not reacted one way or the other to the question or the answer. Surely the Hen would have intervened if . . . And so forth. And so forth.

All true.

The whole episode had lasted not more than one hour, he estimated. In the absence of clocks, time always fooled him, but he would estimate one hour. Perhaps he was wrong or perhaps right. It made no difference, just as it made no difference whether he had been in the Henhouse a total of one hour, one year or ten years. It simply didn't matter.

Now he had to await the verdicts. What was it the Hen had said? That they could come in one hour or one day, three hours or three days? No matter. That didn't matter either.

It was done.

He played some solitaire.

17   The Verdicts

❧

Then they were walking down the corridor in the usual direction. The other doors were opening, the other functionaries waiting to escort their charges. They crowded through the anteroom into the Hen's office. The door was already open. The drapes were still pulled back.

The Hen was waiting for them.

"They have called for us," the Hen told them. "Just one word before we go. It is a requirement of the Committee that all new members remain silent during the delivery of the verdicts. I trust that all of you will cooperate?" He paused, looked from one to the other. "Good. Then I ask that you now follow me."

The Hen led them through the second door at the rear of the second half of his office, a door they had never used before. It opened in turn onto the rear of a large semicircular auditorium which glowed brilliantly from myriad small lights set like stars into its ceiling. Curved rows of seats sloped down gradually toward the front. Set into the curved wall behind the rear row were a number of doors similar to the one through which they had just passed. A din of conversation filled the air.

The Hen led them down one of the aisles which radiated from the front of the auditorium like the spokes of a wheel, past rows of seats filled with people they had never seen before, men and women too, chattering at each other as if at a reunion or festival. The front rows of seats nearest the hub of the wheel were sectioned off from those behind them. They were mostly empty. The Hen led them to one of these front rows, ushered them into seats, sat beside them on the aisle.

In the hub of the wheel, the center of the semicircle, behind a long highly polished table crowded with a variety of papers and files, sat the five members of the Committee. Behind them hung a huge, heavy red curtain. In their middle, presiding, was the man with the tinted spectacles and the stentorian voice. They were served by a battery of assistants who hovered behind them, from time to time darting on errands or leaning forward behind the Committee members to take whispered commands.

As the Hen's group took their seats, six other men stood before the Committee table, partially masking the Committee members from view. They were hearing their verdicts. Against the steady background of noise behind them, the Hen's group could nonetheless hear some of the words uttered by the man with the tinted spectacles. The six new members remained together before the Committee table until the last verdict had been delivered, then, to the applause of the audience, walked, all six, along the first row of seats and disappeared into the clusters of humanity at the rear.

"Dr. Maartens!"

The middle Committee member was standing, calling to

the Hen. He banged a gavel on the table. Almost instantly the hubbub ceased, the auditorium was quiet.

"Dr. Maartens!" The voice rang out in the sudden silence. "Are your cases present, Dr. Maartens?"

The Hen was on his feet, nodding.

"Yes, they are here," he answered.

Then the six members of the Hen's group were standing in a line before the Committee table, before the five Committee members who had resumed their seats, while the Hen himself listened from a position slightly to their rear, at the first row of seats.

"I will ask you first," the man in the tinted spectacles said, his lips thickening as he spoke, his eyes passing up and down the line, his words clipping the air, "to remain standing where you are until all the verdicts have been read. Afterward, those whose pleas are accepted will be free to join this audience until their assignments are ready for them. Those whose pleas are denied will remain here, to await further instructions."

One of his staff assistants then leaned forward and handed him a sheaf of documents which he placed before him on the table. As he began to read the papers, the hum of conversation once more spread through the auditorium.

"Case 24M01?"

Martin, his face serious, took a step forward from the left end of the line.

"Case 24M01, this Committee accepts your plea of guilty. Case 24M02?"

He paused until he received a nod of acknowledgment from Alexander.

"Case 24M02," his voice called out, as he turned over the papers before him, "this Committee accepts your plea of guilty. Case 24M03?"

Again he waited.

"Case 24M03, this Committee accepts your plea of guilty. It notes with pleasure that another member of foreign origin has joined the ranks of the society. Case 24M04?"

He had to bring the gavel down again to silence the mounting din.

"Case 24M04, this Committee accepts your plea of guilty. Case 24M05?"

It was Z's turn. The man with the tinted spectacles turned another page, then looked up, sought Z with his eyes.

"Case 24M05, this Committee accepts your plea of guilty. Case 24M06?"

Just one document remained from the stack of documents.

Simon's turn. He stepped forward from the line. The din rose again in a crescendo. Bright light bounced off the tinted spectacles, forcing him to blink.

"Case 24M06, this Committee denies your plea of guilty and declares you innocent according to its criteria and laws."

He heard a roar of voices in his ears, a cacophony of language. The applause started. Thousands of small lights danced in his eyes, and a whir of faces. The others were moving away from him. He wanted to call to them. He called out, but he could not hear his own voice. He saw Z. Z's face sent him a message of triumph.

The last person he saw, before he was led away, was the Hen, a few steps apart, watching him from the first row of the auditorium, but behind the spectacles, in the large brown eyes, he could detect no expression at all.

18 The Committee's Report

〆

CASE 24MO6

Foreword

    This report, respectfully submitted, replies to the request of the Supervising Authority, Membership, for an investigation of the circumstances surrounding this Committee's disposition of Case 24MO6. Apology is made for its length. The irregular circumstances herein related, the many ramifications of the case, and the unfortunate notoriety it has received in certain sectors of the society, have necessitated an exhaustive study.

Chronology

    The following events are related in the order in which they occurred:

    1. At its regular hearings on the conclusion of the 24th Cycle, the Eleventh Committee of Five received the presentation of Case 24MO6 by its inspecting officer. (Tnscpt cpy attchd hrwth.) Of particular interest in the transcript will be the inspecting officer's procedural methods, which this

Committee deems eccentric, and which are amply reflected
in the inspecting officer's address to the Committee. It
should also be noted that, throughout the 24th Cycle, Case
24MO6 was under this Committee's closest supervision,
through constant conferences with the inspecting officer and
other supervisory techniques (spptg dcmts avlble), and
furthermore that the reasons for the delay in this Committee's contribution to the 24th Cycle are directly attributable
to the inspecting officer's failure to comply with requisite
schedules. (See earlier report on this subject.)

2. Having concluded its deliberations on the cases before
it, this Committee rendered its verdicts on the 24th Cycle in
regular session. (Dcmts ptg Case 24MO6 attchd hrwth.)
Upon occasion, this Committee has seen fit to append brief
explanatory statements to its verdicts, but in Case 24MO6 it
did not choose to do so. While it is not this Committee's practice to justify its findings, and while, in accordance with
established policy, it retains its prerogative of secret deliberation, a discussion of the verdict in Case 24MO6 will be
found below, under *Recommendations*.

3. In accordance with verdict rendered, and following the
normal procedure set forth for the disposition of recipients
of innocent verdicts, Case 24MO6 was processed for release
from the society and returned to Place of Origin.

4. Immediately subsequent to the conclusion of the 24th
Cycle, this Committee received a memorandum of appeal
(cpy attchd hrwth) in Case 24MO6 from its inspecting officer.
If other Committees of Five within the Society are accustomed to hearing appeals from inspecting officers under
their jurisdiction, this Committee is unaware of the practice.
Nonetheless, and though no action could be taken, disposition of Case 24MO6 having already been accomplished,
Membership was convened in special session at which the

memorandum of appeal was considered. It was the unanimous decision of Membership that the memorandum be disregarded and no acknowledgment given. Of special significance will be the exhortative, often petulant language in which the memorandum is written, which this Committee deems improper, the charge that this Committee lacks "humanity," and the eccentric, if not inaccurate picture its author holds of the functions and jurisdictions of inspecting officers and Committees of Five respectively.

Recommendations

Upon adjournment of special session, this Committee considered Case 24MO6 definitely closed.

5. As the Supervising Authority is already aware, considerable time then passed—the work of the 25th Cycle had already begun—the first reports of progress had been received from many of the inspecting officers (a notable exception being the aforementioned inspecting officer)—before this Committee learned, to its surprise, that Case 24MO6 had reappeared in the society. The Chairman of this Committee received an unannounced visit from a receiving officer who, having presented his credentials, informed the Chairman that Case 24MO6 was in his staff's custody. Case 24MO6, the receiving officer reported, was in a state of severe mental and physical agitation, suffering from delusions concerning the nature of the society. According to the officer, he kept demanding to be taken to "the Hen." (Those were his very words. "The Hen" was the name by which, during the preparation of his case, he referred to his inspecting officer—in itself a somewhat piquant commentary on the inspecting officer's case procedures.) He was most insistent about this. He would not leave. He repeated to the point of raving, the receiving officer reported, certain bizarre

fantasies, unintelligible to the officer, but of which, through its supervision of the case, this Committee had prior knowledge. In the judgment of the representative, he was "desperate."

The receiving staff had no experience in disposing of such a case. At first they did not know his identity, only that: 1) he was or had been, in some manner, connected with the society, for he spoke of it knowledgeably, and 2) in all humaneness, a man in his condition could not be released. It was not until he referred to his case by number that they were able to trace him to this Committee, whereupon they sent their representative to consult with the Chairman. The Chairman, cognizant of his responsibilities, asked to interview the man and was escorted for that purpose by the receiving officer. However, the interview was impossible. Upon entering the room in which the man was temporarily held, the Chairman was subjected to violent verbal assault, and it is his belief that, had 24M06 been physically stronger, his safety would have been endangered.

It was thereupon decided by the Chairman, after consultation with a member of the society's medical facility, that 24M06 be placed under sedation, that he be allowed to remain in the society for a limited period of time until he regained some portion of his health, and that he then be remanded to this Committee for further disposition.

These steps were subsequently accomplished. Throughout the very short duration of his seond stay in the society, 24M06 was maintained in seclusion and under sedation. When this Committee received him, the Chairman himself supervised the administration of the disposal series. 24M06 was thereupon returned to Place of Origin.

It is assumed that the Supervising Authority will have solicited and obtained reports corroborating this information from the relevant agencies of the society.

6. Certain rumors, which have been spread through the membership of the society by dissident sectors, have come to this Committee's attention suggesting that the unfortunate outcome of Case 24M06 was caused by this Committee's negligence. It has also been learned, to this Committee's chagrin (which chagrin must also be shared by the society at large) that these certain dissident sectors are demanding a total revision of the current membership system. In reply to the former, this Committee states emphatically and categorically that, after exhaustive study, most particularly of the administration of the disposal series in Case 24M06, no indication or evidence of negligence has been found, and none is believed to exist. In the judgment of this Committee, the reappearance of 24M06 in the society, however improbable, was a fortuitous occurrence. Statistically possible, it is also statistically unlikely, and therefore of no great consequence to the society. This Committee also hastens to remind the above-mentioned dissident sectors that the current membership system exists not because of the dictates of one or more members of the Committees of Five, but because of the nature of the cases themselves with whom the Committees must work.

Recommendations

In submitting the above results of its investigation, this Committee believes that it has adequately clarified the facts in Case 24M06, unusual as they are, and that, for the purpose of the society's records, Case 24M06 can now be considered closed. However, this Committee would consider itself remiss in its duties if it did not explore and describe the larger lessons which are to be deduced from this one case. Case 24M06 is in itself of no importance. Neither this Committee nor the society at large can be concerned with the future welfare of innocents. The charge of "inhumanity" is irrelevant. (It might be pointed out, in this connection, that, although no society in history has yet devised or adapted a totally satisfactory method for the disposal of those candidates it chooses to reject, the disposal series, it is believed, is the most humane and effective yet devised and adapted. It might further be pointed out that Case 24M06 sought membership of his own accord.) The larger lessons of Case 24M06 are, however, of paramount import. Fully cognizant that the Committees of Five are not constituted for theoretical or philosophic inquiries and conclusions, this Committee nonetheless respectfully submits the following recommendations:

1. That a statistical inquiry be initiated to determine whether or not certain types of cases should be barred automatically from membership in the society.

In its deliberations on Case 24M06, this Committee concluded in its best judgment that the subject case was unsuitable for membership by reason of the heresy of innocence. This Committee did not base its conclusions solely upon evidence procured at the trial. On the contrary, it included in its deliberations, and relied heavily upon, evidence obtained throughout the preparation of the case: inspecting officer's reports, written and verbal, transcripts of individual sessions, photostatic copies of the subject's own writings. (Dcmts avlble.) In this Committee's judgment, Case 24M06 was, and remained, a product of typical delusions, which previous authorities have broadly characterized as "the cult of personality" or "the heresy of the individual," but which, in the phrase currently in usage in the society, are called "the heresy of innocence." Certain progress may have been accomplished in the course of the case's preparation (see below), and it is this Committee's opinion that Case 24M06 genuinely sought a verdict which would grant him membership. However, by the time of his trial itself, both in the presentation by his inspecting officer and in direct testimony, Case 24M06 still exhibited ample evidence of delusion. (It should not be wrongly assumed that this Committee based its verdict on the last question and answer in the transcript. On the contrary, it considered the question ill-advised, given the confusion still apparent among many cases over the terms "guilt" and "innocence," and largely discounted 24M06's response in its deliberations.) Case 24M06 clearly remained convinced in the basic fallacy that the self transcends all other social sectors in importance, even to the degree of having already selected for himself a function within the society *before* his verdict. (See Chairman's question and case's response.) This function, it will be noted, is one of high prominence and prerogative. Although this Committee detected mitigating circumstances in Case 24M06 (see below) and therefore considered reopening the case with a new inspecting officer, it concluded that the heresy of innocence was too deeply imbedded within him to be materially affected by any of the techniques of instruction and preparation currently in use, and that, were he granted membership, he would inevitably revert to delusion. It therefore had no choice but to render its verdict.

Though it is not given to useless and time-consuming speculation, and though it disclaims any disrespect toward the more elderly members of the society, this Committee has been aware of a general correlation between types of cases which appear before it and verdicts rendered. Its own data are inadequate for statistical accuracy. Despite previous requests, it has no access to the findings of other Committees of Five.

Lest any such accusation be wrongly made, this Committee disclaims any excessive concern on its part with indi-

viduals. Case 24M06 is closed. This Committee cannot and
does not concern itself with the problems innocents may
encounter in adaptation to Place of Origin. Rather the above
recommendation is proffered because 1) this Committee is
fully cognizant of the desire and, indeed, the necessity of
expanding the society's membership as rapidly as possible,
and 2) this Committee is fully cognizant of the extent to
which the society's physical facilities for the preparation of
new cases are already overtaxed and the schedules of inspecting officers overcrowded.

2. That the Committees of Five be given greater supervisory control over inspecting officers preparing cases within
their jurisdiction.

It will be noted in the documents pertaining to Case
24M06 that, throughout the 24th Cycle, this Committee
repeatedly urged the inspecting officer to release the case to
this Committee's discretion, so that it could either be reopened in a new cycle with a new inspecting officer or
prematurely concluded and abandoned. These measures
were taken by the Committee not only because it considered
the potential of Case 24M06 dubious from the beginning of
the cycle (which judgment, however, did not prejudice the
case in this Committee's eyes when it was finally brought to
trial), but because it feared that, under the highly experimental system of the inspecting officer, the successful com-
pletion of other cases in the 24M group might be impeded.
The inspecting officer, however, consistently rejected this
Committee's advice. He appeared to regard Case 24M06 as a
particular challenge to his professional standing. This Committee was thus powerless to intervene in a case within its
jurisdiction, a case, in its own best judgment, of dubious
content.

Whereas Case 24M06 was admittedly the most difficult

and time-consuming of its cycle, a source of constant contention between inspecting officer and Committee of Five, this Committee makes this recommendation out of concern for the society's best interests, *and for no other reason*. It seeks no personal aggrandizement, no extension of its prerogatives. It seeks only to fulfill its functions and the needs of the society in the most efficient possible manner.

3. That the case of the inspecting officer in Case 24M06 be reopened.

In proposing this recommendation, this Committee realizes that it may be charged with conducting a personal vendetta against the inspecting officer in question (in fact, it has already been so accused: see memorandum of appeal cited above), with excessive and chronic conservatism, and with thwarting experimentation designed to increase the society's membership and advance the society's aims. On the contrary, this Committee has always welcomed and will continue to welcome experimentation, for it understands that the membership must be expanded if the society is to flourish. It also believes, however, that the expression of such needs must be accompanied by constant reminders as to the original purpose of the society, the very foundations of its existence. If this be conservatism, this Committee willingly accepts the charge. The charge of a personal vendetta is easily and simply refuted by an examination of the inspecting officer's record before this Committee. (Dcmts avlble.) This Committee has always sought to be impartial in every respect. It attests herewith, a statement which is statistically verifiable, that the inspecting officer's percentage of successful verdicts is as satisfactory as that of any of his colleagues within this jurisdiction.

In his conduct of Case 24M06, however, and in his general conduct throughout the 24th Cycle, the inspecting officer revealed tendencies which, this Committee believes, endanger the success of future cycles and, by extension, the welfare of the society at large. In attending conferences with this Committee, in filing reports, in completing his contribution to the cycle, the inspecting officer was invariably dilatory. He received all advice tendered him by this Committee in a manner which was petulant and obstructive. He appears to consider this Committee extraneous to the preparation of new cases, to the entire membership system. He presents himself to his cases as a figure of special omnipotence and omniscience, as graphically confirmed by their names for him, the "Hen" and the "Professor" being two such examples, as further confirmed by the highly personal style in which even his own office is furnished. Though such delusions among new cases are to a degree inevitable, given the close and prolonged contact of new cases with inspecting officers, he makes little effort to disabuse his cases of them. His interrogative technique is dangerously psychoanalytic. In this Committee's opinion, Case 24M06, though destined to fail from the first, was actually reinforced in his delusion, his heresy of innocence, by the inspecting officer's example.

Therefore, in the judgment of this Committee, the inspecting officer contradicts, in his personal and professional conduct, the high purpose for which the society was founded: to create, through and for its members, those past and present and the generations of members to follow, a way of life which is life itself, from which the heresy of innocence, and its attendant delusions, have been eliminated. Instead of anonymity, brotherhood, equality, the inspecting officer depicts to his cases a kingdom over which he alone presides. Instead of the profound truth that all members are equally guilty because of the very fact of their existence, he disseminates psychoanalytic misconceptions, fosters differences and foments dissension among his cases. Examples of his deception abound in the documents of the 24th Cycle.

This Committee believes not only that the inspecting officer has outlived his usefulness in his current function, but that he has become a dangerous and dissident element within the society. It thus respectfully urges that his case be reopened, in the hope that such an experienced, valuable and venerable member of the society rediscover the inspiration, the qualities, which first admitted him to membership.

This Committee recognizes the seriousness of these recommendations. Jointly and severally, it assumes full responsibility for them and for the statements made in corroboration.

––––––––––

This report and attendant documents were filed in the records of the Eleventh Committee of Five pertaining to the 24th Cycle. Subsequent to the conclusion of the 25th Cycle, the following notations were added to the file and the records then closed:

1) Rpt. sgnd & dlvrd. No aknldgmt rcvd.

2) As of this date, this Committee recognizes that no action has been taken on the recommendations contained herein.